B.C.
49376

Adventures and Misadventures of
BIG BOTTOM CHURCH

BILL PATTERSON

CROSSBOOKS
PUBLISHING

CrossBooks™
1663 Liberty Drive
Bloomington, IN 47403
www.crossbooks.com
Phone: 1-866-879-0502

©2009 Dr. Bill Patterson. All rights reserved.

No part of this book may be reproduced, stored in a retrieval system, or transmitted by any means without the written permission of the author.

First published by CrossBooks 2/25/2010

ISBN: 978-1-6150-7077-0 (sc)
ISBN: 978-1-6150-7095-4 (hc)

Library of Congress Control Number: 2009940549

Printed in the United States of America
Bloomington, Indiana

This book is printed on acid-free paper.

In Memory of
Bonnie Runnels Patterson
1926-2007
I can still feel the warm hands and hear the tender words of mother.

TABLE OF CONTENTS

SOME PEOPLE DON'T LIKE TO LAUGH	1
HOW I CAME TO BIG BOTTOM CHURCH	11
A MAJOR CONCERN	17
TOSSED ON THE BOTTOM	23
KNICK KNACK PATTY WHACK	28
MEETING JANE WINFIELD	37
ON THE MOVE	44
FOUR DOLLAR BOX	49
GETTING STARTED AT BIG BOTTOM	56
THE MEETING	62
OUT OF THE FRYING PAN	69
INTO THE FIRE	75
FINISHING A TOUGH WEEK	83
TOUCHDOWN	90
SUNDAY STARTS A NEW WEEK	98
JOHN ANDERSON TAKES A STAND	109
DEACONS' MEETING IS NOT OVER	117
W	123
WITCH HUNT	130
CHRIST AND CULTURE	135
VISITING THE WASHBURNS	141
TWICE CAUTIOUS	149
PLEASE ANNOUNCE THIS	155
THE CHURCH IS ALL ABUZZ	164
A HOUSE NEVER VISITED	173
DIRTY PANTS	180
HIT ME AGAIN	186
GRACE	197
PREACHING	204

SUPPER WITH THE OFFICERS	214
MORNING BEFORE THE MISSION TRIP	225
AFTERNOON BEFORE THE MISSION TRIP	233
ALL ABOARD?	244
LEAVING ON A JET PLANE	254

PREFACE

Big Bottom Church shows the adventures and misadventures of Pastor Brent Paulson and the congregation of Big Bottom Baptist. Some are flat-out funny while others touch deep emotions. Although the church and all the characters within these pages are fictional, every pastor has known similar people: the considerate and the crabby, the compassionate and the cantankerous.

One of the characters you'll meet in these pages is Early Washburn. Early speaks in (often mixed-up) clichés. He'd say it like this: "If you keep your chin up and your eyes on the ball you'll see it takes all kinds of people to make the world go round." Or he might say, "Don't count your chickens before they're fried."

Big Bottom Church captures some of life's great issues, yet with an entertaining tone. Last time I looked, it's not a sin to laugh. In fact, the Bible calls laughter a medicine. Help yourself to a healthy dose within these pages. And wash it down with deep gulps of the grace of God.

SOME PEOPLE DON'T LIKE TO LAUGH

In my first week of pastoring Big Bottom Baptist Church, before Darla and I had finished unpacking, I got in trouble with some of Big Bottom's more upstanding members. It happened at a funeral.

The issue? Laughter. I'm one pastor who doesn't subscribe to the idea that a Christian goes around with a face long enough to eat ice cream from a bowl on the floor. As I read the Bible, I see that Jesus came to bring abundant life, and part of that abundance is humor. Because of that, I tell a joke or employ a play on words, or add a zinger in my sermons. I've found most people like a little spice in their food and in their Sunday servings, too.

Deacon H. H. Smith criticized my use of humor. He'd already retired when I met him, but he hadn't aged with grace. A large man with tufts of hair sprouting from his nose and both ears, H. H. smelled of Old Spice. He weighed too much and his hanging jowls added to his somber expression. His jaws waddled back and forth like bowls of shaken jello, especially when he criticized someone.

Seminary hadn't prepared me to handle old men who didn't know what they wanted in life but were mad at everyone who did. After H. H. passed judgment on a friend for fishing the "wrong way," his friend told him, "Your thinking is just like concrete—thoroughly mixed up and permanently set."

H. H. didn't just hold strong opinions; he let them fly toward anyone with opposing views. They exploded from his mouth like rounds from a machine gun. He heard me share a joke when I preached at Big Bottom Church the morning the congregation voted on my coming as pastor. Afterward, he told me the lesson he'd learned as a child from his mother. "A pulpit in a church is like a headstone in a cemetery. It's never a place for laughter." Both sides of his chin continued to shake several seconds after he'd finished his complaint, as if he were still speaking but not opening his mouth. Coming from a deacon officer, his was more than a word of disapproval: it was admonition not to let it happen again.

Far be it from me to correct a mother, but I don't believe H. H.'s mom received her notion from reading the Bible. I'd say she's dead wrong but it wouldn't be funny. Her concept was one of the strangest I'd ever heard. In fairness to her, I'll bet H. H. had been a rambunctious child and she'd tried to keep him quiet in church the day she'd told him that. H. H. was so ornery he had to have gotten started at it in childhood. Meanness doesn't just happen overnight.

H. H. was wrong about laughter. The disciples must've doubled over with guffaws when they visualized the image Jesus used of the man who needed to get the log out of his own eye before he got the sawdust out of someone else's. They howled at Jesus' picture of a hypocrite who strained at a gnat and swallowed a camel. Many sayings in the Bible caused the original readers to hold their sides with laughter.

Having received H. H.'s stern warning not to let it happen again, I began my ministry at Big Bottom Church. Within the first week laughter poured forth like I had never before witnessed.

Two days after I visited shut-in Jane Winfield, a call came from Haslet Funeral Home to inform me of the death of a Miss Winfield. A wave of nausea hit me because I liked Jane so much and thought she'd be a person of wisdom from whom I could learn. I'd only known her two days, but I felt grief like I'd lost a good friend.

I cancelled my appointments and rushed over to Jane's house. Even though she'd lived alone, I thought some extended family might be there and I could give them comfort and a pastoral presence.

Instead of pressing the oval doorbell as I had in my first visit to the home, I knocked on the side door. Footsteps from within the home told me someone was there. Imagine my surprise when Jane opened the door. I said the first thing that came to mind, "I thought you'd died!"

"I don't think so," she replied. "Let me see." She made a big swoop with her arm to create a show and brought it back down to pinch her leg for dramatic flair. After the big production she said, "Nope, I feel pain. Must still be alive. Shucks. I thought I'd died and gone to heaven and God'd given me a husband." She did all this as she looked straight into my eyes, but her broadening smile gave away her sense of humor.

When I got over the initial shock, we had a laugh together and I mentioned to her the call I'd gotten from Haslet Funeral Home. Her sister, June, from New Orleans, had died. Both ladies were in their eighties, both had taught children's classes in Sunday school, and poor health had plagued both. Jane had expected her sister's death for some time. She said, "I'd lost the June I knew a year ago when she had her stroke."

Because of her sister's lingering illness, death came as a relief. Jane scheduled the funeral at Haslet Funeral Home in Hattiesburg with the burial to follow in Metairie, Louisiana. She asked me to conduct the services on Saturday morning, my first Saturday as pastor of Big Bottom Baptist Church.

The funeral home was an ancient, two-story Tudor building in downtown Hattiesburg equipped with fine furnishings and oak floors, darkened with age that creaked with each step. Haslet's was well-known for its motto, displayed on a large sign in front of their building, "The last folks to let you down."

At the funeral two ladies and a man shared about Miss June Winfield's teachings when they'd been children in her Sunday school class. Jane Winfield's two remaining sisters called June an outstanding woman of faith. If she'd been as fun-loving as Jane, I wished I had known her, too. The dear lady hadn't lived in the area for fifty years, however, so most of the people she knew had either died or moved. Only forty people attended the funeral. Half of those were members of Wanda Washburn's Elite Ladies Sunday school class.

Crowds show up for funerals in South Mississippi, but this one was small because June had been gone from the area for decades. I felt for Jane and her sisters because, as a rule, we don't skimp on care when we send folks off to the great beyond. It's one of the things I like so much about Big Bottom. The way people treat the dead tells much about how they value the living. At Big Bottom Church we value the living—at least most of them.

After the funeral the benevolence committee, headed by Carolyn Broome, served a buffet that would rival any in the state. Darla and I had met Carolyn when she served on the Pastor Search Committee. She was fortyish, short and rotund, with a smile that ran from ear to ear and a charm about her that invited Darla and me to join her world. A true Southern lady, she had an obvious gift of hospitality. When she spoke of her tireless work to aid refugees from hurricanes in Florida, Alabama, Mississippi, and Louisiana, she did so with tears in her eyes. She possessed a special knack of making everyone feel cared for and important. Carolyn reached out to touch the arm of anyone with whom she talked. Her hand felt warm and reminded me of my mother's touch when I was sick and needed additional assurance.

The church fellowship hall was lined with at least fifty offerings from some of Big Bottom's finest cooks. The good food and the opportunity for sharing memories around the tables made me proud of the committee and their selfless giving of time to comfort these sisters. I noticed Carolyn took time to speak with the three sisters, touching their arms all the while.

After the meal we drove to Metairie, more than a hundred miles southwest, for the interment. Much of Metairie, a suburb of New Orleans, and the surrounding areas south of Lake Ponchatrain are below sea level. A large levee system and dozens of massive pumps keep the water out. That's the only region I know where bodies are buried four feet deep, not the standard six feet.

The difficulty arrived with a two-inch rain on Friday afternoon, after workmen removed the dirt from the burial plot. The rule of thumb for interments is that the men on the burial crew turn back the soil next to the grave and then the funeral home staff overlay it with green carpet they call "grass." Chairs are situated in front of the gravesite for family members attending the committal service, and a tent is erected for protection from the elements. In this case, however, the rain saturated the dirt before the carpeted turf could be laid or the tent raised. The employees had placed the grass over a mound of mire.

I suspected trouble when we arrived at the grave site. The nearby cemetery building was ringed by huge balloons with the imprinted words, "Gone but not forgotten." I knew New Orleans did funerals in a more celebrative fashion than most of the country, but the festive atmosphere seemed a little much. I later discovered the balloons were remnants of a party thrown that morning for a retiring employee of the cemetery.

I led the processional from the hearse to the grave; but, again, something didn't seem right. I think it was the motto on the black Haslet Funeral Home tent. The tent made a picturesque setting against the green grass and the blue sky, but "Last to let you down" was stitched in large, gold letters on the side facing the hearse.

The Haslet Funeral Home personnel wore snappy suits. I thought it tacky, though, that their suits came with a two-inch, black patch over the right chest, also with the gold stitching, "Last to let you down." Black and gold must've been chosen because they're the colors of the University of Southern Mississippi. I guess the Haslets didn't want to fail to show their support for their athletic teams whether on the artificial turf of the gridiron or the artificial grass of the grave.

The cemetery smelled like a newly plowed field but with a sweet addition—a small sassafras tree had been unearthed from its place over the burial plot and lay beside the mound of mire. Southerners used to make tea by boiling the roots of the sassafras. In this case the damp air kept the odor from being dispersed and so the sweet smell came close to making me queasy.

As soon as I stepped on the carpeted grass, it sank about three inches. The pallbearers, with the added weight of the casket, made valleys of six inches with each step and had to struggle to maintain their balance. Since only three ladies were to sit in the family area for the committal, however, I still hoped the service could be completed without an accident and with the dignity every person deserves.

Haslet's men set up three lightweight, aluminum chairs, attached them to one another for stability, and stationed them in front of the casket for the aged sisters. All three used walkers: Jane for back problems that affected her balance, one sister for a hip surgery, and the other for a knee replacement gone awry. Each needed assistance to her chair.

The Haslet personnel helped Miss Winfield, but were slowed several times when the prongs of her walker needed to be unstuck from the indentions made in the grass. She sat and the connected chairs for a moment swayed onto their back legs, but soon righted. The second sister was assisted in the same way and with the same slowdowns from the impressions in the turf. She sat and the coupled chairs tilted precipitously, but again returned to the upright position.

The third sister weighed as much as the other two combined. Twice she almost fell from the ruts in the grass, despite the help of her walker and two assistants. With considerable effort she made the transition from the walker to the chair. When she sat, however, she didn't ease into the seat. She couldn't. She plopped down. As soon as her weight hit the seat, the three linked chairs flipped backward and landed with a thump. An audible gasp emerged from the assembly. The three sisters still remained in the chairs, but their backs were on the grass and their legs in the air.

Their six legs bicycled the air for fifteen seconds before the funeral home men could collect their wits enough to respond. "What do we do now?" was written with fright on their faces as they shot anxious glances back and forth. One of the men was built like a jockey. He knelt next to the largest sister while the stocky man knelt on the other end by Jane. Both placed one arm over the shoulder of the sister closest to him, and, with difficulty, worked another arm between the chair backs and the grass.

With a "one, two, three, heave," the two attempted to set the three chairs upright again. It would have worked, too, except the small funeral home worker couldn't budge the largest sister. The chairs rose on one end but remained anchored in the six-inch depression the fall had made in the other end. The pallbearers began to snicker. Their volume increased when the big woman wouldn't budge despite the "Ugh" let out by the smaller worker each time he attempted to lift her. The other two sisters, still in their connected chairs, were eased back to the grass.

The two men whispered for thirty seconds, strategizing their next move while the six legs continued to beat the air. At last they switched sides and tried the same tactic with the stronger of the two lifting the heaviest sister. After, "one, two, three, heave," both sides of the chairs lifted from the grass. A loud "thwap" came from the side of the largest sister, a sound similar to that a foot makes when pulled free from the mud. The men raised the chairs upright again and a few of the onlookers clapped. Judgmental looks from the funeral personnel shut down the applause, but merely muffled the laughter, since now it occurred behind hands with handkerchiefs placed over mouths.

Even though the three chair backs were raised they still had a tendency to tilt as if pulled by an invisible mud magnet that wanted to reclaim its victims. To brace them, the larger of the men placed both hands on the back of the largest sister's chair. For the rest of the proceedings he continued to push against it like a football lineman pushes a sled in spring training. In general, funeral home employees are a model of decorum but this one looked funny stretched out behind the chair.

I had a hard time keeping from laughing when the suction made as the chair emerged from the mud pulled a small blob through a seam in the carpeted grass. The muck landed on the patch sewed on the workman's suit so that instead of reading, "last to let you down," it now read, "let you down."

Although the workmen nodded to me to proceed, I worried about the three sisters. They were in poor health, they'd lost their sister, and now they'd suffered an indignity. Jane looked unfazed, but I waited to begin my part until she spoke with her sisters and turned to me with a smile and a nod. Since it was obvious the three sisters were not hurt, I tried to salvage the situation by closing out the cemetery service with the reading of two brief scriptures instead of the five I'd chosen earlier.

After I completed one of the passages and began the other, I looked up. Three of the six pallbearers had covered their mouths to block their laughter. Two others had turned their backs to keep the sisters from seeing their lack of gravity. The last had fallen to the damp ground behind the stands of flowers and held his convulsing side with one hand, but his other hand blocked the swelling reservoir of hilarity threatening to burst from his mouth at any second.

I concealed my face with my uplifted Bible, as if I needed to get the scripture close to my eyes to read, and choked back my own laughter as best I could. I felt the tears trickling down my cheeks. I silently asked God to help me get through this without breaking up. I finished the reading, and concluded with a brief prayer.

Somehow I didn't think Miss Winfield would be upset. Nevertheless, the question lingered in my mind. So I asked her about it when I visited in her parlor the following week. "Don't worry about it," she said. "These things happen. Lighten up and laugh a little. Life is over too soon. Don't take yourself with such seriousness."

Her words struck home because I'd been concerned about H. H.'s criticism of me. Added to that were the strains of moving to a new church and community, leaving our youngest son over five hundred miles away in college, and a graveside service that resembled a pro wrestling match. No doubt about it, I'd allowed worry to seep in. But then Jane told me words I'll never forget.

"Pastor," she said, lifting her left eyebrow like I noticed she'd do as a prelude to a wise saying, "laughter is a control issue."

"What do you mean?"

Jane Winfield raised her left eyebrow again, this time just a fraction of an inch. She sat forward in her chair, patted my left arm, and spoke in a quiet voice as if someone would overhear us, "I worry about people who seldom laugh. They're the same people who try to run everything. We can't control everything that happens in life. And when we laugh it says that we're serious about God but not so much about ourselves and others."

"Hmm," I said, bringing my hand to my chin, "I think you've got something there. How'd you learn that?"

"I've just watched people through the years." She sat back and relaxed. "You can learn a lot if you'll observe how people act and ask God to show you why they do what they do."

"I think I'll start asking God to show me when I don't understand people," I said. I'd already had several opportunities in my first week as pastor of Big Bottom. I'd soon get lots more.

"You'll be surprised when you do. Now about that humor thing, think about it," she said, lifting her left eyebrow a third time. "When parents have a toddler and he's trying to put together words, he'll often mouth funny sounds or make crazy mistakes. What do the parents do? They don't try to discourage him, but they do laugh. If he learns to laugh at himself, as most children do, he'll try again and soon he'll learn. You just watch children. They laugh a lot more than adults do. They also learn a lot more each day. We're God's children. Don't you think He often laughs at us?"

"I think He laughs at some of us a lot more than others."

"Yeah," she replied, a wide smile brightening her face and making her eyes sparkle, "like at the funeral. Have you ever seen anything so funny in all your life? Once we got home and got to talking about it, my sisters and I couldn't stop laughing. There we were, the three of us sisters, still sitting in the chairs with our backs on the ground and our legs kicking in the air." Jane waved with a broad sweep of her arms as if she were wiping out what was in front of her and recreating the scene once more.

"After I got over the shock, it felt like we were all on the kindergarten playground again. Hilarious! I thought I'd never quit laughing. My sister was no stick-in-the-mud. She'd have loved it.

"Yes, when we see our downfalls in life—literal or symbolic—what can we do except trust God and join Him in laughter. Just like that two-year-old does with his parents."

I came to Big Bottom to minister to folks, but I'd already found wise people like Miss Winfield ministering to me. I earned a doctoral degree, but Jane's wisdom far exceeded mine. God seemed to be saying, "Brent, listen to this lady. She tells it like it is. She's wise. She'll teach you some things I want you to learn."

Two-thirds of the people at the cemetery laughed that day—the funeral home employees, the sisters, the pallbearers, the guests, and me. Everyone, except Wanda Washburn, her husband Early, and members of Wanda's Elite Ladies Sunday School Class. They'd made the trip to show respect to Miss Winfield.

When the three chairs fell, I'd heard Early say, "What goes down must come up." When they were lifted, he said, "Up from the grave she arose." He never cracked a smile, though. At the same time Wanda mouthed the words, "Well, I never . . ." Something told me I'd hear from her again.

As I thought about the situation later, I asked God, "Would you help me understand Wanda and Early?"

I didn't hear an audible reply, but I intuited an instant response, "You've been praying to be more like Jesus. Now do you understand how He felt when the Pharisees came around?"

2
HOW I CAME TO BIG BOTTOM CHURCH

"How'd you like to move to a church near where you grew up?" Curt asked. I'd answered the phone call from a pastor friend.

"I'm fine, Curt; thanks for asking. How are you? How's Sandra? And the kids?"

"No," he said. "I didn't call for niceties. We've got enough of those at church. We're okay, but I called to tell you I've heard about a church in Lamar County, near Hattiesburg. They've lost their pastor. Aren't you from that part of Mississippi?"

"Well, yeah, Curt, but you know I'm happy here at First Baptist." I hadn't told the entire truth. The church was doing well, but I was beginning to struggle—a kind of undefined unease that came when God wanted to teach me something, or when I got out of touch with Him, or when I became competent with a job but a little bored with the routine. Maybe God did want me to move.

Curt knew how I felt because he and I had met every few weeks since a rally of Promise Keepers in our state. We'd shared things we told no one else, except our wives. Most men, even pastors, have a hard time talking about personal thoughts and feelings, but the PK group gave us impetus to try.

"Besides that, when'd you ever get together with your old buddy for golf or prayer if I moved two states south?"

Curt had a flat-top haircut, a throwback to the 1960s. He also had a 1960s no-nonsense approach to ministry that left him with little time for hobbies except an occasional golf game. "I hate to get all spiritual on you, Brent, but when I prayed for you the other day, this idea popped into my mind—to submit your resume to that church. I took it the Holy Spirit put that on my heart. You going to obey the Holy Spirit or not?"

"You're hitting below the belt, aren't you?" One reason I liked Curt Jones was his directness. I never had to guess where I stood with him.

"Tell you what, you pray about it and see if God's leading you."

"Ok, I'll do it. And thanks for thinking about me."

"Sure. We pastors need each another. In the meantime, while you're praying, try to imagine all that fried catfish down in Mississippi."

"You rascal. You know how much I love catfish. By the way, Curt, what's the name of that church?" It'd been thirty years since I moved from my home state of Mississippi; but occasional visits and phone calls several times a week with my parents, who still lived near Hattiesburg, kept me up to date with the area.

"I think it's Sit Down Baptist or something like that," Curt said. "Man at the preaching conference told me about it. Name sounded funny, but he said it's a good church and Hattiesburg is growing out that way, so it's got potential."

"You mean Big Bottom Baptist?"

"Yeah, that's it. Sorry about that; must've conjured up something."

"I'll pray about it and talk with Darla and get back with you on Monday when we meet for the men's group."

The name does sound funny, doesn't it? There's an old saying, "a rose by any other name would smell as sweet." Least, that's how I think

Shakespeare said it. Would the people of Big Bottom Baptist be as obese as the church name indicated?

Darla and I didn't want to refuse to go to a place just because the name was unusual. After all, God sent one of King Saul's grandsons to Lo Debar and that name sounds like what people used to say in a limbo contest. Jonah took a ship towards Tarshish. That city sounds like the combination of the tartar sauce spread on a fish sandwich and the relish put on a hot dog. One of the churches in Revelation is called Smyrna. That sounds like one of those jellies Smuckers would market.

Unusual names of churches began to pop into my mind. Harmony Baptist Church No. 2 is in central Kentucky. The No. 2 distinguishes it from the original Harmony Church. Story goes they split because of disharmony. I once told about those names in a revival meeting to emphasize the necessity of getting along. After the meeting a man who'd moved from Eastern Kentucky told me of three churches near where he grew up: Unity Baptist No. 3, Unity Baptist No. 2, and Unity Baptist. They'd split three ways—because of disunity.

It's not easy to live up to a name. I've not always lived up to mine. I wear the name "Christian." I find joy and purpose in Christ. And I believe the Bible. I've found it's easier to believe than to live, though. I'm still on the journey. So how could I discriminate against a church just because their name sounds odd?

A church with a strange name called my friend Dirk James. He became pastor of Rock Star Baptist Church. We called him the leader of the Rock Star band of believers. He later found the church took her name from the community and the community took its name from an explorer who'd chiseled a star into a large rock. Why didn't they call it Star Rock instead of Rock Star? I suppose rock stars were not around years ago when the church and community were named. At any rate, my friend had eight wonderful years there. That gave me hope a pastor could thrive in a church with an odd name.

From having grown up in the area, I knew Big Bottom took its name from a family of earlier settlers who'd established a stopping off place for trains between New Orleans and Atlanta. When the area was surveyed one stifling July, the surveyor wrote in pencil with a sweaty hand. He'd labeled a low place around Black Creek as "bc;" however, his pencil smeared and it looked like "bb." The people of the area assumed he was referring to the low, swampy area as "Big Bottom." A pencil and perspiration gave a name that was taken up by the train depot, a store, and the local church.

It struck me that the people could have named the area "Bare Bottom," because that's what it looked like after the swamp was drained and the trees died. I envisioned a church sign for Bare Bottom Baptist Church featuring the church logo of the Coppertone Sun Screen child with the dog pulling off the bathing suit. If the name kept people away from Big Bottom Church, imagine how it would keep people away from Bare Bottom.

The original surveyor later moved to the area and told the people of their error about the name from his survey notes. By that time, though, the train depot, the church, and the store had signs denoting their names, so they figured it easier to run the man out of town than to change the name of their signs. And that's what they did.

In time the trains were rerouted. Only a store, the church, and a few scattered homes remained. The railroad tracks remained, too, but they were paved over a few years ago and turned into Long Leaf Trace, a running and bike trail. The area is five miles west of Hattiesburg, not far off Highway 98. Hattiesburg's growth spilled into Big Bottom and beyond.

When I was growing up, the region centered on Lake Shady, a recreational area run by the Hennington family. The owner, Henry, and my dad were friends. We hunted deer and fished on land he leased along the Chickasawhay River in Greene County and we sometimes visited Lake Shady on Sunday afternoons. I recalled the brown recreational center with its concrete floor and long, screened porch perched on a hill overlooking the sandy beach. Lake Shady had been renamed Lake Serene and now held over a thousand homes in subdivisions on both sides of Highway 98.

While single family homes composed the majority of housing in the area, students from the nearby University of Southern Mississippi and William Carey University lived in multiple apartment buildings. The region mixed hospital personnel and home health aides, lawyers and laborers, construction workers and computer geeks, school teachers and social workers, business people and bus drivers. Urban professionals and landed gentry blended with day laborers and immigrants. Who'd have ever thought Big Bottom would become so multicultural? Singles and married folks, the educated and the uneducated, the wealthy and the impoverished all called it home. Country, city, and suburbia blended. Darla and I found the mix refreshing.

We faced a problem. We didn't want to leave the folks I'd pastored in Kentucky for the last ten years. We'd raised our boys there. We loved the people. Many of them were like family. Could we ever be as close to another group of people as we were to them? The church in Kentucky was unified and the staff was strong.

We struggled with the decision. We would have to leave our second son in college at nearby University of Southern Indiana. Although he was independent, he'd miss our being close and without a doubt we'd miss him. We didn't worry as much about our older son because he was married and practicing law in Memphis and would be about as close to us in Mississippi as in Kentucky. The thought of leaving our granddaughter, Claire, however, seemed more than we could bear. How could we make it without seeing her smile, blond hair, and precious dimple or holding her in our arms every day or two?

Yet there was this pull inside. I didn't know if it was my pull to a church that had more potential to grow or if it was my own greed to provide better for my family. It could be sinful pride, the desire to pastor a larger church. I struggled with the decision for weeks. One day I'd feel a definite leading of the Lord. The next I'd second guess the decision and feel under conviction for being selfish.

We decided not to turn in my resume. Instead, we'd pray. We asked the Lord to have a second person contact us within the next three months to request a resume, if that was what He wanted. Although we didn't want to miss God's leadership, we didn't want to get ahead of His leading, either.

The day after we raised that specific prayer, an old friend from seminary called to say he wanted to submit my name to a search committee from a church outside Hattiesburg if we would allow him to do so. God had answered our specific prayer so I couldn't refuse. I sent him my resume to give to the committee.

My life verses are Proverbs 3: 5-6. "Trust in the Lord with all your heart and do not lean on your own understanding. In all your ways acknowledge Him, and He will direct your paths." We prayed, "God, if you have Big Bottom in mind for a new stage in our journey with You, continue to show us and we'll follow; but if not, please close the door."

Two weeks later I received a call from S. A. Tanner, an outgoing man who described himself as "a friend to almost everyone." He also chaired the pastor search committee. We talked for at least an hour.

It turned out that he grew up in the area, as I had and, also like me, had played basketball for Oak Grove High School. S. A. told me he'd even been chosen by his team as "Most Offensive Player."

"You mean Best Offensive Player, don't you?" I asked.

"No, that may have been what they called it when you graduated, but I've got the trophy to prove I was elected Most Offensive Player."

He asked me about several neighbors I'd had growing up in the Lamar Parks subdivision west of Hattiesburg. We also made a connection with quite a few people both he and I knew from Oak Grove School. He asked about my relatives in the Big Bottom area. Satisfied with our common associations, he hinted he'd call back.

The next day I received phone calls from some of the people we'd talked about. Tanner had phoned each one to check me out. This indicated thoroughness to me and made me glad that committee chairman Tanner performed his task well. In three days he called again. And that's how Darla and I began our journey back to our home state and to Big Bottom Baptist Church. We didn't know serious trouble awaited us. We would soon find out S. A. Tanner deserved his trophy.

A MAJOR CONCERN 3

Darla and I had met at the University of Southern Mississippi in a gathering of Inter-Varsity Christian Fellowship. I led the group that year, and at one meeting a beautiful, red-haired girl swept in with other co-eds who shared her apartment. I don't remember either the guest speaker or the topic that night; couldn't remember, my mind had turned to mush. I could think of nothing but Darla. After the meeting I followed the girls to their apartment where Darla and I talked for hours. That began an intense year of growing in the Lord and in love with one another. We married three months before going to Southern Baptist Theological Seminary in Louisville, Kentucky.

We had apprehensions about moving back to Mississippi. Darla had grown up in Pascagoula, on the Mississippi coast. I'd grown up in a suburb just outside Hattiesburg and two miles east of Big Bottom. We'd spent the first twenty-three years of our lives in a culture of racial prejudice. We loved our parents and relatives and enjoyed spending a week or two with them back in Mississippi each year. However, we couldn't deny a darkness hung over the area, a darkness we could feel like a heavy blanket that dropped over us when we'd return, a darkness brought on by inequality.

Mississippi is a great state. It's beautiful. Tall pines, giant live oaks, magnolias, open fields, and woods. Gorgeous lakes and beaches. Its writers, musicians, artisans, and ball players compare well with those of other states. And you can't beat the friendliness and courtesy of the people. It's just that we remembered our growing-up years when that friendliness and courtesy didn't extend to people whose skin wasn't white.

I remembered riding the school bus from the suburbs west of Hattiesburg to Oak Grove School, five miles away. Along the route we passed two homes of black families. The children from those homes had to travel to their own school, eleven miles away. Even as a child, despite what I heard from my elders, I didn't think that was right.

Even though Darla's area wasn't as bigoted as mine, she'd seen plenty of examples of injustice, too. Mississippi had improved by leaps and bounds over the years—in some ways more than other states—but we knew the area still had a long way to go. Could we minister in this setting?

We knew no place is perfect and we knew we weren't either. After praying together one night, Darla asked me, "Do you think one of the reasons God might be sending us back to Mississippi is to share His love for all people?"

I remembered driving along Highway 98 late one night as a freshman in college. I saw a car at my uncle's grocery and gas station. All the lights were out. I knew my uncle and aunt had gone to bed hours earlier, so I suspected someone had had car trouble. Sure enough, as I pulled into the graveled entrance I saw a young black lady standing beside a car with its hood up.

I knew nothing about how to fix a car but I could see the young lady's hands shaking. I would have been scared, too, if I had been a black lady whose car had stopped late at night in rural Mississippi during the height of civil unrest. The only thing worse for her than to have had her car stop would have been to have seen a white boy drive up. Back in the days before cell phones people had to depend on prayer and the help of others. I'll bet she got serious with God that night.

The first thing I said when I drove up was, "Don't worry, Ma'am. I'm a Christian. I'm not going to hurt you. I just thought you might have had some car trouble and you might need some help."

She said, "Hallelujah. There's a God in heaven who still answers the prayers of His children!"

We couldn't start the car, so we pushed it to the side and left a note on it for my uncle and aunt to read the next day. Then I drove her the seven miles to her home. Similar scenes happened about ten times during my college years. I hadn't stopped only to help in a temporary distress but to show one more person, and another, and then another, that all white Christians weren't prejudiced.

The Lord taught me through these situations. He'd taught me people in need don't care about the skin color of the one who helps. Imagine my surprise when I had a flat and the first person to help change my tire was a person of color. Our needs go deeper than our prejudices.

What is true in the physical realm is also true in the spiritual. The first person I had the privilege of leading to receive the Savior was Valerie, a black coed at USM. I'd seen Valerie at our Inter-Varsity Christian Fellowship meeting the previous week and saw her again getting a cola at the student union. When I asked permission, she allowed me to pull up one of the bentwood chairs to the round table to talk with her. There was a buzz of activity, as the "Hub" was always alive with students coming and going.

Valerie was a slender beauty from the Laurel, Mississippi, area. She'd grown up in a devout home and had a cavernous desire for the Lord; but, "How do you know Him for yourself?" was her question. We talked about Jesus for some time and then crossed the street to the Danforth Chapel.

Once inside the twelve-foot-tall poplar doors, we sat on the pews and talked another few minutes. When it was obvious she wanted to become a Christian, we made our way to the front where we kneeled for prayer. I heard Valerie say, "Dear Lord Jesus, I know I am a sinner. I've tried to do things on my own but they haven't worked out. I need you, Lord. Please forgive my sin and come live inside my heart and help me live for you."

Valerie knelt unforgiven, but stood as a brand new person. Her face glowed. Her smile radiated. She walked taller. It was as if a fifty-pound load had been lifted from her shoulders. I was just as excited for her. We left the chapel and raced along the concrete sidewalks until we found some other Christians. She shared the good news that she'd come to know the Lord Jesus, and we rejoiced all over again.

Last I heard Valerie was preparing for missions overseas. Her openness to Christ helped me become a cross-cultural witness. Years later, that enabled Darla and me to move with our two boys and serve five years as missionaries in South Korea.

Maybe the Lord was sending us back to our home state to encourage people to be a witness to all folks, regardless of color. Would the people of Big Bottom Baptist Church welcome black people and internationals into their congregation? I couldn't be their pastor if they wouldn't. It was a high-priority question.

Imagine my surprise when Darla and I met with the pastor search committee after their visit to the First Baptist Church where I pastored. Eight members comprised the committee and one would soon become a good friend. Dr. Samuel Jones was the first black professor of philosophy and religion at the University of Southern Mississippi and vice-chairman of the committee.

Later I found the church hosted a Spanish-speaking mission. Also, of twenty-five hundred members of Big Bottom, about forty were black and another fifty were from countries other than the United States. While still small in percentage, the triple facts of the church having numerous minority members, having a cross-cultural mission, and electing Dr. Jones to the search committee spoke to me of an openness to reach all people for Christ. So this was the new Mississippi? We just might like it.

S. A. Tanner, the chairman of the search committee, had asked me about the committee's coming to visit the two morning worship services of First Baptist on the second Sunday in January. They did, and stuck out like a sore thumb. Although they chose seats in various parts of our hundred-year-old building and split their attendance between the first morning worship and the second, Darla and I still feared they'd be conspicuous.

Baptist churches are congregational in polity and choose their pastors by committees elected by the individual churches. This sounds good because the selection involves the free choice of the committee, the pastor and his family, and the congregation. The reality can be frightening. Inexperienced committee members come into a worship service of a prospective pastor to visit. When welcomed by church members and asked if they're new in town, search committees sometimes lie. "In a Christian way, of course," as committee member Betta Lovett said, "only to protect the church."

If a search committee is recognized and the pastor doesn't leave soon, he becomes a "lame duck" pastor because the congregation knows he's thinking about leaving. My friend, Curt, came close to that experience. He loved the church he pastored and wanted to stay. He grew troubled one Sunday morning, however, when he saw a search committee, uninvited, and seated together in his morning worship service. Curt spoke with boldness at the end of the service and told the parishioners he couldn't control who attended the services, but that he loved them and wouldn't think of leaving them for another church.

Another pastor noticed a decided decline in attendance and spirit among the members of the church he pastored. After several weeks of this he asked some close friends, "What's up?" They told him of a committee who'd visited the large church a month earlier without his approval or knowledge, and noted word had gotten around he'd be leaving soon. Search committees can play havoc with a pastor who wishes to stay.

Despite this, the committee from Big Bottom decided the truthful thing to do would be to say they were from "out of town." I appreciated the honesty but they may as well have parked in front of the church in a van with Big Bottom Baptist Church stenciled on the side and hung a sign around their necks, "PASTOR SEARCH COMMITTEE." Flashing, neon lights above their seats wouldn't have been clearer. Darla and I believed the entire choir and most of the other attendees knew they were present. A light snow had begun falling outside the building. I thought it symbolic of the coolness toward the visitors within.

In times like these pastors rely on two verses of scripture. One is from Paul, "Be instant in season and out of season." Lots of days in Baptist churches are "out of season." The other is from John, "This too shall pass." And it did.

S. A. had asked me to arrange a luncheon "where we can talk" after our morning services at First Baptist. Darla and I set up the meeting in a side room of a famous barbeque restaurant forty miles away and prayed none of our members or friends would be making the trip for lunch that day. The light snow and God kept our members from risking the drive.

We piled into my old Ford van and one of their vehicles and drove to Moonlight Bar-B-Que. We admired the horse paraphernalia and the scales of an old cotton gin decorating the outside of the rustic building. Some on the committee leaned against the side of a narrow, iron-wheeled wagon and talked of the way things were when they grew up on their farms, two states away but with similar equipment.

The hickory smell of the restaurant filled the air. We waited in line while two of the older members of the committee sat in rocking chairs placed to help people take a load off their feet while they waited for good barbeque. After forty-five minutes, a hostess escorted us all to the side room and seated us at a long, rectangular table with a yellow-and-white-checkered table cloth.

We welcomed a committee from Mississippi with great Kentucky barbeque, carrot and raisin salad, a local Brunswick stew called burgoo, flat beans, corn, fried okra, mashed potatoes, English peas, corn bread, and a choice of lemon meringue pie or blackberry cobbler. I get hungry just thinking about it.

TOSSED ON THE BOTTOM

Darla and I liked most of the committee members and they liked us. No surprise. Over the years numerous people have told us we have "people" gifts. We enjoy meeting folks. I've met some who aren't my favorites, but I've never met a person from whom I couldn't learn something. I should've been alert to one of the questions asked, however.

"Pastor, do you always use humor in your sermons?" The question came from a thin-lipped lady with a slight frown and a wrinkle deepening between her eyebrows.

I'd told a joke during the sermon to help the congregation warm up. It'd worked with the congregation, but not with the most wooden member of the committee, Wanda Washburn. There's a fine line between being proper and being stilted. She'd crossed the line years ago.

Wanda was tall and slender with graying hair pulled in a bun behind her head. Her black, pleated dress adorned with simple, white buttons hung down to her ankles. I'd have guessed she belonged to the Pentecostal church had it not been for the single strand of pearls and the dab of make-up. Since she didn't ride in my van to the restaurant, Darla and I hadn't met her yet. I'd thought it a little strange when she introduced herself with a hand extended only six inches from her side, "I'm Wanda W. Washburn from the old line of families in Lamar County." The emphasis was on the "W" as if some people forget but I'd better not.

"Pleased to meet you," I said as I squeezed her hand. "It's nice of you folks to come all the way to Kentucky to visit with us." Her hand fell limp as if I'd dishonored her by too cordial a shake from a newcomer into her circle. Dr. Jones rushed in to hurry us into the buffet line where the smell of hickory-smoked barbeque called us.

The other committee members acted thrilled to see us. Darla and I asked about each person, about their families, and in what area each served the church. We found some interesting things. For one thing, the committee members had some of the strangest names we'd ever heard.

For another, we discovered that S. A. Tanner never meets a stranger. How do you spell e-x-t-r-o-v-e-r-t? He had an odd habit, though: trying to make connections with everyone he met by tracing their families to find some connection with his family or friends. Dr. Jones had to reel him in when S. A. continued a ten minute conversation with the waitress.

We were in Western Kentucky, but he found the waitress had roots three hundred miles away in the mountains of Eastern Kentucky. S. A. stood six-feet-two and weighed about 220 pounds. He seized the diminutive waitress' arm and pinned her wrist to the table. She squirmed under the pressure as Tanner droned on. Tanner traced his family tree on his mother's side into eastern Kentucky and found his great grandparents, the Jeffersons, were also in her family line.

Because of this unusual connection, S. A. announced to the committee, "We don't need to look any further. I prayed for a sign that Brent and Darla Paulson are the people for our church, and God's just given me a sign."

Compatibility with the committee wasn't the main issue for Darla and me. The question for us? "Is God in this?" That is, did our gifts and abilities fit what Big Bottom needed, and did God want us to move our ministry to Big Bottom Baptist Church? The fact the chairman found his sign in such an unusual way gave us concern. If such a tenuous connection signaled to S. A. we should come, would some other nebulous thing indicate to him we should leave?

It wasn't that I never paid attention to signs or coincidences. Big Bottom has similar initials to my name, B. P. I got chill bumps when I realized it. The thought ran through my head that B. P. (Brent Paulson) is for B. B. (Big Bottom). I dismissed this, however, knowing that blood pressure and BlackBerries also have similar initials but that learning how to use my BlackBerry had not been good for my blood pressure. God would confirm it in other ways if He wanted us there.

We found S. A. an active deacon who sometimes taught Sunday school, sang in the choir, and served as a greeter for the Wednesday night meal and for the prayer service. The church must've respected S. A. to elect him as chairman of the search committee; however, it troubled us when we found he had six grown children but that none were active in Big Bottom Church. Three lived in other states. One felt destined to membership in the local Presbyterian church, and the other two didn't consider themselves Christians. "But pastor, I'm not worried about them because God promises they'll come back around if we raise them right." He wasn't worried, but now we were.

Samuel Jones headed Big Bottom's international ministry, an active one for college students. USM, a school of fourteen thousand students, was just five miles away from Big Bottom. Samuel could have passed as a double for Tiger Woods. Students who were new to Southern Miss often asked him for an autograph, thinking Tiger had come to Hattiesburg for a tournament at Cane Creek or one of the other nearby golf courses.

In his late thirties, Samuel had wisdom far beyond his years. For over forty years his dad had pastored the Greater Corinth Baptist Church in Tyler, Texas. Samuel grew up in a home that stressed education and following Christ as ways of advancement. After graduating valedictorian of his class, Samuel went to Vanderbilt University for undergraduate work and to Yale for his doctorate in philosophy. The Dean of the College of Liberal Arts considered it a coup to land Samuel on the faculty of the Department of Religion and Philosophy. I found Samuel to be one of those rare individuals who could talk philosophy or fishing with equal zeal.

Wanda Washburn warmed up somewhat when I asked her role in the church. She lifted her chin and spoke with distinction, pausing after each word, "I teach the Elite Ladies' Bible Class." Wanda spoke the word "elite" with a higher pitch than the others.

"That's an unusual name, Wanda. How did the class arrive at the honor of such a distinguished name?" I asked.

"We wanted a descriptive title," she said, lifting her chin still higher, "and <u>everyone</u> knows the elite ladies."

I had to excuse myself for a few minutes, saying the barbeque or something wasn't sitting well with my stomach. This wasn't a deal breaker, but it was close. At the very least I knew if Darla and I went to Big Bottom I'd be doing a lot of preaching from James on practical Christianity and from First John about loving one another. How a Sunday school class, started to reach ladies, could exclude other ladies by its choice of name was beyond me. When Wanda spoke I caught glimpses of disgust on the faces of several committee members and knew something unsaid was happening.

Later I found the church elected the committee by secret ballot. Each church member could write up to eight names on their copy. The top vote getter would be the chairman, the second would be vice-chairman, and the next six would be on the committee. Wanda's Elite Ladies Bible Class had determined that all class members should vote for one and only one person. That way their votes would not be diluted and their candidate, teacher Wanda W. Washburn, would be a sure member of the search committee.

Some of the standards of the church had been dropping, they felt, and the Elite Ladies could help if they could bring in the right pastoral leadership to back them up. There were twenty-nine "Elite Ladies" present on the day of the ballot and Wanda received all those votes plus eight more from family members and friends, one more than enough to be the eighth person elected to the committee—and enough to shut out a more deserving nominee.

When I returned I found Darla conversing with the committee members. She's a good counterbalance to me. Things can get under my skin, but Darla has a deep inner peace, an ability to ride the waves above the stormy sea. I love my wife for it. She often reminds me of God's grace. If I want God to extend His grace to me, I've got to extend it to others, too.

Somehow the whole conversation had turned while I was gone. The committee now talked about the constituency of the congregation and what they wanted in a pastor. Their community had changed from rural to suburban. The church had changed with it, becoming diverse to a surprising degree. However, there were several sizable groups of people the church felt it should be reaching to a larger extent in order to reflect their proportion in the area's population. They wanted a pastor who could preach the word of God with accuracy, minister to the people, and lead the people and staff with passion to reach eastern Lamar County.

My gifts from God are encouragement, preaching, teaching, and evangelism. I have them, but I can't brag about them because I didn't earn them. God gave them to me. When the search committee explained the kind of pastor they wanted, I felt they described a picture of the passion and gifts God placed in my heart. After the meeting, Darla and I made our decision. Despite a couple of red flags, we believed God was in this. If the church called us, we'd have no choice but to go.

5
KNICK KNACK PATTY WHACK

The committee asked me to preach at Big Bottom Church in view of a call on the first Sunday of February. That's the typical way Baptist churches do things. The committee and prospective pastor agree God's will is for him to come. Then they hash out particulars about his role, salary and benefits. After they've come to terms, he preaches before the congregation. The congregation then votes for or against the new man to become their pastor.

Since the congregation elects the committee, as a rule they trust them enough to vote for the man the committee suggests. Notable exceptions occur. For instance, the church might have major problems of which the committee is unaware. Or, maybe there is friction about who is on the committee. In those cases even Jesus wouldn't receive a favorable vote. If a pastor receives many negative votes, just ten percent or so, he'll think long and hard before coming to the new church. To come with that many votes against him would mean he'd begin with a sizable block of folks opposing him before he even began.

Another thing that can happen is for the pastor to stumble his way through a sermon that doesn't touch the people or show vision for the future. I know some pastors who'd rather have a tooth pulled than go through this method of changing churches. They prefer the Methodist route where a pastor is appointed to a church by the district superintendent. They think it foolish to vote on a potential pastor based on a thirty-minute sermon. They know a pastor's time is given to many concerns and he shouldn't be judged by his pulpit performance alone.

I like the Baptist way, though. After all, week after week, a pastor touches more people with his Sunday sermons than in any other way. A congregational vote gives each member a voice in what each believes is God's will. Early in a new ministry, a pastor can count on the support of those who felt led to vote for him.

We drove down to Lamar County on Friday and rejoiced because the temperature was at least twenty degrees warmer and the sunshine highlighted the green needles on the pines. We spent a restful night with my parents. They were thrilled we might move much closer to them.

We awoke on Saturday morning to the smells of pork chops with biscuits and tomato gravy. Don't tell Darla, but nobody on earth can match Mom's biscuits or gravy cooked in her old iron skillet. It's obvious we'd have to get into some exercise regime or the penchant for terrific Southern foods would swell our waistlines. Big Bottom would describe more than a geographic area.

There's a reason Mississippi leads the nation in percentage of population with obesity. Many think it is because poverty forces people to eat things that are inexpensive and full of fat, like fried chicken. There may be some truth in that. Many of us in Mississippi don't know what cholesterol is. If we had some, though, we'd fry it. The part about fat-causing foods being inexpensive, however, is wrong. Have you paid for a meal in a catfish house or a KFC in the last few months? You may have had to take out a loan to do so. Some of us native Mississippians think the reason more from our state are overweight is that the cooking is better here. Plain and simple, food in Mississippi may not be better for you, but it sure does taste better.

Darla looked for houses while I met, one at a time, with the staff members of Big Bottom Church at the lake home of Sam and Denise Jones. Under the grand pines rising over a hundred feet above a well-manicured lawn and surrounding Sam's redwood deck, I needed only a light jacket on that warm winter day. We sat at the patio table while I asked each staff member about his or her ministry and spent a lot of time listening. I tried to hear what was said and what wasn't.

I found Carter Ross, above all others, interesting. He served as Associate Pastor and has had that role for well over a decade. He stood at least six feet, two inches and must have weighed close to three hundred pounds. He leaned forward whenever anyone talked and listened with great care, often reflecting back their words. He had a curious habit, though. Once in a while he would mix up his words and jerk his head at the same time.

I chalked it up to anxiety. It's a scary thing for a staff member when a new pastor comes. The new pastor might not desire their ministry in the church or he may wish to radically alter their roles. I'd picked up nothing from the pastor search committee that indicated any staff member needed to depart or that they should be doing something other than what they were doing. I wanted to assure each minister that I was no authoritarian leader. I wanted them to know I'd value and need their opinions and ministries, as long as we worked together as a team. I also wanted to express my expectation that each would take a leadership role in the outreach work of the church.

I was pleased with these initial meetings. I believed I'd fit in well with the staff. Having been through a change in senior pastors before, Carter had briefed the staff that change was possible and they needed to be prepared to support their new pastor. Each staff member seemed relieved that I hadn't wanted to change things right away. I picked up nothing negative.

On the first Sunday morning in February Darla and I got in the car early enough to arrive at Big Bottom more than forty minutes before the worship service. Having grown up in the vicinity I thought I knew exactly where to go. Fifteen minutes later it was obvious I'd taken a wrong turn. I would've cursed myself for not driving by the facilities earlier, except that I'm a Christian and cursing is not a fitting thing for a preacher to do on Sunday mornings prior to preaching.

Everything had grown up with shopping centers, subdivisions, and apartments everywhere. Nothing looked the same. I swallowed my pride and stopped to ask directions at a Gulf station on the corner of Oak Grove Road and Highway 98. We arrived flustered, but still twenty minutes before the service.

Darla and I parked in one of the spaces designated "Visitor Parking," since we had Kentucky plates on our car. Whether the church called us or not, this would be our last time to park in a visitor's spot. It felt good to park one building away from the sanctuary, as our church in Kentucky was downtown and parking there was at a premium.

We walked up the concrete sidewalk by the preschool building toward the sanctuary. We saw two couples ahead of us stop to pat a young child on the head. When we got to the child, we saw he was a boy about two years old and crying. There were no other adults around. Assuming he'd gotten out of his classroom by mistake and was lost, Darla and I stooped to talk with him.

He wouldn't tell us his name and he seemed frustrated. I took him by the hand to lead him back to the preschool area. He began to wail. Darla talked softly to him and he calmed down. I scooped him into my arms and held him for a moment. That seemed to be what he wanted. He didn't object when I took him into the door of the preschool building. I used soothing words with him all the way.

A lady in the preschool reception area looked at me with a curious stare. I noticed the pupils of her eyes widen. She said, "Mister, what are you doing with Alex Reynolds? Are you one of those preverts or something?"

I replied, "I think the word you are looking for is pervert but. . ."

Before I could finish my thought she jumped in again, this time in a loud voice. "Yeah, a pervert. Ladies we got us a pervert here. He said it himself."

Darla and I were flabbergasted. Before we could reply one of the children's teachers said, "Well, he's picked on the wrong child this time. Mister, you may not know it but Alex's dad is a deacon and an attorney. He won't just put you in jail; he'll throw you under it!" She reached for Alex and headed with him toward one of the nearby class rooms. As Alex was hurried away, I saw him turn his head back toward us and laugh, pleased he'd caused a disturbance.

"No, no, no. There's been a mistake. If I were a child molester, my wife wouldn't be by my side while I brought the child to you."

"Yeah," the receptionist said and I imagined the wheels turning inside her head. "I guess that's right. But how'd you come to have Alex when he's supposed to be in his room?"

"Darla and I were walking up the sidewalk. We saw the boy crying and figured he'd somehow gotten out of his room and needed to be brought back."

"Thank you, mister. Sorry about the confusion. Little Alex is a rounder. I don't think the room's ever been built that'll keep him in. There's not enough d's in A. D. D. to describe him."

Darla and I left with as little commotion as we could but felt every eye was on us. We stopped just outside the door of the preschool building. We were both breathing hard. Darla's red face now matched her red hair. "Brent, let's go home. There's no way we're ever going to recover from this. Let's just get in the car and drive back to Kentucky and pretend this never happened."

"Baby, we can't go now. It's ten minutes until the service time. They'd never find a preacher to fill in. There'll be a thousand people or so here. Who knows, maybe someone will be saved today. Satan may be trying to throw a roadblock in our path just before something good happens." I used every explanation I could think of to keep her from bolting. The unfounded accusation had disgusted us.

By then sweat was pouring from my forehead and my stomach ached. I excused myself to enter the bathroom just outside the sanctuary. I stepped into the men's restroom, entered the stall, and closed the door. Soon I heard a young man enter the outer door, talking with his friends.

"Hey, dudes, you staying for the worship service?" he said.

"Yeah, man, they're voting for a new pastor today and I'm gonna vote against him."

"Dawg, that's wrong. Why you do like that?"

"My Grandma's in the Elite Ladies Class, and she told me her teacher's not sure they got the right guy."

"For real?"

"That's what she said."

"Well, dude, you better pray about that. The committee's presenting him, and you don't wanna go against what God wants."

"I'll pray about it, but he'd better preach the Bible or I'll vote against him."

"You won't be the only one, either," another young voice said. "I heard an older man in the hallway say that he's going to vote against him, too. He said something about no Baptist vote should be unanimous, just to keep the leadership on their toes."

Hearing this didn't keep me on my toes, but it did keep me in the bathroom. I heard the water from the faucet turn off, the door close, and the footsteps trail away. My stomach hurt. When I eased out of the restroom door, my face must've looked pale, because Darla said, "Brent, are you sick? What's wrong, honey?"

I didn't have the heart to tell her. I just said, "Darla, we want to be sure this is the right place. Just pray, pray, pray during the service. We don't want to get out of the will of God."

I preached a message on prayer. We know Jesus had a three-year ministry; but when we put the events of His adult life side by side, we have only sixty distinct days of those three years. Yet Jesus had a dozen major teachings on prayer during that time. He often prayed and He taught His followers to pray and not give up.

I shared how the disciples could have asked Jesus to teach them how to witness or how to organize or how to advertise, but they didn't. They asked Him, "Teach us to pray." The reason, I believe, is they understood the power and wisdom of Jesus came from prayer.

I can't explain it, but something happened in the middle of the sermon. God took over. I felt great freedom to preach His word. The congregation must have felt it, too. They sat still enough to hear a pin drop. Three people joined the church that morning. Others came to kneel at the altar for prayer. When the secret ballots were counted, the vote came in 714 for and eight against.

Sam Jones came to the podium bearing a USM football jersey for me and a belt embossed with grits dyed with several colors and glued to the buckle to form a southern landscape. He gave a hat for Darla that displayed the acronym G.R.I.T.S. (Girls Raised in the South.) We celebrated and the church rejoiced with us.

After we moved in the fourth week of February, Sam Jones told me he'd found out about the restroom incident from some college students who overheard some teens bragging about what they'd done. The voices I'd heard were those of mischievous teens who'd learned their new pastor-to-be had stepped into the bathroom. By common consent, they'd decided to "turn up the heat on the new guy." They even placed dollar bets on whether or not they'd see me sweat.

They'd succeeded both in turning up the heat and in making me sweat. Though they meant it as a prank, I'm convinced God used it to force me to depend on Him. He has a way of doing that in my life. Though I've failed Him at times, when I seek Him and depend on Him, He's never failed me.

I didn't blame the young men. If their parents had found out, they'd either not be able to sit for a few days or wouldn't have car keys for a month. As I think about it, they were downright clever. I'd have done the same thing as a teen if I'd have thought of it or had possessed the nerve.

At any rate, we moved back home to Mississippi. Now we could try to apply the principles of church growth in a suburban setting. These had worked in a rural setting, in a small town, in a small city, and in a metropolitan area, but would they work in suburban Mississippi?

Furthermore, would they work among some people who'd known me before I became a pastor? We'd met at least thirty folks in church who remembered me from playing basketball at Oak Grove High School or from other events in my growing-up years. Jesus said a prophet is not without honor except in his hometown. Would these let me be their spiritual leader?

People from our home state had poured their lives into Darla and me while we were growing up. Now we could pour our lives into others from Mississippi. There was a sense of repaying a dept; this time paying it forward.

And, for the first time in years, we'd live close to our parents. Darla's dad had Alzheimer's. She'd be a hundred miles away, but that was far closer than the six hundred miles away we'd been living. Before, if our parents needed us, it took a day to drive home. Now we could drive to Darla's folks in two hours and to mine in ten minutes. We were even closer to many of my aunts and uncles who'd played pivotal roles in my life when I was growing up.

There is something about coming home that speaks to every heart. The offer to come back to Mississippi included benefits that couldn't be written into a financial package from a search committee. It included an offer to make my home near my relatives again. It meant moving back to my home county where some of the old trees, lakes, buildings, and farms were still familiar. It meant seeing my cousins' grandkids learn how to ride their bikes and play "alligator" in the old Black Creek swim hole.

Part of it was shelling butterbeans and talking for hours under the live oak trees. Fresh tomato sandwiches, deer sausage, yellow squash, watermelons, butterbeans, black-eyed peas, cantaloupes, and grits would be regular customers at our table. Now when we'd eat shrimp, they might be fresh from the Gulf; and when we'd eat okra, it would come fresh from the garden. It meant being with my relatives when they were in the hospital and praying for them face-to-face, not just over the phone, when they needed physical or spiritual help.

It meant cool drinks of water on hot summer days and deer hunts in November. It meant the smell of the plowed earth during planting season. It meant picking peas in the summer and throwing bass lures under willow trees overhanging the lakes. It meant pine trees and azaleas, magnolias and mistletoe, walnuts and wisteria, catalpas and crepe myrtles, hickories and honeysuckles. It meant red-throated hummingbirds, red-headed woodpeckers, and red-winged blackbirds. It meant seven-layered coconut cakes and fig preserves. It meant class reunions and hugging family and old friends. It meant hearing that wonderful Southun drawl. It meant feeling at home while driving down the street because I'd know many people along the way and their kids, and some of their grandkids. It meant roots and wings at the same time.

When I was growing up we used to sing page 237 of the old Baptist Hymnal, "Lord, I'm Coming Home." The refrain goes like this:

"Coming home, coming home,
Nevermore to roam,
Open wide Thine arms of love,
Lord, I'm coming home."

MEETING JANE WINFIELD

My first official act as pastor of Big Bottom Baptist Church was a visit to the home of Jane Winfield. That was on Monday, two days before her sister died and four days before the burial in Metairie. Miss Winfield's physical problems limited her mobility, but I'd heard from the pastor search committee of her significant role in the church in her healthier years. Wanda Washburn stated that if I accepted the pastorate of Big Bottom Baptist Church, one of my first duties should be to visit Miss Winfield because, "She's done so much for the church over the years, and now, when she's confined to her home most of the time, no pastor'd ever dropped in to comfort her."

I wish I could say my first visit to Jane Winfield's home came as a result of pure intentions—to minister to a shut-in member of the church. That wouldn't be entirely true. I also went to meet the expectations of search committee member Wanda Washburn and to get off to a good start with her, sort of like paying the rent. If pastors pay the rent by doing basic things as expected, they can then give the rest of their work time to things they see as productive for the church. Despite the poor motive, I'm glad I made the visit.

I drove to her home and found a sign on the front porch, "Come to the side door." I did and pressed what I thought was the doorbell under the carport. I heard the grinding of the chains lowering the garage door. Embarrassed, I reversed the door. I imagined an aged lady thinking some strange man was trying to break into her home. I located a small oval below the first button, pressed it and received an electrical shock on my finger; however, I heard a distinct "ding-dong."

A few moments later Jane Winfield opened the door and caught me flailing my hand in an attempt to get the sting out. She wore a flowered housecoat over a pair of black slacks and a tucked-in, blue blouse. Her smile and the warmth of her reception put me at ease from my blunder. "Don't you worry about the garage door, sir; people make that mistake all the time. I ought to put a sign beside the doorbell that says, 'Press here.'"

"It might shock them," I muttered.

"Yes, I suppose another sign on my old house would shock people since I already have that one on the front door. Maybe I'll just leave it like it is. They'll figure it out," she said.

"Miss Winfield, I'm you new pastor. I thought I'd drop by to get to know you."

"Oh, my pastor's come to visit," she said. "You must come in."

I followed Miss Winfield as little by little she made her way, walker in hand, through the pine-paneled den. Each time she turned her back, I shook my tingling hand again. We walked up one step into the kitchen where the smell of fresh oatmeal cookies filled the air, down the narrow hall, and into the parlor of her 1950s era home. The parlor smelled a bit musty, as if seldom used. Peeling paint marked large spots on two walls.

I sat, as she suggested, in the recliner beside what appeared to be an ancient Tiffany lamp. It threw off a multitude of colors through its stained glass shade onto the light blue walls. A burgundy Victorian couch with walnut trim was next to the recliner and blocked the sealed front door. I noticed the color of the couch when Miss Winfield removed the white sheet from it just before she sat in the straight chair nearby.

She stood her aluminum walker beside the chair, but the rubber tip of one leg caught on the leg of the sofa. The walker tipped and hummed with a dull ringing of the metal that seemed to drone on for thirty seconds. "Confounded thing," she mumbled. She left it where it fell. "Can I offer you a glass of iced tea and a cookie?"

"No, thank you. I just wanted to visit a while to get to know you and to pray for you," I answered. I wanted some iced tea and without a doubt I'd try one of her oatmeal cookies when I left. Jane Winfield, however, walked with her back bent over her walker, as if she had osteoporosis or some back injury. I didn't want to put her to the trouble to get tea and cookies, even though she already had them prepared.

Other than her physical problems, Miss Winfield was like most middle-aged men wished their mother to be. Her shoulder-length grey hair sparkled when light fell on it and surrounded a round face lined with wrinkles. She smiled often with full lips and her eyes lit up when she did. I felt at ease. I couldn't tell if Miss Winfield had on make-up, but she didn't need any. An inner beauty shone through her face and calm demeanor. Except for her walker, I sensed she was at peace with herself.

"I'm so glad you came by to visit me," she said again with a smile so broad it deepened the wrinkles around her eyes.

"Miss Winfield, someone on the pastor search committee told me you'd taught Sunday school at the church for several years but weren't able to get out much any more. Is that right?"

"Who told you that?"

"I believe it was Wanda Washburn."

"W., huh?" With that she dropped her head and diverted her eyes.

"Is there something I should know?"

"Well. . ." She looked for a moment as if she'd tell me but changed her mind. "You'll find out soon enough. But just remember, Wanda does some good things, too." Her emphasis was on "some."

"At any rate, I'm afraid it's true. And I miss going to church so much. When I was young and active, I didn't realize how much it meant to be on mission with people you love," she said.

I nodded.

"We didn't just go to church, we were on a journey together, and God used us to help grow the church as this area grew. It was so exciting to see all those boys and girls begin the year in the four-year-old class. They'd run to the door with their new shoes. I can still hear the squeaks and see the black marks their soles made on the linoleum. I can still feel the tugs of their hands when they wanted to sit in my lap." Miss Winfield got a far-away look in her brown eyes, as if she were not with me. She was at the door of the four-year-old Sunday school department welcoming the children as the young couples brought them for the first time.

As she spoke, I imagined the tension of the young mothers and fathers who lingered at the door with their children. "Will Johnny be okay? Will he like the teacher? Will he cry? Will he learn something? Will he want to come back?" They'd have those and a dozen other questions. At least Darla and I did when we brought our boys.

In my mind's eye I could see a thirty-year-old Miss Winfield, with a strong back, bending down to welcome each child with a hug and to invite them inside to color at the table while at the same time giving a word of assurance to the parents. She seemed the kind of warm person children love to be near, and for a moment I felt I was a child entering her classroom.

"They grow so much in a year's time, you know," Miss Winfield said, breaking that magical moment that had transferred us back in time fifty years.

"Yes, ma'am, I'll bet you enjoyed teaching the children," I replied.

"Sure did. I sure did. I began teaching the four-year-olds when I was sixteen. I led that department long enough to teach some of the children of the ones I'd earlier taught and later, even some grandchildren. I miss those kids. Sometimes I wonder if the Lord will let me hold and teach children in heaven," she said as tears began to trickle down her cheek.

"Some nights I lay my head on my pillow thinking about one child or another. I might dream about that child and I take it as a sign from God I'm supposed to pray for her. Do you think God is asking me to pray for those children that way? I call them children, but now they're grown up and most of them have their own kids."

"You may have something there. God communicates with us in the Bible, but I think His Spirit also prompts us from time to time, like when we're supposed to pray for someone," I answered.

Jane nodded.

"I read about a missionary in the Amazon jungle whose son Jim had a high fever, but they didn't have access to a doctor. Their few medicines didn't seem to help. He worsened day after day and Jim's parents feared he would die. One bad night they stayed up with him and prayed and the fever broke, all of a sudden, around two o'clock in the morning. By the next day the boy seemed back to normal. Two weeks later they got a letter from a friend in the States who said she'd awakened out of the blue with the thought she must pray for little Jim. She'd knelt and done just that. The burden left her about one a.m. her time and that would have been two in the morning their time. The letter asked if anything had happened for Jim to need prayer that particular night."

"I believe it," she said. "That's what I do. Then I write them a note and remind them of a lesson or two we learned in the four-year-old class."

"You write them? And you still remember the lessons from the classes you taught?" I asked, astonished.

"Well, of course I do. I write them or call them on the phone. I can't get out much any more, but I like to think God still uses me to touch some of those kids. Is it okay to call them kids? I still think of them all as my kids.

"And as far as those lessons—you bet I remember them. The best lessons in life are learned early: God loves you. God puts people in your path who love you and want to help you. You can't do much without others. You must help other people, in particular those less fortunate.

Confess and ask forgiveness when you do something wrong. Cough into a tissue. Wipe your nose, but not on your sleeve. Work hard. Laugh a lot. Cooperate. Tell the truth. Tie your shoes. Give a tithe to the Lord. Wash your hands after you use the bathroom.

"By the way, I don't write them about that one." We laughed together. "Yeah, I'm sure they've learned that one by now. Those lessons we learn near the beginning of our lives are the foundations for successful living. We'll never live long enough to outlive their usefulness," she said.

After a while I glanced at my watch and was surprised to find a visit I'd planned to last thirty minutes had stretched into an hour-and-a-half. Yet I felt I'd just entered Miss Winfield's classroom and had received her hug and some life lessons. I didn't want to leave, but I had an appointment at the church.

It thrilled her I cared enough to come by, and it thrilled me that a person with physical restrictions hadn't become sour with life. I knew I'd come back from time to time to seek her advice and prayer. I asked, "Miss Winfield, I'd like to pray before I leave. For what would you like me to pray?"

Jane Winfield furrowed her brow and brought her hand to her forehead as if deep in thought. She didn't speak for thirty seconds but I didn't rush her because it was obvious she took my request seriously. I wondered if she'd ask for relief from the pain in her back, a pain I'd heard was her constant companion.

She spoke in a softer voice when she replied. "I'll mention a couple of things—first, to stay positive. It's not always easy, you know. And then for God to show me how I can reach out to others even when I can't leave home most days."

"God tells us in Psalms 37 if we delight in Him, He'll give us the desires of our heart. It seems to me you're delighting in Him."

"Oh, I hope so." Miss Winfield straightened her back and sat a little taller. "In fact, I know so. I talk with Him all day long as I amble around this old house. Spending time with Him is my greatest joy. You know that old hymn don't you, 'He walks with me and He talks with me and He tells me I am His own?' That's the way I've found it."

Despite my amazement at Miss Winfield's unselfishness, I prayed as she'd asked. And I had no doubt God would answer.

After I said, "Amen," Miss Winfield said, "Thank you, pastor; now, how can I pray for you?"

"Pray for me? You, you want to pray for me?" I asked. She astounded me. I asked her to pray for my wife and me to settle in well, to find new friends, to get off to a good start in ministry with the church, to lead my staff responsibly, and to help me balance church work with family life. And she did—with an intensity that told me I wanted Jane Winfield on my side because she's surely on God's side!

She touched my arm lightly on the way out and I felt a surge of electricity, but different from the doorbell shock. It emanated from the warmth of her hand. It was curative, like the touch of a mother. She'd given hundreds of preschoolers that warm touch through the years. I floated out of her house feeling I'd dropped in on one of the Lord's closest disciples, right up there with Mother Theresa.

Miss Winfield insisted I take a couple of cookies as we passed through the kitchen. The taste brought back memories of my Mom's goodies. I wondered how many times Miss Winfield baked cookies for the four-year-olds of Big Bottom Baptist Church. Lots of love, sound wisdom, and good cookies are a sure-fire recipe for success with children—and with the child needing to be loved inside every adult.

7
ON THE MOVE

Stuff. It amazed me how much stuff we'd accumulated. Darla and I moved quite a bit in our earlier years, but hadn't in ten years. Richard Foster's advice about simplicity came back to me over and over—each time I moved a heavy box. We pay for stuff when we buy it. We pay again when we store it. And we pay a third time when we move it. A friend told me people need to move every three years just to get rid of clutter and center down to the important.

Big Bottom Church called me, but that necessitated Darla's moving. I felt a little guilty asking her to leave a job she loved, a Sunday school class she'd started and taught, and good friends. To top it all, Darla has better organizational skills than I. She took to packing up our things into boxes and labeling them according to the contents and the rooms into which they'd go. I was the "gofer." I'd go for this and go for that, whatever the need might be to complete the job of moving.

How could I complain about an excess of goods to a woman who'd put up with me? Let's just suffice it to say Darla and I don't share the same views on simplicity. You know, the whole "Men are from Mars,

Women are from Venus" thing, or is it the other way around? To be fair to Darla, I guess I should state it from her standpoint: we value different things.

One time I mentioned her closet contained three times as many shoes and clothes as mine. For Darla, clothes tell who she is or how she feels. Clothes for me tell who's had a sale a few years ago. And so she said, "Well, why don't I just jump out of bed and throw on the same pair of slacks and the same shoes every day for a week like you do? If you like, I can wear a blouse to work one day and if it isn't too dirty or wrinkled, I can wear it again the next day. Or, maybe you'd rather me ask you, 'Sweetheart, does this shirt smell too much to wear again?'"

I replied, "No, honey, you must have misunderstood. I'm not complaining. I just wanted to compliment you on having just the right thing to wear whatever the occasion."

She wasn't buying it. Darla's intuition kicked in and she knew I hadn't told the truth, the whole truth, and nothing but the truth. But she'd made her point and, in the interest of peace, let the matter drop. So did I. After all, she's gorgeous and a wonderful mother to our boys and I'm fortunate to be her husband. I considered myself lucky to get out of the discussion without a major argument, one I'd never win.

A man-versus-woman battle often surrounds material possessions. Women feather their nests with things and men go crazy. Scott, a youth minister serving our former church, lived in his own small home. As the day of his marriage approached he began seeking advice. Some of the best he received came from a good buddy who'd married two months earlier.

"Scott," he said, "the space you now claim for yours—don't even try. The chest of drawers is hers. The counter tops are hers. The refrigerator is hers. Yes, the whole kitchen is hers. The floor is hers. The bed is hers. The bathrooms are hers. The closets are hers. The cabinets are hers. In fact, the whole house is hers. If you're lucky, you can claim part of the garage. The sooner you get your head wrapped around the fact that it's all hers and you're just living in her space, the happier you'll be."

Most couples compromise. A few arguments occur over space; then they hash things out and come to a more-or-less common agreement. If they can afford separate closets, they do better. However, to say there's no difference in the way males and females look at things would be naïve.

I accused Darla of having a Freudian slip when labeling the boxes of our household goods. On a large cardboard box of quilts she'd written, "Guilts." In her rush to label everything, she'd misspelled the word. We laughed together about it, though. I told her if Christians could just box up our guilts and sell the boxes, I'd be out of a job. There's something about going to a new location that allows us to leave the old behind—both the guilts of things undone that ought to have been done and the wonderful people we'd miss.

The pastor search committee checked on the cost of moving Darla and me and found moving companies would charge around seven thousand dollars. They decided to give us five thousand dollars and let us move ourselves. They reasoned it would save the church two thousand dollars. Also, if we could rent a U-Haul and move for less than five thousand, we could keep the left-over money for the necessary items every move entails, like new curtains, payment for our Mississippi car taxes and tags, drivers' licenses, etc. Their decision became a symbol of our first months at Big Bottom, good intentions but not quite right.

The Mississippi good-ole-boy way of moving is to gather a few friends, throw your stuff into the back of a couple of pick-ups, and boogie on down the road. The committee wanted us to have a few dollars left over for other expenses, and we appreciated their thoughtfulness. They hadn't factored in the fact that gas now sold for three dollars a gallon and it was too much to ask people from our former church to drive six hundred miles with our goods and then turn around the next day and drive back home, another six hundred miles.

We soon realized the largest U-Hauls we could rent were not as tall, wide, or deep as the sixteen-wheeled moving vans used by professionals. It took two U-Haul trucks to move our stuff. After paying for the trucks, some specialty boxes, tape, gasoline, meals, a night's lodging, and for someone to drive one of the trucks, we lost money on the deal. We didn't dare tell anyone, though, because it would've been complaining. Complaining is no way to begin a new ministry. Besides, we felt a little guilty because of all the stuff we'd accumulated when Jesus had no place to lay His head. If we forgot, the big box labeled "Guilts" reminded us.

Darla and I noticed times of major change in our lives have been very important. Moving, for instance. Feelings are heightened. Someone may give a cake on an ordinary day and we'd be grateful. When neighbors, Dr. Ben and Glenna Dover, brought over a pecan pie and other goodies soon after we moved in, though, we knew we'd remember their thoughtfulness forever.

Darla and I have some strong memories of our moving. Staying up night after night packing and stacking boxes left our muscles sore, and missing sleep left us dog-tired. We remember having to look for empty boxes day after day. We remember how it felt when our muscles strained to lift the boxes onto the top of the stacks. We remember the cold front that moved through Kentucky in late January. The icy wind felt like a slap in the face every time I stepped out of the seventy-degree house into the fifteen-degree outdoors to load another carton into the U-Haul.

The strongest recollections, however, are of people who came over to help us. Friends took off work to put in a day of loading the trucks. Others came by for a few minutes to run errands, to bring colas, or just to see what we needed. Our friend Carl had lots of experience with U-Hauls and showed us how to pack tightly so the goods would make the journey unscathed. When he saw we weren't too good at it, Carl took off work two days and helped.

In my mind's eye I can still see him measuring the boxes to ensure a tight fit or tying cords to the inner sides of the U-Hauls to keep the furniture and boxes from moving. Christianity in overhauls, that's what we called it. Even though we were leaving, the help of these amazing folks said, "We love you and want to help you." What do people do without strong Christian friends? Their help reminded us of God's grace. Unmerited. Undeserved. And yet so wonderful.

Our next greatest memories are of the people who met us at our new home in Big Bottom Subdivision. They, too, got busy. The trucks had taken two full days to load but just four hours to unload. S. A. and a number of the young adults and youth he'd recruited from the church appeared. It touched us that S. A. had enlisted folks to help us.

One of the boys, Marcus, had a voice that sounded familiar. I mentioned this to him and asked him if we'd ever met. He pulled on my coat sleeve, and I followed him into a room off the hallway where no one else could hear.

Marcus looked around to ensure no one else could hear. He said, "You recognize my voice because I was in the restroom when you came for the trial sermon. You got to promise not to tell my mother." He peeked down the hall again. When no one was in sight, he continued. "The other guys who pulled that restroom stunt are here, too. We wanted to help you move in. Seemed like the least we could do after the trouble we'd caused you."

A tall and somewhat clumsy young man, Marcus wiped the sweat from his forehead as he began to beg: "She'd kill me, pastor. She'd kill me. I mean I'd be grounded for a year, maybe more. You won't tell, will you?"

"I don't know," I replied. "You boys did a serious thing. It upset my stomach so much I almost didn't make it out of the restroom in time to preach," I said. I had no intentions of ratting on the boys, but now the tide had turned and it was fun having them on the spot.

"Please don't, pastor. You don't know our parents yet. They'd kill us. Pleeease don't tell them."

"Well, I don't know. Marcus, why don't you bring in the other boys and we'll talk it over," I said.

Within one minute four boys appeared at the door. By then, I'd found the box labeled "Guilts" and brought it in, too.

"Come in, young men," I said with a smile, "We've got some talking to do."

FOUR DOLLAR BOX

"Now pastor," the young man who appeared to be the oldest spoke, "you aren't thinking of turning us in, are you?" He stood six feet tall with blond hair and wore a Southern Miss athletic jersey. His brown hair hung over his eyes, and his face was marked with acne.

"What's your name, son?" I asked.

"Mike."

"Mike, you read my mind. I thought I'd inform your parents." By now all four of the boys were wiping sweat from their faces and prancing back and forth. Two were wringing their hands.

"Please don't, pastor, it'll get us in all kinds of trouble," one of the boys said as he wiped his hands on his pants.

"Well, you did help me move in today," I said, with hesitation.

"Yeah, that ought to count for something," Marcus said, jumping into the conversation.

"But we've got this problem, boys. See the box?" I asked. "What's it say?"

"Uh, 'Guilts,'" Mike replied.

"Yeah, how do you deal with your guilts?"

"I guess we could just box them up and shove them under the bed like it appears you're doing with your guilts," Mike said as he turned and snickered. The other boys caught it and began to chuckle, too.

"But there's a problem with that approach," I said. Proverbs says when we cover up a wrongdoing, it'll just come out later; but if we confess and leave it behind, we'll have peace within. And since you told me today about that restroom stunt and you helped me move in, I guess the least I could do is keep quiet about your shenanigans." As I spoke as I turned over the box labeled "Guilts" so that the label could no longer be read. "Especially when I consider the four dollars you put in my pocket."

"Wha. . . what four dollars? We haven't put any money in your pocket," Mike said.

"It's the bet that we could make him sweat," Marcus said. "He wants us to give him the four dollars we won." They started fishing in their pockets.

"No, boys. You keep your money. I didn't move to Mississippi to take money from you. I'm talking about the four dollars I bet my wife."

"You bet your wife four bucks?" Mike asked with an obvious look of shock.

"Sure did. She's supposed to give me one dollar for each one of you boys I can make sweat. Let's see—one, two, three, four." I stared at one young man and then another until I'd looked at each of them and insured perspiration flowed. "I'd say I'm up four dollars today. Thanks."

They looked at one another and then Mike burst out laughing. Soon all four laughed and I did, too. They sat on the floor and I sat on the guilt box and we all drank colas and laughed and got to know one another. I found Mike is a senior and made a 31 on his ACT test. He's planning to enter USM with a full ride in the honor's college. Marcus is a sophomore and unsure of himself, but mischievous. The other two are brothers from the Rawls family. They are on the cross country team and live six doors down the street from my home.

I think I made four friends. Who knows? Maybe God will call one of them into ministry. When I was their age, I'd behaved like they had; it's just that I wasn't as creative or bold about it, and God called me. He seems to delight in taking the rebellious ones like the Apostle Paul and me and making something out of us.

Carolyn Broome taped rolls of paper on all the floors to keep the crew from tracking in mud or scraping the wood floors with heavy furniture. They all threw themselves into the task of setting up our new home. The house filled with grunts as the heavy pieces moved in. They even pieced the heavy, dining room table together, connected the phones and computers, and set up the beds. Wow! What a reception!

Some neighbors who are church members, Dr. Ben and Glenna Dover, brought in eight pizzas and a case of cold, diet colas. We took a break to share our first full meal since the move with our new friends from Big Bottom.

On our visit in view of a call to Big Bottom Church, Darla'd found a house that seemed just right. It had been built on Lake Serene twenty years earlier, and the owners had renovated it two years earlier. They loved the place but a promotion out of state made the sale necessary. The fact it was all brick and almost maintenance-free sold me on it. I have no abilities maintaining a home, other than cutting the grass. If everybody had my carpentry and mechanical skills, people would still live in grass huts and lean-tos.

I'd always dreamed of a home on a lake. I'd loved to fish from the days my granddad took me as a boy. He loved it, I loved him, and so I soon grew to love fishing, too. I seldom got to fish now, due to church responsibilities. A dock on the lake would make it easy to be on the water ten minutes after arriving home from work on that one day a week or so when I caught a few extra minutes.

Already I could smell the wonderful freshness the ozone adds to the lakefront. I could envision buying a small bass boat. I knew I'd name it "visitation." That way, if someone called the office in the spring when the bass are about to bed and are eating every lure thrown their way, the secretary could say, "The pastor will return your call tomorrow. He's out on 'visitation' today." Besides, I might be able to reach some men for ministry if I could get them out in my boat, fishing. At least, that's how I justified the purchase to Darla.

This home featured a swimming pool. A pool meant more repairs, upkeep, expense, and things I didn't understand about keeping the ph of water right. These proved a negative for me, but Darla'd always wanted one. She'd been on the swim team at Pascagoula High School and could imagine hosting Sunday school classes around the pool. She sold me on the idea when she mentioned that we'd need a drawing card for grandkids one day, something to attract them to stay over a few days at Nana and Poppa's.

It also had a porch and a study, both overlooking the lake. I pictured writing sermons about God's creation while viewing the sun setting on Lake Serene. We felt so blessed of God to move into our dream home.

My parents lived five miles further west and two more miles north of Highway 98 on North Black Creek Road. Thirty years ago, a few years before retiring, they'd moved from the subdivision to a farm near where Dad grew up. We were now close enough to be handy, but not close enough to interrupt them or vice versa.

Big Bottom Church was a little over a mile east of our home. When Curt Jones, my pastor friend, called, I described it to him as, "just close enough to get to work and worship in five minutes, but far enough away not to be disturbed twice a night by someone wanting a key to get in the church after office hours."

Despite the pool and dock on Lake Serene, the home was otherwise modest, with two bathrooms and two bedrooms, a sewing room and a study. We put a sleeper sofa into the study to allow for extra room when both our boys came at the same time. Renovations had added additional wiring and opened space between the kitchen and living room. Our furniture fit well, and window treatments and carpet cleaning were the only added expenses before moving in.

Dr. Ben Dover asked me the difference between the Lake Shady I remembered as a boy and Lake Serene. I answered, "About forty thousand dollars per lot." In fact, homes in the area cost about the same, per square foot, as those in western Kentucky. Since the bank rates had fallen, we moved in with only a small increase from the note than we'd carried in the Bluegrass state, an amount covered by a small increase in salary.

Best of all, Darla seemed happy. I'd been concerned about that. She'd loved her Sunday school class and her job at the doctor's office in Kentucky. And, she'd once said she didn't think she could ever move back to Mississippi.

A sign in a church member's kitchen read, "If Momma ain't happy, ain't nobody happy." With all my heart, I wanted her happiness, but not just for my own. I love her. Her concerns are mine and I want her to feel comfortable, secure, and settled—well-nested. I can be ok most any place as long as Darla feels good about it.

After the departure of the young adults and teens who'd come to help us move, boxes were everywhere. We shuffled back and forth like a dog or cat out of place. At last bedtime came. I tried to smooch, since it was our first night in our new home, but she'd have none of it since she was too exhausted. Darla said I looked for any opportunity. Since I'm a red-blooded American boy, I'm glad to admit she's right—but only with my wife.

Darla awoke in the middle of our first night back in Mississippi burning up and arose to turn down the electric blanket. I woke up soon afterward. I was cold so I turned it back up. She soon turned the dial down again. All night long it was like that. Up and down. Up and down. In the morning, we both rose, but angry rather than rested.

"Why'd you turn that blanket up?" Darla asked with a voice that sounded more like a supervisor's demand than a sweetheart's question.

"I got cold. Why'd you turn it down?" I asked.

"Brent Paulson, you'd burn up the house if the thermometer stayed where you wanted it."

To say we were a happily married couple that day would've stretched the truth. In our dream home, when we should have been most content, we were like competing puppies, snipping back and forth all morning.

Several months later, I mentioned it to Jane Winfield during one of our long talks. She said, "Brent, that's how life is. When everything's going great and you ought to be most content, you may not be; but when things are going wrong sometimes God surrounds you with an incredible peace, and you know all will be ok."

I think that was the same day I also mentioned how stern Wanda Washburn seemed to be. Jane said, "Brent, your biggest troublemaker watches you from the mirror every morning."

I said, "Miss Jane, how did you know my wife watches me shave every morning?" She chuckled.

"You're a natural kidder, but you know who I'm talking about," she said as she lifted her left eyebrow.

I did. Jane was right. She'd nailed me.

Around two in the afternoon, in our first full day in our new home, unpleasantness still in the air, Darla wanted my help storing some suitcases and boxes under the bed. While storing the "Guilts" box, we discovered the cord to the electric blanket. It had never been plugged in. We'd wasted all that energy and emotion turning it up and down and had blamed one another and we were both wrong. Many disagreements are like that, at least in the Paulson home.

We laughed so hard we cried, and even rolled around on the carpet with the thought of how we'd blamed one another for what was neither's fault. Then we lay down on the fresh-made bed and apologized to one another. The clean sheets felt good against my skin and putting our guilts away made my conscience feel clean, too.

We prayed, dedicating our new home to God. We asked His help to make it more than just a house, but a joyful home for us and for others we'd invite in for meals or board games or Bible study. We held one another for a long time, reveling in the joy of being alive and in love and back home in Mississippi. And then we dedicated our new home in our own, special way.

GETTING STARTED AT BIG BOTTOM

I began my first Monday at work like a mosquito in a nudist colony—I knew what to do but where should I start? I decided to begin with the visit to Miss Jane Winfield I mentioned in an earlier chapter and to two other members in frail health. They appreciated the ministry visits and I appreciated the wisdom and love I found in Jane.

Then I spent time with the staff ministers. I'd grown to understand an approach to ministry I'd never dreamed possible in earlier years. If I gave about a quarter of my work time to the ministerial staff, I could multiply the ministry far beyond what I could hope to accomplish by taking an "every man for himself" approach. Part of this time came in the thirty minutes we'd spend most mornings for staff prayer time and in the couple of hours given each week for the full staff to meet. In addition, I met often with individual staff members.

The get-together with the college pastor, Bart Richards, and the associate pastor, Carter Ross, were memorable. Richards wore a pull-over shirt and jeans, casual attire that improved his chances to reach college students. He offered Hershey's Kisses while we talked. We melted the chocolate in our mouths and had sweet conversation about the needs and hopes of the college ministry. I found Bart full of passion for the Lord Jesus and the college students to whom he'd been called.

The visit with Ross set the tone for our regular visits to come. We determined that first day to meet each Monday for lunch and to hash over any upcoming or needed items concerning the staff. Ross dressed in a business suit and looked the part of a chief operating officer. He was my chief-of-staff and, judging by what I'd heard and by the order with which he kept his desk and bookcases, had solid administrative abilities. This would fit in well with my people skills, I decided, because it would allow me to shuffle off to Ross most of the administrative duties while I concentrated on the area where God had gifted me. I noticed again the strange peculiarity about Ross. Every so often he'd misplace a word and then yank his head to the right. If he became nervous about something, these tendencies seemed to increase.

I'd never asked a staff member to resign nor have I had to threaten dismissal. One time several years ago I should have taken steps to have one staff member, Alex, dismissed, but didn't. Somehow he and I worked things out and the church prospered. In my first afternoon at Big Bottom, however, I received a call from deacon J. Rayford Madden requesting I cancel whatever else I had on my schedule the rest of the afternoon. He wanted to visit with me about an impropriety in a staff member. I swallowed hard.

J. R. had been on the pastor search committee. A long-time land owner and developer, J. R. was a patriarch in the area. In his mid-seventies, he stood six-feet-three-inches. J. R. had the aura of a man who didn't like to waste time. Nevertheless, he never pushed or prodded to get his way. Distinguished, he was a true Southern gentleman and represented the senior adults on the search committee.

During the search process I remember his saying, "Big Bottom has a good staff. They might need a little direction and motivation, but they do good work." Now, however, in my critical, first week, he spoke of an "impropriety." I felt like I'd been deceived, but it wasn't so. J. Rayford had just discovered something.

A line of splendid live oaks bordering a long, paved drive greeted me on arriving at J. Rayford and Susanna Madden's home. The house itself looked like an antebellum mansion with two stories fronted by six white columns and a set of massive oak doors opening onto a substantial entryway and revealing a broad, curving staircase. I imagined Melody greeting me at the door with Scarlet and Rhett sweeping down the stairway close behind. Hundreds of acres of fields where soybeans had grown the previous summer surrounded the home. A white fence reminiscent of a Kentucky horse farm bordered the entire property.

Susanna greeted me at the door with one of the kindest welcomes I'd received in a long time. "Oh, pastor, what an honor to have you visit our home on your first week at the church." Mrs. Madden wore a checkered gingham dress with a white apron covering much of the front. She smiled broadly and seemed glad I'd come. She must not have known about J. R.'s summons.

"Thank you, Mrs. Madden," I replied. "What a terrific Southern mansion you have. It must be a fine home for entertaining."

"Oh, yes, it is. We love it. And, we try to have J. R.'s Sunday school class and mine come over often. But pastor, it feels empty, sometimes. You know how a large home can be when no kids are around." Susanna's radiant smile faded. "The best times in our home were the days our children were growing up."

"You have two children, don't you?" I asked.

"Yes, and they both live out of state. J. R., Jr. is a lawyer on Peachtree Street in Atlanta, and Caroline is a fashion designer on Fifth Avenue in New York. They don't get to come much, but I'm telling you, when they get home with those grandchildren, this big ole house springs to life again. For a little while, it's just like the days when our two were growing up."

After several more niceties, I stuck my foot in my mouth by asking about the Elite Ladies class. Susanna told me, "I guess you've asked the wrong person. I could never be a member of a class not trying to reach out to everyone with the Gospel. For several years now, I've been part of a team that starts a new, young couples' class each year."

What a gracious lady. And to think, I'd labeled her just because she was almost old enough to be my mother and lived in a well-appointed home. I know God can forgive a down-and-out person, but can He forgive a pastor who judges people before getting to know them? Without a sound I asked Him. I also decided Susanna Madden was a jewel.

Soon J. Redford came in from a meeting and ushered me into the library, a walnut-paneled room with a twelve-foot ceiling, lined with bookshelves holding the writings of Hawthorne, Dickens, Thoreau, and O'Henry. Alongside them were the complete works of Homer, Plato, Herodotus, Xenophon, Aristotle, Pliny, and Josephus.

The room offered upholstered, red leather chairs. A tapestry similar to one in Biltmore mansion in Ashville covered most of one wall, and a stuffed, black bear stood seven feet tall in one corner, paws outstretched. An immense, mahogany desk was angled to catch the light from the floor-to-ceiling window. A world globe rested on one corner of the desk. Books and papers laid in a way that suggested the room was not just for show but also served as J. R.'s office.

J. R. thanked me for coming to see him on such short notice. "I'll get right to the point, pastor. It's the Hispanic minister. I've received some information you'd better read."

I'd known Big Bottom Church sponsored a Spanish-speaking mission. The hope was to reach a growing people group in the area with a worship service in their own language. Big Bottom had paid the mission's way until a few years earlier. As it had grown, it'd become more self-sufficient and, while still meeting in Big Bottom's chapel, was collecting money to buy land to build its own facilities a few miles closer to the center of most of the Hispanic population of the Hattiesburg area.

From a cursory look at the budget, it appeared to me that the mission was paying its own way except for the salary of the pastor. Pastor Manual Reyes, a Mexican man educated at Southwestern Baptist Theological Seminary in Ft. Worth, where I'd completed my doctoral work, showed much promise in helping the church become a self-supporting congregation. In his thirties, he struck me as energetic and visionary. Until the church became self-supporting, he'd remain a staff member of Big Bottom Baptist Church and under the supervision of the church mission committee and me.

"This is what I'm talking about."

J. Rayford pushed in front of me copies of several emails he'd received from a young lady who worked in his home and also attended the mission. The pastor of the mission had filled these emails with the most profane suggestions imaginable. I knew that if these were from Pastor Reyes, we'd have to act. If a mistake had been made and they weren't from him, he needed to have his name cleared.

Since five o'clock had already arrived this Monday, I called an emergency, joint meeting of Big Bottom's personnel committee and the mission committee for the next night and tried to contact the pastor to request his attendance. I'd hoped we could get together in private before the meeting, but I was unable to reach him all day on Tuesday and had to leave a voice message. I knew the committee meeting would be one of the toughest I'd attended in thirty years as a pastor.

Pastor Reyes arrived ten minutes before the meeting. He stood almost six feet tall, stocky with black hair and brown skin. His beautiful wife, Maria, who stood beside him, appeared to have been crying, and suspended the corner of a handkerchief from her left hand. Reyes requested we step inside a Sunday school classroom.

Right away he began asking me to give him another chance. Maria nodded her approval of his requests. I inquired if he'd sent the emails and he confessed he had. I prayed for God to show His grace to Pastor Reyes and Maria, to grant His help for healing, and to help the mission. We left to attend the called meeting.

S. A. Tanner chaired the personnel committee and Sam Jones the mission committee. They and eight other committee members who were able to adjust their schedules on one day's notice, sat stoned-faced around the conference table. Because the personnel committee members didn't know the story, several were angry at a called meeting in my first week as pastor. I later learned they thought I was trying to "clean house" of loved staff ministers. "What was going to happen tonight? How would it affect our church and our mission? How would it affect us?" We all had questions.

10
THE MEETING

S. A. Tanner began the meeting by thanking Pastor Manual Reyes and Maria and the members of the two committees for attending. He then dismissed Reyes from the proceedings but requested him to stay close by so as to meet with the committee later. S. A. led those who'd attended that night, but his actions showed no empathy. He acted with a matter-of-factness that surprised me, since Tanner possessed great people skills. He asked Carolyn Broome to lead in prayer.

After the prayer, Tanner rambled on for ten minutes about someone from Lamar County he'd met in the Amsterdam airport last year. When a committee member broke in to ask why they'd been called to attend a special meeting, Tanner apologized and said he was "just trying to open a difficult subject with some lighter conversation." He then lifted high the copies of the emails, changed the expression on his face from pleasant to somber, and said, "We've got some serious business to deal with."

When the emails went around the room and the committee received assurances they'd, in fact, come from Pastor Reyes, they were angry.

"Just imagine, we're paying him a good salary to get that new church established and he's spending his time in ungodliness." The consensus was strong for an immediate dismissal.

Pastor Reyes was called in. S. A. asked him to take a seat at the table. As soon as he did, S. A. said, "Reyes, I've just got one question for you: did you send these emails?"

Pastor Reyes lowered his head and sobbed in silence. His hand carried a handkerchief and he often brought it to his eyes. He confessed. He cried some more. He begged forgiveness. He asked for a second chance. It was obvious he was a broken man. My unspoken question was whether he was broken because he was repentant or because he'd gotten caught. Either way it hurt to see the results of sin.

Carolyn Broome, the person in the room I'd least expect to judge another person, spoke. "Pastor Reyes, before today have you ever been accused of anything inappropriate?"

Reyes put his head in his hands. "How'd you know?" he asked.

"Know what?" Carolyn asked.

"About the other times," Reyes replied. "Three other times. But with prayer I thought I had the problem cured. I'm sure if you'll give me just one more chance, I'll do better. You'll see."

We were stunned. After a few seconds of silence Carolyn resumed her questioning. "Pastor Reyes, were these other times since you accepted the staff position at Big Bottom or before you came here?"

"Two of them were before."

"Pastor Reyes, it is not easy for me to ask this of you, but I feel I must. Have you made any inappropriate advances to anyone else in the Hispanic mission or to anyone in the area?" Carolyn asked.

Reyes put his head in his hands and continued to sob. He never answered the question. S. A. asked Reyes to absent himself while the committees deliberated.

Carolyn Broome moved and the committee voted to declare Pastor Reyes no longer an employee of Big Bottom Church or pastor of the mission. There were no dissenting votes. Then S. A. asked him to return to the room.

Pastor Reyes requested, and we granted, permission to write out an immediate resignation so as not to be considered "fired." Right away he whipped out a piece of paper from his inner coat pocket with the resignation already signed as if he'd anticipated this and wanted to be prepared. He shoved it in front of Tanner and walked away.

By this time half of us were crying over our hurt for Manual, Maria, the mission, and his victims. Innocence left Big Bottom that night. Maybe it already had. But now we were aware of a spiritual battle of immense proportions.

Sam Jones moved and the committee voted to ask the Mississippi State Baptist Convention office for help in filling the pulpit of the Spanish mission.

Next, Jones moved and the gathering voted, seven to four, for me to call a breakfast meeting of leaders of the mission the next morning to explain the situation, to request their patience, and to reassure these devout men and women that Big Bottom Church still wanted the mission to succeed. For the life of me, I couldn't understand why anyone would vote against that motion, but four did.

Jones recommended and it passed the joint meeting, seven to four, to pay for up to ten counseling sessions for Pastor Reyes in USM's behavioral modification unit or with a Christian counselor of his choosing. Pastor Reyes, of course, must first agree to counseling.

Four members, all from the personnel committee, as in the previous motion, voted against it. Because Rev. Reyes had harmed the reputation of the mission and of Big Bottom Church, they wanted to punish him. S. A. Tanner, among the four, had an odd smirk on his face, almost a look of satisfaction, and muttered something about "destroying his ministry." I didn't understand it and marked it in my mind as unusual. I talk over unusual things with Darla because she has a gift of discernment, but she didn't understand S. A., either. All five members of the mission committee, one from the personnel committee, and I voted for the motion, just as we had in the prior motion.

The joint committee also voted to make our findings public to Big Bottom Church and the mission. This vote once again split seven to four, along the same lines as the previous votes. The minority viewed this as something to hush up so as not to bring negative attention to the church.

The majority also didn't want to blow this out of proportion, but we felt we'd learned a lesson from the well-publicized difficulties within U. S. Catholicism a few years back. We wouldn't try to sweep it under the rug. If there'd been some illegality on the part of Pastor Reyes, we wanted the victim(s) to come forward and accept our offer of counseling and of legal alternatives. We considered ourselves in the business of helping families, not of being complicit by enabling or secreting the wrongdoer. I knew I'd receive questions from television and newspaper reporters, but I was too drained to think of it that night.

Carolyn Broom suggested we pray, and we didn't need to take that motion to a vote. We dropped to our knees around the conference table. I remember few prayer meetings as powerful as that one. We prayed fervently for the Hispanic mission, for Pastor Reyes and Maria, and that nothing like this would ever be necessary in Big Bottom Church again. God hears the prayers of the contrite and the broken-hearted, and we were both. The things we'd had to deal with shouldn't occur among God's people. I could hear gulps for air because some were sobbing. Scripture says, "Humble yourselves before the Lord, and He will lift you up." And He did.

The people had voted for me to be their pastor no more than a month earlier, but it takes more than a vote to become pastor of a people. That night, that fateful night, in the furnace of hardship, I became the pastor of six of these committee members as we struggled through difficult decisions together. I didn't know it at the time, but the four who voted in the minority became my adversaries. In one powerful night a seven-to-four vote spelled out for me what much of my next few years would be like.

Men, even ministers, have strong temptations and can fail in our sex-saturated society. I was glad the committee dealt with resolve in handling an awkward situation. Christians cannot wink at sin. God is love but He is righteous also. It also pleased me that they dealt with redemption by providing counseling for Pastor Reyes.

I wondered what had happened to the committee that called him. Why hadn't they searched out his references and past friendships and work experiences and found out about his past? Did the committee try but fail to find anything wrong? Did they drop the ball by not examining his background? Could all this have been avoided? And did the church have liability if other wrongdoings surface and it comes out that the proper investigative work hadn't been performed by the committee that recommended him as mission minister of Big Bottom? I had a lot to pray about.

After a furious round of phone calls to mission leaders upon arriving home, I dropped beside my bed for another lengthy time of prayer before falling asleep a few hours before dawn. At seven a.m. Sam Jones and I met with seven mission leaders and poured out our hearts to them about the situation and our hopes for a mission that would stay strong.

Although the mission leaders were crushed, they seemed to understand the positions we had taken. They apologized for failing the mother church and feared it would mean people in the area would look down on Hispanics. Sam and I both assured them that nothing of the sort would happen in Big Bottom and that we saw it as a problem with their mission pastor, but not with the people.

Over and over again the mission leaders expressed their deep appreciation at being consulted about the situation before it leaked out to the congregation or to the media. They asked about the funds they'd collected for a building. We gave the leaders our assurances both that the mission owned these funds and that Big Bottom Church still wanted to do our part to help the mission succeed.

These godly men and women pledged to double their efforts of prayer and outreach. Their dedication moved me. They also decided that each of them would call five families from the mission to explain and to ask for their prayers and continued attendance.

Sam and I concluded we had done the right thing by consulting with the mission leadership. We hoped a renewed interest and zeal by these leaders could strengthen the mission's work.

I called Carter Ross and asked him to gather a special staff meeting on Wednesday morning so I could give details about the problem and the committee's solution and to ask them to hold the story until I got some legal advice. When I shared the details with them on Wednesday, the news shocked the staff. Within thirty minutes I had a message from my secretary to return a call to WMAD television station. I figured Reyes hadn't wanted the story out nor did I suspect the committee. How had they found out so soon?

Dr. Jones mentioned that he'd been on an administrative committee at USM that had to deal with a similar impropriety. Before calling the reporter back, I thought I'd better call Sam. My friend advised me to talk to an attorney from Big Bottom before proceeding.

I put in a call to R. M. Parsons, a long-time attorney from Hattiesburg who served as a deacon at Big Bottom.

While waiting for his return call, I phoned Neville Wright, chairman of deacons of Big Bottom Baptist Church. Since I knew him from the pastor search committee, I felt he'd understand the vote and appreciate the heads-up.

Neville Wright, Nev for short, had joined Big Bottom Baptist Church sixty years earlier as a child when he'd received Christ and had never been a member anywhere else. The most notable thing about Nev was his smell. Darla and I both noticed it during the first search committee meeting. His clothes reeked of moth balls. We'd smelled it above the hickory-cooked barbeque we'd eaten in Kentucky with the search committee. Nev and S. A. sat beside one another during the meal and talked together while other members of the committee asked Darla and me questions or responded to our questions. We'd thought their actions strange, but since it was our first face-to-face meeting, we'd decided not to judge the two before getting to know them better.

"Nev, this is Brent Paulson. Do you have a few minutes to talk?" I asked.

"Well, Dr. Paulson, I wondered when you'd ever get around to calling." The way he'd drawled out "doctor," with added emphasis on the first half of the word, told me something wasn't right. I decided to ignore it for now and get to the matter at hand.

"Nev, something's come up here at the church, and I thought you'd want to know about it," I said.

"Yeah, I already know something about it, Dr. Paulson" he said. I detected the same emphasis on my title.

"You do?" I asked. A look of astonishment must've come across my face.

"Oh, yeah, pastor" he said. "I got a phone call from deacon Tanner last night and from one of your staff ministers this morning, and that set me to wondering why my pastor hadn't called me first."

"There goes staff loyalty," I thought.

"Nev, let me assure you I haven't been trying to keep anything from you. We had a death in the church this morning; it was just last night when the joint personnel committee and mission committee met and made their decision; and now I've got reporters calling. Neville, you'll get to know me in the days ahead. I'll make some mistakes, but you'll find out I always try to keep key leaders informed. To tell the truth, today, well. . . I don't know how to put this other than to say I've been up to my armpits in alligators."

Neville seemed to settle down after that and ended up saying not to worry because "Big Bottom's been in messes before. We've always come out of them and we'll come out of this one too."

His saying so didn't comfort me. It made me wonder what messes Big Bottom had before and why I, as a new pastor, hadn't been informed of them by the pastor search committee.

Most pastors, when they begin a ministry in a new location, enjoy a "honeymoon," a time of six months—maybe even a year or more—when all works well, everyone's happy, and almost everyone follows their lead. My church honeymoon had lasted two days. I phoned Darla and surprised her and myself when the words came out, "Honey, do you think we made a mistake by coming to Big Bottom?"

11
OUT OF THE FRYING PAN

Soon afterwards the *Hattiesburg Advocate* called. The reporter said the story would be headlined in Thursday's paper, barring some unforeseen catastrophe, and the deadline would come in two hours. The note from the secretary said if I wanted to be quoted in the article, I'd need to return his call within ninety minutes.

I'd already waited several hours for the lawyer's return call. Any lawyer worth his salt would be busy, but, hey, I was dying. I could feel all my hopes and dreams for Big Bottom bundled up into a roll, laid on an altar, and sacrificed before the god of public opinion prior to completing a full week as pastor of Big Bottom. I called again. And again.

For some reason lawyer jokes began going through my head. I thought of the attorney whose millionaire client stood trial for murder. "Do you think I'll go to jail?" the client asked.

"Not with all your money," the lawyer replied. Sure enough, after several expensive appeals, the hiring of a number of "expert" witnesses, and posh legal fees, the man went to jail—without any money.

My son Tom, an attorney in Memphis, asked me what you call a group of lawyers who parachute over a field. I didn't know. He answered, "Skeet." Sounded to me like that one came from a man who'd lost all his worldly goods with the help of a lawyer.

At last attorney Parsons called. His advice was excellent: say as little as possible and don't say anything about Pastor Reyes that could get Big Bottom Church sued. Tell the paper and television station it was a sensitive personnel matter and we'd hold a press conference tomorrow afternoon. With that strategy he and I would have a day to collect our wits. Parsons had wisdom to deal with a situation I'd never faced. I thanked God for placing him in Big Bottom Church and for raising him up for this need. I thought I'd enjoy pastoring a Parson.

When I called WMAD, Jill Adamson answered the phone. Jill asked for an on-air interview, but I declined, saying, "R. M. Parsons and I will hold a press conference in the lobby of Big Bottom Baptist Church tomorrow afternoon at three." Jill told me, off the record, that she's a strong Christian and an active member at Temple Baptist Church, just two miles further west of Big Bottom. Without saying it, I knew she'd give Big Bottom Church as favorable a spin as possible, under the circumstances.

The *Hattiesburg Advocate* called back before I could return their call. This paper competed with the larger circulation paper in the area, and they were aggressive in trying to get the scoop. Something inside told me not to talk with them, but it's not my nature to snub anyone.

I'd learned from my parents that, in their rush for a story, the *Advocate* often made mistakes. A single issue of the paper ran what people called, "the dropsies." One article had the headline, "Farmer Bill drops in House." Another headline read, "Local high school dropouts cut in half." Another, "Hattiesburg residents can drop off trees." Still another read, "Eye drops off shelf." By the end of the day, rumor had it that five families had dropped their subscriptions.

Reporter Kyle Hampton sounded like a young man, but he must've come from a hard-nosed journalism school or else had it in for churches. I told him the same thing I'd told Jill from the TV station, but he wasn't satisfied to wait until the press conference. He probed.

"Did Pastor Manual Reyes commit adultery?"

"Mr. Hampton, I'll neither confirm nor deny anything you ask. The conference is tomorrow at three p.m." I said.

"Tell me this, is he a child pornographer?" he asked.

"Mr. Hampton, I think you'll find your allegations go far beyond the truth. I'm reserving any comments until tomorrow at the press conference."

"Well, then, you don't deny he's a pornographer?" he said.

"I didn't say that at all. You are making up things, young man, and you ought to be ashamed of yourself," I said. "After all, a man's reputation's at stake. Give the man some dignity like you or anyone else would want."

"Ah ha," he replied. "You're getting defensive. I must be closing in on the truth," he said.

"Mr. Hampton, I'll talk with you tomorrow at the press conference. Let me remind you a man's future hangs in the balance. Please don't take liberties with what I've told you," I excused myself with courtesy and hung up. I felt lucky, given his tactics, to get away with saying as little as I had.

Several radio and out-of-town TV stations called. I declined interviews, saying there'd be a press conference tomorrow afternoon at three o'clock at Big Bottom Church.

That night I held my first Wednesday night prayer meeting as pastor of Big Bottom. Prayer meeting, I'd been told, consisted of a small group of adults, more often than not older adults, who'd sing a hymn and then pray for twenty-five minutes about various ministries of the church and for sick people. After that the pastor would deliver a brief, verse-by-verse exposition of his choice of Scripture. About forty people attended.

The reason for such a small group was the huge senior high worship service in the youth building and the large college service in the chapel. These two energetic meetings required more than fifty adults to counsel and to lead the small clusters that assembled after the group meetings. Also, the middle school, children, and preschool choirs and mission meetings necessitated more than eighty adults. Given those on-going programs, I felt fortunate the church could gather forty additional adults to pray and study God's Word on Wednesday nights.

Since their new pastor was conducting his first prayer meeting at Big Bottom, the usual crowd had swelled to over a hundred. I was thrilled because we needed all the prayer we could get. Sam Jones made sure there were no reporters present.

I began the meeting by saying that tonight prayer meeting would differ from the usual pattern. With so much evil going on, I hadn't had time to prepare a lengthy biblical talk. Also, with so much evil going on, I hadn't needed to. There are times to study the Bible and there are times to pray. Prayer time had come. I shared for ten minutes from biblical passages about how God's people turned to prayer in a time of need. Then I handed the meeting over to Dr. Jones, chairman of the mission committee.

Sam stood over six feet tall and dressed impeccably with a brown suit, blue shirt, and matching brown-and-blue striped tie. He carried himself with the dignity of a professor. He looked confident but, more importantly, he had the trust of the people. It thrilled me the church had a lay leader of his caliber during this crises.

Sam told the people about a "sensitive personnel issue with Pastor Manual Reyes of our mission." He said all he could without getting into details, including the fact there was an issue of immorality and Reyes had resigned. He stated there would be a news conference at the church the next afternoon at three and, "Our new pastor needs prayer for God to protect him, our church, and the mission." He told the folks that, despite being new, I'd handled the problem with, "forthrightness, decency, and compassion for all concerned. I'm glad God brought Pastor Paulson here for such a time as this."

Several of the folks present had worked to help start the mission, and they were curious and stunned. They began to ask questions. "Might we be mistaken?" "Were any other staff involved?" "Was the church being sued?" "How did you discover the impropriety?" The folks wanted to know and I couldn't blame them.

We answered all we dared, without getting into too many details. We wanted to show the committee had moved with haste, due to the gravity of the issue, but also with compassion. The people seemed to grasp the seriousness of the matter and we had a lengthy time of Spirit-filled praying. Some even prayed God would work a miracle to bring good to Big Bottom Church and the mission out of this bad event.

I knew there would be some trying days ahead, but these folks sure could pray. I believed God would come to the aid of any people who'd pray like that. However, I didn't see how God could bring good out of these matters.

On the ten pm edition of the local news, with pictures of the Big Bottom Church sanctuary in the background, WMAD ran a brief clip about a local church that would, "hold a news conference about a personnel issue tomorrow afternoon. Be sure to listen to tomorrow night's news for full details." I thanked God for Jill Adamson and her sensitivity and patience in reporting.

The next morning the *Hattiesburg Advocate* ran an article on the front page, just below the fold, with the heading, "New pastor won't deny immorality by staff." It also promised further details after the news conference. I was angry. Their approach reeked of the old question asked of a presidential candidate, "Do you still beat your wife?" Even if the candidate said no, he'd still be branded as someone who had in the past.

I called R. M. Parsons. This time he took my call and suggested I contact the editor to complain. He reasoned if the editor disagreed with me about unfairness, he'd still caution the reporter about his tact. If he agreed with me, maybe he'd jerk the young man off the story and replace him with someone more sympathetic.

I called the editor and told him of the conversation I'd had with his reporter the previous day. I told him I'd taken notes of our conversation and knew he'd slanted the story. The editor mumbled something about this being the fourth time and how he'd never again hire someone from the journalism department of a certain northeastern university. He said he'd cautioned the young man not to get "the Bob Woodward syndrome" because, "for heaven's sakes, you're in South Mississippi, not South Washington, D. C."

Later I found that the editor, because he'd given Hampton several previous warnings, fired him over this sensationalized report. Hampton didn't appear at the news conference, but his bias had already damaged the reputation of the church. Even if the paper ran a retraction, we'd be branded as a church whose staff practiced indecency.

I learned about a priest who heard the confession of a man who'd slandered his neighbor. For penance, the priest suggested the man tear a hole in his feather pillow, pour the feathers on his own front porch, and then come back the next day for further instruction.

The man agreed. The next day the priest asked the penitent man to pick up the feathers and put them back into the pillowcase and sew it closed again. The man objected, "But, Father, by now the wind will have blown the feathers all over the area. Some will be miles away. It'll be impossible to gather them all."

The wise priest said, "Yes, and neither can you undo slander once it's left your mouth and entered another's ears. It soon blows with the wind."

I remembered the prayers from the meeting the day before. Some had prayed God would do something that would bring Him great glory. Others asked God to do something that would help, not hinder, the work of Big Bottom Church and the mission. With the slanted newspaper article, those now seemed impossible. However, I knew God specializes in what seems impossible. I kept praying, over and over, "God, use our extremity as Your opportunity."

INTO THE FIRE

R. M. Parsons and I scheduled lunch on Thursday at the Crescent City Grill on Hardy Street in Hattiesburg. I decided to go by Jane Winfield's home first, since it was only six blocks north of Hardy. Truth be known, I felt I'd let Jane down because I'd only contacted her by phone since the death of her sister. Things happened so fast at Big Bottom after discovery of the Manual Reyes incident, I considered myself fortunate even to get a few minutes to make a phone call. I wanted to pray for her and see what the church could do to minister to her. Also, she'd scheduled the funeral for Saturday, and I knew I'd better learn about her sister so I could tailor the funeral to fit her sister's life.

Jane accepted her sister's death with calm composure. "Age crept up on her and she couldn't do the things she used to do. It's tough getting old, you know it?" Jane's shoulders bent a little more than normal and her eyes had lost some of their sparkle.

"I'm learning fast, Miss Jane."

"Yes, I read the newspaper. How'd you get time to come by here? I figured you'd be tied up all day with the news conference and reporters calling for quotes," Jane said.

"Miss Jane, I'd decided I wouldn't speak of my troubles today, since you've lost your sister. I just came by to learn about her life and to pray with you."

"That's nice of you, but I want you to remember something," she said as she lifted her left eyebrow. "If God let everything run smoothly all the time, we might lose our sense of dependence on Him. You know what I mean?"

"I think so, but tell me more," I said.

"You know all this from your theological studies, but I've learned it from decades of practice in trying to live for Jesus. Just when we think things are going well, boom! Something comes along that devastates us and forces us back to our knees to seek His power, His protection, and His help. Without Him, we can do nothing.

"Now don't get me wrong, I'm not saying God causes things like a sister's death or a staff member's wrongdoing, but I'm saying He works even through those things to strengthen our faith if we'll let Him," she said. "You know what I mean?"

"I do, and you can't know how much you've helped me today," I said. "I came over here to comfort you; instead, you've helped me."

Jane Winfield placed her hand on my shoulder. It felt like the hand of blessing I'd remembered from my ordination service thirty years earlier and chill bumps arose on my neck. I believed she was transferring power from her well of deep spirituality. "Why does God leave us old folks on this earth unless it's to share some of our prayers and insights to help others along?" Jane said.

In my book, Jane Winfield ranks as one of God's choicest servants. I'd only met her on Monday of this week and already felt like I'd known her for years. Before I left, she gave me a good dose of "don't let those folks get under your skin, pastor. God's going to see you through this. I'm going to be praying for you here in my house while you're at that news conference." The best medicine doesn't always come from the pharmacy.

At eleven thirty, the agreed-upon meeting time, I pulled in the parking lot of the Crescent City Grill. After ensuring R. M. was nowhere in sight, I asked the waiter for a corner table to assure privacy, but it was too late for that. There was a wait of twenty minutes or more unless I wanted a place at the bar. He assured me the food would be the same and there would be no wait. So, knowing how hard it would be to reach R. M. Parsons for a change of plans, I reluctantly agreed and followed the waiter to the large mahogany bar. Twelve could sit at the high stools and there were only two open spaces together so I grabbed one and threw my coat over the other for R. M.

Parsons had suggested the place because of the excellent food, the proximity to his office, and the high noise level. We didn't want to risk being overheard planning our strategy. He'd chosen well. The tables behind the bar were full, and the people's chatting away raised the volume so that hearing beyond our table would be difficult. USM was only a half mile up Hardy Street. Students, many with folks I'd assumed to be their parents, filled the restaurant. They made the eatery lively with their smiles, laughter, and the ways of youth.

I'll admit I felt out of place at the bar. While waiting I noticed the framed sayings along every wall. They had witticisms like, "Always be careful about lending money to a friend . . . it can destroy his memory." Another said, "Talk is cheap because supply always exceeds demand."

I sat there sipping a diet coke while looking at the offerings behind the bartender. Johnny Walker and Jack Daniels whiskeys, Smirnoff Vodka, and wines whose names weren't familiar to me lined the wall. I imagined a reporter for the *Hattiesburg Advocate* snapping my picture and writing a story with the caption, "Your sins will catch up to you."

The Bible does say, "Take a little wine for your stomach," and I've discovered many Baptists have lots of stomach trouble. However, I'm a teetotaler and this certainly wasn't the time for a battle on the issue. I get stronger against the stuff every time I have a funeral for a person killed by a drunk driver. Still, I recognize I'd do better cutting down on my food portions, so I don't try to make the issue of drink the unpardonable sin.

After I'd glanced at my watch a dozen times, Parsons arrived, forty minutes late and excusing himself for tardiness due to a client whose case was scheduled for court the next day. The blended smells of cooking fish, shrimp, oysters, gumbo, breads, and seasonings had whetted my appetite, and I'd just summoned the waiter to order when R. M. rushed in. He kept the waiter at the table to save time, as if he'd done this often, and ordered tuna steak on a bun. I ordered the grilled amberjack. I wasn't sorry he'd been late. I'd drawn energy from watching the students and young adults fill the café with joyous laughter and the uplifting sounds of youth. Over fresh fish drowned with diet cokes refilled twice, we decided our approach for the news conference.

Thirty minutes before the conference began, I checked out the church lobby to guarantee proper set up. It surprised me to see two hundred folks, most of whom I assumed to be members; eleven microphones; news crews from three radio stations; WMAD; two Jackson television stations; and several newspapers. Overkill, I thought. Must be a slow news day.

As the crowds continued to arrive, I saw we'd have to move the conference into the only place on campus large enough to support the numbers, the sanctuary. I hadn't wanted to do this because I wanted Big Bottom members to associate the sanctuary with worship, not the confession of wrongdoing. Then it occurred to me that "sanctuary" meant "holy place," and confession before God and man is one of the holiest things we can do when we appear in His sanctuary.

With cameras rolling, I asked those who attended to excuse our forcing them to set up in one place and then move, but I'd not expected so many people. Then I opened our conference with prayer, extolling the holiness of God and asking His forgiveness for the times each of us fail Him, not only the one whose actions caused the news conference, but the rest of us as well.

The newspapers, of course, weren't live and said nothing about the prayer putting all of us on level ground. The television stations also edited their coverage. The radio stations had chosen to cover the event live, however, and therefore broadcast the prayer along with the rest of the conference. Weeks afterward people were still calling in to the church office to set up counseling appointments because they'd heard the prayer and realized they were as guilty as Pastor Reyes, hadn't yet been caught, and wanted a way out.

R. M. Parsons hadn't arrived and it was fifteen minutes after the hour. I was learning that although God is never late His Parsons often are. With Dr. Sam Jones and long-time associate pastor Carter Ross by my side, I decided to begin the meeting. I shared the things Parsons and I'd agreed upon. With the clicks of camera taking pictures in the background, I began with a brief history of Big Bottom Baptist Church. I told how the church had been founded to minister to people in the area and to reach others with the Gospel. I listed a number of areas of community outreach Big Bottom Church sponsors and how we were thrilled to offer services for our members and others.

Then I told how the Lord had led Big Bottom Baptist to begin a Hispanic ministry to serve a people group new to our region. I shared how the relationships between the church and the Hispanics who attended the mission meetings had grown, how the church had provided vital services to Hispanic members, and how the church desired to continue the good relationships with the entire community, including Hispanic people.

At that point, I shared the chief reason for the called news conference. "The Big Bottom Hispanic staff member, Pastor Manual Reyes, has resigned for personal reasons," I said. "These reasons included inappropriate suggestions to a lady who attended the Hispanic worship services. Big Bottom Church does not now and has not ever condoned immoral or inappropriate actions by her staff or members. We believe in a redeemed fellowship. We believe God can and will save anyone who comes to Him, and we believe that coming to the Lord includes genuine repentance and turning from sin.

"The reason for a public news conference is that, although we do not believe Pastor Reyes' actions were widespread, we wanted to offer counseling and advice on how to follow up with appropriate legal action if anyone else has been harmed by Pastor Reyes. Big Bottom Church exists to help, not to hurt, individuals and families; and we want to maintain integrity by helping people even if the publicity may damage the church."

I then opened the floor for questions. A flood of hands rose. Associate Pastor Ross knew most of the people present and began to call them by name to come to the microphone to ask their question.

"How many women has Pastor Reyes molested?" was asked first, by a long-time member.

"We are not saying he has molested women, only that there was the appearance and some evidence of wrongdoing," I answered.

The next question quickly followed, "Then are you saying he molested men or boys?" An audible gasp emerged from the group.

"No," I replied, "I'm not saying he molested anyone."

The next questioner asked, "Then why did you call the news conference?" I heard a chorus of "Yeah" emerge.

I replied, "Because openness and honesty ought to be a mark of God's people. Big Bottom Church has nothing to hide. We want to be transparent before the community. And we want anyone who believes injury came to them personally by Pastor Reyes to make it known to us at the church so that we can offer counseling and legal advice."

Betta Lovett, a member of the personnel committee who had attended the meetings with Pastor Reyes and had voted against making the findings of the committee public, spoke next. I knew Betta from the pastor search committee. Betta Lovett had represented the choir and the large singles' ministries when on the search committee. She was attractive, in her thirties, with blond hair that fell down to her shoulders only to flip upward an inch in perfect symmetry. Betta is short for Elizabeth, but we found her accurately named for the ministries she represents.

During the search committee meetings, Darla, who has a spiritual gift of discernment, said she felt Betta Lovett would be intensely for us or just as intensely against us, depending on her mood and the pressure of others. After only a few minutes in Darla's presence, she'd complained about the previous pastor who "never so much as stuck his head into the door of the singles' department," about her previous husband, and about the trends in congregational music. "Why, we may as well sell the pipe organ, for all the use it's getting these days." When I thought of Betta afterwards, what came to mind was the child who prayed, "Lord make the bad people good and the good people easier to live with."

Her comments during the news conference surprised me, "Pastor Paulson, if you aren't going to tell us what Pastor Reyes did wrong, then why did you call this meeting?" Out of the corner of my eye I saw a number of folks nodding in agreement and several could still be heard saying, "Yeah."

I don't know why, maybe it was the lights from the television cameras, but for the first time that afternoon I saw S. A. Tanner. S. A. spoke his "Yeah," loudly enough from his place two-thirds back in the assembly to be heard above the rest. The combination of the question from one who knew and the appearance of S. A. to instigate dissent during the news conference stunned me. I stood on stage, mouth open in astonishment, but no words coming.

Sam Jones must have sized up what had just happened and quickly took the microphone. "As Pastor Paulson said, we've called the conference in order to be transparent with our community and to open the way for any people hurt by Pastor Manual Reyes' actions to contact the church so we can provide competent professional and legal counseling.

"We also have met with the leaders of the Hispanic mission. We want Hispanics in this area to know Big Bottom stands squarely in support of the mission, but also against sin of any kind. The leaders of the Hispanic mission feel the same way and wanted to express their solidarity with us in these actions. In fact, the moderator of the mission, deacon Jesus Gonzales, stands on the platform with us today," Sam said.

Other questions centered around how much we could say about what Reyes did, about the damage we thought it might cause the mission church, about harming the image of Big Bottom Church, and whether we'd "bought off Pastor Reyes to keep his mouth shut."

Sam and I were surprised that the hardest questions and those that could have put the church in a bad light came not from the media but from some long-time members.

A little over an hour after the conference began, and just as R. M. Parsons entered, we ended as we'd begun, with prayer. I'd asked Jesus Gonzales before the meeting began and he closed by taking us to God's throne with moving words of heart-felt contrition and pleas of Divine assistance.

After the meeting I invited all those present to the church fellowship hall and treated those who came to coffee, cookies, and sweet fellowship, as if they'd just joined the church. In the months to come I realized God had shown His grace by providing this time so I could get to know several key members of the media in a less formal setting. Secretly, I figured if we'd just dismissed, gripe groups would have assembled in the parking lot and plotted future strategy against me or the church.

Years ago I heard a little poem that expressed my views:

"They drew a line and shut us out,
Heretic, rebel, a thing to flout;
But love and I had a will to win.
We drew a circle and took them in."

13

FINISHING A TOUGH WEEK

I took the morning off on Friday. After a month of packing and moving, a night of tossing and turning, and the roughest start to a pastorate I'd ever had, when I woke up Friday morning I could barely move. By eight o'clock, Darla finished her breakfast and came back into the bedroom to check on me.

"Sleepyhead, you'd better get up," she said.

"I'm not getting up yet, Darla," I said.

"Why? Are you sick?" she asked.

"Not exactly," I answered.

"Oh, I know. You're feeling down, aren't you?" she asked.

"You might say that."

"It's all that trouble from Pastor Reyes and the newspaper, isn't it?" she asked.

"Maybe," I replied.

"Well, I know what to do to fix you up," she said as she crawled in bed beside me and began rubbing my shoulders. Her soft hands felt wonderful as they worked out the knots caused by the stress of the past few days. "You know if you'll get up and get busy you'll feel better," she said. Darla's soft suggestions coupled with her touch were manna from heaven. She always knows what to do to encourage me. It worked and I began to open up to her.

"Darla, do you realize we haven't had a moment's rest since we came here? I have to prepare a funeral sermon today, preach it tomorrow, and think about what I'll preach at church on Sunday morning and evening. I've hardly had time to catch my breath all week, and I've got three messages to prepare before Sunday," I said. I'd readied my first month of sermons before moving but somehow Bluegrass sermons didn't feel right for the Magnolia state. Since we'd had all the trouble, the messages didn't seem to fit.

The great fear of pastors is what some call, "the relentless return of Sunday." No matter what happens during the week, Sunday soon arrives and the pastor'd better have a word from God for the people. It's terrible to have to say something and not have something to say.

When I first began preaching, I said everything I knew—twice—in the first six months. I wondered where in the world pastors got all their material week after week for fifty years. Then I began to get more deeply into God's Word. Soon I realized that fifty lifetimes wouldn't be sufficient for teaching all the Word. For the pastor who studies, there's always more to say than years to say it. The Bible is a bottomless treasure.

I asked Darla if she'd mind calling the office to let them know I'd not be in that day but they could reach me on my cell phone if they needed me. She also, at my request, asked Associate Pastor Ross to handle any questions that came from the church or news media. I trusted Carter Ross, and furthermore the people of Big Bottom Church trusted him. He'd proved himself with faithful service over fifteen years under the leadership of three pastors.

I finally got up, ate a bowl of Darla's hot, homemade vegetable soup for breakfast to clear my sinuses and get half my veggie intake for the day. I read a little from the Bible; and then I took my prayer reminder cards to the deck overlooking Lake Serene. After a few minutes with the Lord, I felt better, but still not ready to face another day of Big Bottom troubles. There had to be something going on behind the scenes, an underlying mischief motivating some of the members to ask the questions they did in the news conference, but I'd not yet figured it out.

I piddled around a few minutes and found myself in the garage where I picked up two fishing rods and my tackle box and headed to the dock. The cool air striking my cheeks and the smell of fresh water invigorated me. From the time my granddad Paulson took me fishing at his pond when I was a boy, I've loved being around a fishing lake. It refreshed me to hear the splash of the lure and to see the ripples as the artificial bait progressed along its journey back to the rod. I spent a quiet hour tossing lures and talking with the Lord. Although I didn't catch a fish, within an hour I knew what to say at the funeral and what passages of Scripture I felt the Lord wanted me to preach in the services on Sunday.

I'd gladly have stayed all morning, just being alone with the Lord and the lake. After all these years of being a Christian, I still find it amazing how I can start a day with the doldrums, but take a few minutes with the Lord and He fills me with get-up-and-go. He proves Himself to me over and over again.

I decided to preach on Sunday morning from Matthew 11 where Jesus issued His Great Invitation, "Come unto Me all you who labor and are heavy laden and I will give you rest." I knew from studying the passage and from personal experience that the kind of rest Jesus referenced is not that found in an easy chair. No, it's the refreshment of doing something that has purpose and meaning, the kind of supernatural energy that comes from being part of something bigger than we are.

As I rejoiced at what the Lord had just done in my life—replacing the pits with a pizzazz—a water moccasin caught my attention. He was a big one, warmed out of hibernation by two weeks of above average temperatures and by the February sun. He swam toward me to see what the splashing lure was all about. I reeled in and made two mental notes: one, that the serpent always interrupts God's work, and two, that I'd need to bring a heavy stick with me each time I came to the dock. At any rate I had joy, real joy, again. No wonder some bumper stickers down South say, "A bad day fishing is better than a good day at work." Yes, especially when Jesus is your fishing buddy.

I visited the funeral home on Friday afternoon and, in addition to praying for Miss Winfield and her two sisters, I met a number of other elderly members of Big Bottom Baptist Church. Early Washburn, in particular, caught my interest because of his name and uncanny proclivity to speak in clichés. Although I'd not yet met him, I'd heard of Early and his unusual name. As his wife, Wanda, reminded me within fifteen seconds of our initial meeting, his family was one of the early settlers of the area and had owned thousands of acres.

Early received his unusual name when his mother delivered him after thirty weeks of pregnancy. The Washburns hadn't decided on a name. When a nurse stuck her head in the hospital room to ask Mrs. Washburn, the reply was, "He's early." Before Mrs. Washburn could explain further, the nurse was called away and the Washburns later discovered, to their horror, "Early Washburn" had been typed on the birth certificate. Back then not many people went through the legal steps to change a name, so the baby became Early Washburn. I've been told he's lived up to his name and almost always arrives fifteen to thirty minutes before any meeting.

I'd come before the set time so I could pray with the sisters, and I stayed until the doors of the funeral home's inner parlor were opened for guests. The Washburns were first in line. Wanda hurried Early over to me, presumably to introduce him.

"Pastor Paulson, I'm so glad you're here. And, I've heard you've been over to Miss Jane Winfield's home earlier this week. Thank you," Wanda said.

"Yes, Mrs. Washburn," I replied, careful not to offer my hand as I had when I'd offended her on our first meeting. "And I've got to thank you. I went because you suggested it. Miss Winfield is such a delightful woman and so wise."

"Well, I wouldn't go that far, pastor, but it was good of you to go. There are lots of elderly folks at Big Bottom who've given their best years in service, and we just can't forget them. I know any pastor worth his salt will make time for the saints who built this church," she said.

Wanda Washburn is one of the small sorority who apparently meet often to practice verbally slapping people while giving compliments. A flattering remark is offered with one hand, a person reaches out to grasp it, and POW! The other hand smacks with force. Wanting to change the subject, I asked, "And is this Mr. Washburn? A pleasure to meet you, sir," I said, extending my hand.

Early Washburn stood about six feet tall, two inches taller than I. Like his wife he was slim, but unlike her, Early was red-faced with a bulbous nose that shined even redder, as if he'd imbibed a few drinks in his day. He dressed in a black suit with a white shirt and grey tie. A white handkerchief with crisp folds protruded from the front left pocket. He looked the part of the landed gentry. He grasped my hand firmly and shook while saying, "Don't put your foot in your mouth, pastor."

"Pardon?" I asked.

"I said, 'Put your best foot forward, but don't put it in your mouth, or it'll be a bitter pill to swallow.'"

"Oh," I said. "I thought I hadn't understood you. What do you do for a living, Mr. Washburn?"

"Oh, a little of this and a little of that. I've worked like a dog all my life, but when your back's up against the wall, what can you do? You can't put all your eggs in one basket, now can you?" he said.

Wanda gazed intently at him. "I just love to hear my husband speak, pastor. Isn't he something?"

With a straight face and one-hundred-percent truthfulness I replied, "Mrs. Washburn, any man with you must be something special."

"Well, thank you," Wanda Washburn said, turning slightly. She blushed and the thought occurred to me that she does belong to the human race, after all.

Early turned to me and said, "Of course she likes to hear me; after all, you can't bite the hand that feeds you."

Judging him to be around seventy, I asked, "Are you retired, Early?"

"Curiosity killed the cat, you know. But since you asked, I'll tell you that ever since I was knee-high to a grasshopper, I've been taking the bull by the horns and getting with it. But Rome wasn't built in a day, and you can take that to the bank because, after all, you drive for show and pick up the spare for dough."

We continued like this for several minutes and I suddenly realized I didn't know anything more about Early than I did when we'd first started speaking, except that he was married to Wanda and spoke in clichés, presumably to avoid being real. All the while Wanda looked on at him with a gaze that neared worship. I'd been called to be Early's pastor, but I didn't know how to relate to him, except to practice transparency myself.

While we were talking I breathed a silent prayer asking the Lord to help me understand Early and to be a good pastor to him. It came to me that, over the years, he may have invented this way of relating to avoid having to be authentic with his judgmental wife. Or, did she become like she is in reaction to him? Family systems are fascinating, and sometimes deadly.

The funeral and the meal afterwards went better than expected, but then came the fiasco of the flipping chairs at the graveside service. I spent the next two hours driving back from Metairie on Interstate 59 alternating between laughing at a once-in-a-lifetime occurrence and speaking out my morning message.

I practice the "oral manuscript" method of preparation and it helped to have two hours on the highway, without interruptions. I had a few stares from some people who'd pull alongside when I'd come to a more animated part of the sermon and raise my hands with gestures. Steering with knees isn't that unusual, is it?

My neighbor, Ben Dover, told me he'd driven to work recently along his customary route on Highway 98 and had received the shock of his life at a traffic light. He glanced into the car beside him and observed the driver reading the newspaper and watching a program on the video screen mounted on the passenger-side console. When the light changed, the man roared off with his paper still obstructing half the windshield. Dr. Dover said it scared him so much, "I almost dropped my electric razor into my cup of coffee!"

The folks who passed me probably thought they'd seen a madman. They didn't know they were observing a dress rehearsal for Big Bottom Baptist Church's morning worship service.

Darkness fell more than an hour before my arrival in Hattiesburg. I was exhausted. I went to bed early that Saturday night before my first Sunday morning sermon as pastor of Big Bottom. My mind ponged back and forth between the morning sermon, the moral failure of Pastor Reyes, the subterfuge of S. A. Tanner, the newspaper article, the news conference, the wisdom of Jane Winfield, the clichés of Early and the lack of humor in Wanda Washburn.

I'd had a tough first week. I also had an assurance within, given by the Holy Spirit, that God raised me up for just such a time as this, to help others and point them to the God of grace who never fails us.

14

TOUCHDOWN

Sunday is the first day of the week. I needed a new week to roll around. The last one had been disastrous. I knew, however, God doesn't always view things like I do. Darla sensed that God may want to do some housecleaning at our church. I joked about taking a mop into the sanctuary; but she said, with all seriousness, "No, Brent, you know what I mean. I hate to put it to you this way, but when you find ungodliness in one place there may have been an open door for other ungodliness to travel in; you know, like train cars follow an engine."

"Thanks, Darla, that's just what I need. It'll take me a year to get over the Reyes incident, and now you're telling me that I may have a train load full of them."

"Well, honey, I just don't want you caught off guard. Will you promise me you'll pray for God to help you through this?" she asked.

"That'll be the easiest promise I've ever made," I said. "But will you promise me you'll be praying, too? One more incident like last week and I'm afraid Big Bottom will have long-term damage."

"Well, God's the One who builds up and the One who allows a tearing down. If we'll just stay right with Him, He'll see us through this. He'll help the church, too. He knew what He was doing when He brought you here," she said.

I love my wife. How could I help but love her? As a man I ought to be the one protecting her, but I felt ashamed I'd had us move and now we had to deal with all this mess. Yet, she not only wasn't complaining, but she was also praying for me and giving me spiritual wisdom. God threw away the mold when He made Darla.

I felt fortunate the church received no more reports about any other wrongdoing by Pastor Reyes. It may be the lady who works for the Maddens is the only one he bothered. Also, the news media had been kind to the church, with the exception of the opening salvo by the *Hattiesburg Advocate*.

WMAD had used Big Bottom's news conference as its opening story and spun it as, "Local church shows rare transparency." There had been an editorial at the end of the telecast to praise the church for not trying to hide wrongdoing and for offering help to any victims. The station manager closed his remarks by saying, "We're only human and we fail sometimes—even those of us in church—but we can be honest when we fail. Our hats are off to Big Bottom Baptist Church and her leadership for not trying to cover things up when they ought to be confessed up. Here's one church where people can be real with God and one another."

I expected Sunday morning's attendance to be off and to hear several families were beginning their search for a new church home. When I drove into the parking lot an hour before Sunday school, however, I found it odd that the lot was already beginning to fill. I later learned that the orchestra, praise team, some teachers, and the pastor's prayer partners always come early.

The deacon officers also had a special meeting, without inviting me. I learned that later, too. I should've guessed it when I smelled moth balls upon entering the main hallway, but I didn't see Nev anywhere around.

Six pastor's prayer partners met with me in the pastor's study, as they had with the previous pastor. This group rotated responsibilities so that each prayer partner had the early duty only one Sunday a month. My predecessor had done a great job in helping the church become more prayerful. After all, Jesus said, "My house shall be a called a house of prayer," and "Without Me you can do nothing."

I felt His strong presence as we knelt around my desk and each prayed for God's protection over the church and His power for the pastor and staff. I received a strong sense that the God Who created heaven and earth had chosen to answer those prayers.   The verse from Jeremiah 29:11 came to me, "I know the plans I have for you, plans for welfare and not calamity, plans for a future and a hope."

I got the Sunday school report shortly before exiting the pastor's study for the baptismal pool. Attendance was ten per cent higher than normal, and the Hispanic mission's attendance was also up. Perhaps the incident wouldn't hurt the church or the mission, after all.

When the stained glass window slid to the side along a track to open the baptismal area for congregational viewing, what I saw surprised me. I looked out on a packed church building and chairs being brought into the aisles. More than two hundred people above the normal crowd attended. A sense of excitement filled the air.

One man, accompanied by his family, met me after the service. "We've been looking for a good church. We saw on TV how Big Bottom was honest about a problem staff member. We like the way you handled the problem openly." Echoing the words of WMAD's editorial, he said, "We want a church where we can be real. We think we've found it."

That morning I brought the opening welcome to the worship service from the baptismal water and then baptized two youth who'd accepted Christ during the youth Power Hour on Wednesday night. After the baptisms, I dressed to go back into the worship service, while feeling the power of God on His church. We'd tried to do the right thing, the open and honest and redemptive thing, despite the wrongdoing of a staff member. God had honored it.

The congregation sang, with vigor, the praises of the Lord and I preached with an unusual anointing from God about a rest that is found only in Jesus. Four families joined that morning. Two of the families had never stepped foot in the church before that service. They'd not come expecting to join that day, but sensed a strong leadership of the Lord to do so and obeyed Him.

The offering was received, the announcements were made, and I readied myself for the benediction when deacon chairman Nev Wright quickly rose from the first bench, made his way up to the podium, leaving behind a scent of moth balls, and paused for dramatic effect. After a few seconds he announced the deacon officers had met that morning and decided to call a special meeting of the deacons at nine that night.

Talk about a major downer. I've never been more surprised because I knew nothing of the intention or the background of the meeting. Instead of the people leaving the sanctuary praising God, they left wondering what was wrong. Darla and I shook hands with people at one of the exit doors as has been our custom my entire ministry. At least fifteen people asked why the deacons had called a special meeting. "Must be some little business matter, I suppose," I answered, but the response didn't satisfy them or me.

I called Nev as soon as I got home. "Nev, this is Brent Paulson." As soon as we finished the niceties, I got down to business. "A number of people at the door today asked me why the deacons called a special meeting. I couldn't tell them and it felt awkward. I like to keep in close touch with leaders in the church and support you folks in front of the people. When I don't know what is going on, though, I don't know what to say."

"Well, then, Dr. Paulson," Nev said, emphasizing the title again. "I guess you know how I felt when all the stuff about Pastor Reyes came up."

"Nev," I said, "I thought I'd explained that to you. I called you just as soon as I had a spare minute. I always keep in touch with leaders in the church. You'll see as time goes on. I don't like surprises and I won't surprise you or the other church leaders, if I can help it."

"Yeah, Dr. Paulson," Nev drawled slowly, still emphasizing the "Doctor." "It's the same way with me, too. I was just about to call you. It's the first time I had a spare minute." I didn't believe him. I wanted to believe him but somehow I didn't and that's not like me. I'm so gullible that it's gotten me in trouble. Yet, when Nev spoke with such sarcasm, my spirit received a strong check.

"And if you last here, you'll see that I keep in touch, too; course, I don't know if you'll last," he said.

I made no reply; I couldn't say anything. I couldn't even breathe. I must've gone into a psychotic break or something. It felt like I moved through a fog, or maybe it was my double, an apparition. I know it couldn't have been more than a few seconds, yet it seemed like everything was in slow motion. I seemed to have leaped from the conservation with Nev to an event that happened years earlier.

I was in a football game, suited up at the defensive cornerback position I played when a junior at Oak Grove High School. Since I lettered in football three years at Oak Grove, I remember a number of games, like I suppose every has-been player does. However, in over thirty years of remembrances, I don't believe I'd ever recalled this particular game. Maybe the reason was this game taxed me physically and emotionally more than any I'd ever played. Nev's words brought back something I'd buried deep inside.

The colors of the uniforms were vivid, ours gold and black, and the visiting team's maroon with white stripes and numbers. The turf was wet and tearing up in places, making the footing unsure, despite our inch-long plastic cleats with steel tips. A slight fog hung in the air, the result of a rainy day and a falling temperature. The fans yelled from the stands. I could see it all, exactly as I played the game more than thirty years earlier—the field, the fans, the sidelines, the coaches, the refs, and the players. The temperature was in the forties, but it was humid and steam rose from the players. I was right there, in the game, on the field. The visitors were up by a touchdown and running the ball almost every down.

The team we played wasn't a finesse football team. Richton didn't have slashing runners and pass receivers who'd win with their speed or proficiency in catching the ball. No siree. Their strategy capitalized on their strength and size. These were big, strong boys, made muscular by hauling pulpwood in the summer, at least that's what we'd been told. They wore down their opponents and physically man-handled them, especially as a game wound down. It had worked all season with them and it would work with Oak Grove, too, because we were smaller than most teams in our division. I weighed one-hundred-and-thirty-five pounds. And this was rock 'em, sock 'em, ground and pound, grind it out, smash-mouth football.

They had a two-hundred-pound fullback and often pulled their big guards to get in front of him for sweeps around the end. I used whatever speed, agility, and deception I could to weasel between the guards. Ultimately, though, the tackle had to be made and that meant strong contact. Again and again I fought off the guards only to be run over by the fullback. I'd tackle him every time—I had to, since it was up to me and the defensive end to contain the outside run, but he'd gain five to seven yards a carry. We couldn't stop their running attack and lost by two touchdowns.

It felt helpless to know what they'd do, but still not be able to stop them. And time after time collisions knocked the breath out of me. I hadn't felt that way in years. I could feel the excitement of the run coming my way and knew I'd have to respond, but I also intuited that it didn't make much difference how I responded because the situation was beyond my ability to manage. Still, I had to try.

After several seconds of flashback that must have seemed like silence to Nev, he said, "Did you hear me?"

I saw the guard pull and knew the sweep would soon follow. I sidestepped him and he managed only a glancing block. "Yes, Nev, I heard you. May I make a suggestion?"

"Sure, sure you can. We always want to know what our pastor thinks."

Insincerity rang in his voice. "Nev, we seem to have gotten off on the wrong foot. May I take you to lunch tomorrow? I've always had a good association with the deacon chairman at the churches I've pastored, and I suggest we start all over. Let's make our working relationship one of mutual admiration and support."

"Well, pastor, after the deacons' get-together tonight, you might not want to meet with me," he said.

The other guard bore down on me and I knew I must evade him or else the big fullback would have no one to stop him for at least ten more yards. "Whap," he popped me strongly on the shoulder pads, but I managed to turn to the side so that I bounced off and stayed on my feet. "Yeah, uh, yeah, the meeting. Nev, I wanted to ask you what the meeting concerns," I said.

"Concerns?" he parroted.

"Yeah, what's up? What's going on?" I asked.

"Haven't you guessed? It's about you and the dissatisfaction the deacon officers have with you."

I looked up from the block of the second guard to see the fullback, now with a full head of steam, bearing down on me. I lowered my helmet just in time; he'd already lowered his. "Crack!" It sounded like two rams meeting head on. We both fell hard but five yards beyond the line of scrimmage. For a moment I was oblivious to the world.

"You there? You there? What's a matter, has the call dropped? Has a bird flown between your cell phone and the tower?" He was being facetious, almost taunting, but his words stunned me too deeply to reply.

That kind of thing happened to other pastors, but never before to me. After all, I was easy going. I always got along well with others. It wasn't difficult for me to admit when I was wrong. I've always been okay with doing most anything church leaders felt they needed to do, as long as it fit the mission of the church, would honor the Lord, and could be done with integrity and excellence. But now it appeared my job was at stake. Only weeks after signing a heavy mortgage and moving my family from a loving church, and only one week into my ministry at Big Bottom, It appeared I'd be struggling to keep my job. I knew further talk would be like trying to convince that two-hundred-pound fullback to shake my hand instead of running over me.

"Well, I guess I'll see you at nine, tonight." I said.

"Oh, you don't need to worry about that; you aren't invited to this meeting. You'll be hearing from us, though," he answered.

The crowd in the visitors' stands roared and I looked up to see the referee signaling touchdown. Several plays had passed without my awareness. The last I remembered they'd been on the forty yard line.

"Tell you what, Nev. I'm pastor of Big Bottom Church and I can come to the meeting if I think I need to, but I'll certainly pray about it and do what the Lord directs me to do. I'm asking you to pray about the meeting, too, and do only what He tells you to do."

"Oh, I've already prayed," he said. "Me, S. A. Tanner, H. H. Smith, Early Washburn, and the former officers."

15
SUNDAY STARTS A NEW WEEK

When I hung up the phone in my office, the football game vanished but the fog remained. I'd counseled enough people who'd had a significant loss to realize I was in shock. A family member hadn't died, but my hopes for a peaceful ministry and my respect in Big Bottom Church had. I'd just arrived at Big Bottom and already disaster threatened. It blew my mind.

Some have questioned God in times like these and I don't judge them. Each person is different, and God is big enough to handle it when people do question Him, but I didn't. I felt His Presence with me and wondered if this is what Paul referenced in Philippians Chapter Four as, "peace that passes understanding." I prayed until words would not form in my mind. Then I sat for a long time. At last I asked God for a scripture to help me through the rough times to come. In my heart I intuited—no, "apprehended" is a better word because it seemed to come to me from the outside, from supernatural realms—"Psalm 37." It couldn't have been plainer if I'd heard a voice.

I picked up my study Bible, turned to Psalm 37, and began to read,

> Do not fret because of evildoers,
> Be not envious toward wrongdoers.
> For they will wither quickly like the grass,
> And fade like the green herb.
> Trust in the Lord and do good;
> Dwell in the land and cultivate faithfulness.
> Delight yourself in the Lord;
> And He will give you the desires of your heart.
> Commit your way to the Lord,
> Trust also in Him, and He will do it.

I grasped this was a spiritual battle and I didn't need to worry about it. What I needed was to stay close to Him, trust Him, and let Him fight the battle for me.

I talked with Darla. It hurt to have to tell her of the troubles. We needed prayer, however. There was no getting around it. She had to know. I asked her to sit down.

Darla sat in a kitchen chair. I moved another one close by, sat down beside her, and held her hand. I looked in the eyes of the woman I loved more than life itself. Darla intuits so many things that she knew something was wrong, seriously wrong, before I'd asked her to sit. Her eyes widened, her skin turned pale, and she grasped the edge of our oak table so hard her knuckles turned white.

I'd seen this look on Darla's face twice before. More than twenty years earlier when she heard her brother had died in a car wreck she looked that way. She'd also appeared that ashen when she'd heard of a friend's losing her husband. He'd left for work doing fine that morning but he'd had a massive heart attack that afternoon. Darla's pupils dilated. She'd released one hand from the table and was twirling her auburn hair. She'd guessed the news to come. The hurt I saw on her face deepened my own.

I also felt ashamed since I bore responsibility for bringing her back to Mississippi. I wished I could shield her from the hurt. When I told her what Nev had said, she nodded with understanding.

"From the first time I met him, I knew something was wrong in his life. Be careful around him, Brent. He's capable of great evil. We've got to get some prayer warriors lifting us to God." With those simple words she rose, headed for the phone, and called a friend. From her former Sunday school class Darla knew Joy to be strong in prayer. Joy promised to call the other class members to enlist their prayer support, too.

In the meantime I used my cell phone to call S. A. Tanner. "Hello, S. A., this is Brent Paulson. I hope I'm not disturbing you this afternoon."

"No, Brent, glad you called. You feel free to call anytime. Matter of fact, I was just thinking about you." With that he unwound like a spring, telling about some person he'd met in the Firestone Tire Store the previous day while getting the oil changed in his car, a person who'd known me from junior high days. He went on like this, citing four people he'd met at Firestone, Wal Mart, and Kroger.

Fifteen minutes later, I grabbed the first opening I dared and reminded S. A. that I'd asked the pastor search committee to serve as a pastor support committee for the first year of my pastorate at Big Bottom Church. He remembered.

I mentioned the announcement of Nev Wright that morning at the conclusion of worship and that, since S. A. served as a deacon officer, he must've known about it. He hemmed and hawed but, at last, acknowledged it.

"What's going on, S. A.?" I asked.

"Oh, I wouldn't worry too much, pastor," he exclaimed in a jovial tone of voice. "You won't lose your job over this. Least I don't think you will. The deacons will reprimand you for not keeping them informed and watch you a little closer, that's all."

"Reprimand me? Watch me a little closer? For heaven's sake, I've been here a week and we've had all this trouble with the Hispanic mission. Now you tell me the deacons will watch me closer and want me to keep them more fully informed?" I felt my face flush and my jaw tighten. "S. A., If I wasn't doing something right, why in the world didn't you say something before it got to this point? I had no idea about all this."

"You pastors are all alike," he replied. "The last pastor claimed he didn't know, either, but we clipped his wings, too. And the one before that. I wouldn't worry about it. We'll work it out."

"S. A., you told me you wanted a servant leader, but you didn't say you wanted a servant to follow your leading."

"Now don't get all worked up. These things happen in every family and we'll work it out."

"Well, tell me this," I said. "When did you begin to suspect I wasn't keeping you or the other deacons informed?"

"That's easy," he replied. "When the votes began during the time the personnel and mission committees met with Pastor Reyes. Couldn't you see my votes were different than most of the committee members'? That should've been a clue to you to back off and delay those votes," he said.

"Let me get this straight, S. A. Are you saying I should have ignored the majority of the committee members to do what you wanted?" I asked, astonished.

"You said it, not me; but, after all, I was the one who brought you here and you owe me that much, don't you think?" he answered.

I was too shocked to say much at that point. After a few seconds of silence I managed, "It appears you and I have different perceptions of a pastor and to whom he owes his allegiance, but let's talk this out some time soon." I began to feel overwhelmed again. Something inside told me this would be a problem for months to come. Something also told me this wasn't the main problem, just the lightning rod for some other difficulty. I could smell the coffee brewing but didn't know where to find the pot.

I heard Darla still talking on the phone with her friend, so I decided to call Sam Jones. Sam apologized on behalf of the church and the search committee and said he hurt for Darla and me, in particular because the service had gone so well before the ill-timed announcement of the called deacons' meeting. Then he told me similar things had happened to the previous two pastors. He said the committee had recognized I had strong communication skills and felt the problem wouldn't come up with me; therefore, they hadn't wanted to taint the search process by sharing with me the difficulties with the previous pastors. "In hindsight," he said, "we blew that call and that's why I can't apologize enough."

I heard the hesitation in his voice, a sign of embarrassment and contrition.

"You see, in the past, we had pastors with aggressive management styles who hadn't always kept the people informed. The committee thought it best not to mention it to you because they felt, with new leadership and a different mix of spiritual gifts, no problem would emerge. Now I realize the difficulty didn't rest in the pastor, but in the deacon officers who wanted to run the church."

Sam went on to explain the church had an antiquated system of electing deacon officers, with the present officers forming the nominating committee for new officers each year. The importance of this couldn't be overestimated because in Big Bottom Church the officers set the agenda and tone for the deacons. For at least fifteen years the deacon officers had rotated among six men. When anyone mentioned a need to bring in new leaders, they replied, "Well, the church is growing and we seem to be doing okay." Then Early would add, "Why upset the applecart by adding some watermelons?"

According to church by-laws, after three years of service, a deacon must wait a year before being selected by the church to serve another three-year term. However, among the six, at least three were always active deacons. The spots seemed to rotate back and forth among the six, according to which men were serving a three-year term as a deacon and were available. Even though there were only three officers at a time, these were so entrenched that all six met in the deacon officer gatherings whether or not they served as active deacons.

I heard his voice begin to quiver as Sam said, "Four of the men are on the deacon body now, but all six participated this morning in the decision to call the special meeting. It took me most of the afternoon to get to the root of the problem, and I'm flat-out mad.

"These shenanigans have happened enough at the university that I've come to expect them, but I just don't expect them at church. I guess it's just the nature of people to want power. I'm telling you I'm not going to stand for it. This stuff has got to stop. You come to the meeting if you want, or if you want to let me handle it, I think we've got the votes to take care of it. The officers were using you as the catalyst, but the problem predates you. I now know this power play would have come up no matter who our pastor had been."

"I'm coming to the meeting; but if you don't mind doing it, I'll just stay on the sidelines and let you carry the ball, since you know the men."

"I'll do it, Brent. You can count on me."

Darla was still on the phone when I finished talking with Sam just after four o'clock, so I called Jane Winfield to enlist her prayer support. She promised it and told me she'd already heard of the problem from Tell Connie Barksdale who'd called her after the church services. It shouldn't have surprised me she'd heard form Tell Connie because Darla and I'd gotten a whiff of her penchant for spreading stories from meeting her on the pastor search committee.

At twenty-seven, the youngest on the committee, she worked in the youth ministry. Darla and I enjoyed Tell Connie's enthusiasm. Like Darla she had red hair and freckles. Like Darla also, she had the fun and zeal of one who'd not come to the conclusion that life is sad. Tell Connie could pass for a co-ed at Southern Miss; yet she hadn't let the distinguished or aged members of the committee intimidate her.

I asked how she came by her name. She told the story with graciousness; as if it'd been the first time she'd ever been asked. Her father, Dr. Clifford Barksdale, taught archaeology in the Biblical Studies Department at William Carey University, a Baptist institution only ten miles from Big Bottom. For many years Dr. Barksdale took students to the sites of ancient cities for archaeological digs. The cities are built on mounds overlooking their surrounding plains, and the sites are called, "tels." Tel Aviv, Israel's capital, retains the "Tel" in its name.

The fact her father loved these digs so much led him to name his daughter, Tell. He spelled her name "Tel" but few others knew what a tel was and so at Oak Grove Elementary she'd been forced to add the additional letter and spell her name, "Tell Connie Barksdale." Rumor had an alternate view: Connie had heard a family secret and let it slip in an embarrassing place and from then on was known as "Tell Connie."

At any rate, after letting me know from whom she'd heard the news, Jane said, "I've got something to say to you." She hesitated a moment before launching in again. "I don't want you to think I'm a clairvoyant or anything. I don't get visions; no, nothing of the sort. I'm not like that woman on television who sees ghosts."

"Miss Winfield, I don't think that or I wouldn't have called you."

"Well, let me ask you. Are you sitting down?"

"Yes, matter of fact, I am. Why?" I asked.

"I took a little nap right after Tell Connie called me. I had the situation at church heavy on my heart. And I guess the Lord gave me a dream. I don't understand it all but I knew I should tell you."

My interest piqued. "What'd you dream?"

"I dreamed that there were six deer on the front yard of the church. You don't think I'm strange, do you?" she asked but didn't wait for an answer.

"These bucks had big antlers and one in particular had huge horns. The strangest thing, though. Their horns interlocked. They rushed towards the church when it was full, all six of them linked together, and it seemed they'd run over people. Some folks were scattering to get out of their way. You were in the front and they were heading straight for you. About that time, I saw a hand from heaven appear in the clouds and drop a sheet between the church and the six, a sheet invisible to the people, but I had no trouble seeing it. Those six bucks ran into the invisible sheet and fell down. They got up and tried again and again and again. Each time they'd hit the sheet God dropped from heaven and they couldn't progress any further.

"After several tries one set of horns came unhooked from the others and the buck shed his antlers. The curtain lifted and he walked under. He'd become a person just like the other church members, and he was no longer a threat.

"The others just kept on trying, but they couldn't get beyond the sheet. It seemed to me God was shielding His people—and you—from harm. I didn't understand what the number six means. I also don't understand what it meant that one became like us. I don't understand the horns, either, but I had the strongest sensation that I must tell you. I couldn't not tell you. I've tried to figure it out, but I can't unless God is saying He's protecting His church. Does all this mean anything to you?" she asked.

"It sure does. It sure does. It means you're in touch with God. And it means I'm going to call on you whenever I have a prayer concern."

"Oh, you're just trying to flatter me," she said.

"No, no, no. It's true. You can't know how much your dream means to me. I was so worried about the deacons' meeting coming up, but now I'm just going to look over my sermon for tonight and take a little nap," I said.

"Good deal. If you can take a nap that'll do you a world of good, least it always does for me. It's amazing how a problem will come up and I'll feel all down but a little nap and a little trust in the Lord will perk me right up again," she said. Although I couldn't see her, I'll bet she raised her left eyebrow as she said it.

I shared with Darla, and we embraced, rejoicing in the fact God seemed to have shown us His answer already. Reassured, I looked over my evening sermon and did just as Jane Winfield had suggested, I lay down for a little nap.

Darla lay beside me. It felt good to have her arms around me and mine around her as we prayed for God's protection for us and for His church. We also asked His assistance in the deacons' meeting to do what needed to be done to help the church. The next thing I knew the alarm clock rang its shrill wake-up call. Darla had gotten up to pray and to find promises in her Bible. She complained that I could sleep for twenty minutes and be refreshed when twenty minutes of siesta for her would leave her too sluggish to do anything except sleep some more.

I felt refreshed for the evening services. While Darla dressed for the worship, I looked over the message. Soon we drove to church, talking along the way about the strange events that had transpired that day and trying to make sense of it all. We concluded that God must want to do something powerful in Big Bottom Church for Satan to raise an uproar so soon after I'd become pastor.

I was told the crowd of five hundred people at evening worship was a great deal larger than normal. With the deacons' meeting and the anticipation of what might happen, I'd expected a crowd. The Lord had led me to preach from Joshua 3:5 where Joshua advises God's people to "consecrate yourselves today, for tomorrow I will do wonders among you."

In the middle of the message a man got up from his pew near the front center of the sanctuary and began to walk around the building. I'd noticed his wife dive to catch his arm when he first rose, but she was a moment too late and he made it into the aisle. Some of the people began to chuckle and I lost their attention. After three trips up and down various aisles, he approached his former seat and his wife waved as if hailing a cab. As he neared her, she managed to grab his arm. He sat by her side with consideration again. At the conclusion of the service, they came out the door where Darla and I stood to greet people. They looked about seventy years old.

"Pastor, we're the Hartfields, Robert and Sue, and we've got to apologize about Robert's getting up. I hope it didn't disturb you." I noticed Sue acted as spokesperson for the two.

"Mrs. Hartfield, it is a delight to meet you two. I'm glad to be your pastor." I avoided the subject of Robert's moment of fame.

Sue continued, "We're so sorry, but Robert can't help it. When he goes to sleep, it just comes over him and he doesn't know it. He takes heart medicine and it makes him drowsy. He's liable to fall off to sleep anywhere and . . ." with this Sue lowered her voice as if telling me a secret. "Sometimes he walks in his sleep. We sit so that I'm on the outside of the aisle most of the time, but Robert had a nap today and I didn't think he'd doze again. We're so sorry. We feel so ashamed. Maybe we shouldn't come to church anymore. Please accept our apologies and we won't be back." She hesitated a moment and examined my face as if she were waiting to see how I'd react.

"Wait a minute, Sue. I know some folks take medicine or have medical conditions and go to sleep when they'd rather be awake. Please don't stop coming because of this. Besides, if everyone stopped coming for every medical condition, I'd have no one to preach to." They chuckled. I hadn't notice the two slumping before but now I detected their shoulders straighten and they stood taller.

After a few more niceties the Hartfields left. The next person in line was Mike, the young man who'd pulled the restroom prank and who'd helped me move in. I could see he'd been laughing, but with his hand over his mouth to keep the Hartfields from seeing him. When they walked beyond hearing range he snickered as he shook my hand, "You're some pastor, you know it? You help people."

He must have noticed my look because he said, "No, I mean it, you do. As a result of the sermon tonight two people rededicated their lives to Christ during the invitation." Then he paused for effect. "Also tonight, one man went to sleep. Ha, you put some to sleep and you wake some up!" With that he stepped away, laughing as he went.

I decided then and there I liked that young man. He had spunk. And creativity. Yes, the Lord might call him into ministry one day.

The incident reminded me of my friend Curt whose sermons were edited for cassette tapes and CDs and made available to the public. Curt told me a lady called his church and requested a half-dozen of his sermons because she'd, "been having trouble going to sleep." He didn't know if she wanted to substitute his sermons as a sleep aid, a little like counting sheep, or if she wanted to make productive use of her time while awake.

And that's the trouble with much of a pastor's ministry. It's hard to know if growth occurs in people's lives. A carpenter knows each day what he's done—he can see the progress. We pastors can measure bricks and bucks and baptisms—but how do you measure real development in people's lives? We have to lean on Proverbs 3:5-6, "Trust in the Lord with all your heart and lean not on your own understanding; in all your ways acknowledge Him and He will direct your paths." In other words, we commit ourselves to the Lord, try to follow His leading, and then trust Him with the outcome. Come to think of it, that's pretty much the way all of us have to live the Christian life.

Darla and I went home after church, ate chicken noodle soup and crackers and shed a few tears as we talked. We were tired, tired from the moving and setting up a new house, tired from the funeral and the chair flipping episode, tired from the Reyes incident and the news conference, tired from deacon officers' fiasco, and tired from everything being so new and so different.

Even though we knew God was in control, we felt cheated by some of the events. The deacon officers had robbed us of the excitement that moving home, starting a new job, and meeting new people should bring. Instead of being refreshed and invigorated, we felt exhausted; yet we knew we'd have to spend more days like this one before the problems were overcome. We also knew, no matter what happened in the deacons' meeting, we still had God, our integrity, and one another. And so we lay on the bed and prayed, putting it all in His capable hands. Darla fell asleep in my arms. I kissed her on the forehead, tucked a pillow under her head, and pulled the sheet over her. I rose from the bed, straightened my shirt, brushed my teeth, put on a tie and coat, grabbed my car keys, and headed for the lions' den. As I left I whispered a prayer that Darla would dream of a kinder, gentler tomorrow.

JOHN ANDERSON TAKES A STAND

On the way to the meeting I wondered if the officers would try to bar my entrance. Although I hate conflict, I'd fight if they tried to block me. The closer I got to the church grounds the more my stomach churned. I didn't want a showdown but if the OK Corral occurred, I'd shoot it out with the best of them. I had to be there to see it and participate if needed.

At 8:50 pm I walked toward the classroom where we met and heard men talking inside. I entered a rear door and took a seat in the back. It surprised me there were no deacons already in the room, except for the officers in the front talking with such excitement that they'd missed my arrival. I could pick up only bits and pieces of their conversation since the room was large and they were huddled like a football team about to run a play. At last I heard S. A. say, "Can you believe he'd do that?"

About that time other men began to arrive. The officers, glancing at the influx, saw me. "There he is now," S. A. said.

I breathed a prayer and gave S. A. a smile. He peered back with a face of stone but lifted his right foot and put it down several times. He also took out his handkerchief and snorted. The cumulative effect made me think of a bull deciding whether to charge. I had to ask God to forgive me for seeing myself as a matador wanting to insert the sword, especially when it felt so good to see the image in my mind.

Other men filled the room. Some had somber faces. They hadn't wanted to be called away from their families for this late meeting. Perhaps, like me, they despised conflict but knew it was about to come. Sam Jones entered, saw me, and flashed a thumbs-up sign. Yeah, Sam's going to be a good friend.

Nev Wright called the meeting to order and said, "Take a seat, gentlemen. We've got some serious business to conduct tonight and we'd just as well get to it." The men hastened to find a chair, and all sat except for one of the older deacons, a man who looked familiar. It dawned on me it was Robert Hartfield, the man who'd walked in his sleep in the evening service.

Hartfield spoke up, "Men, you know I seldom say anything in these meetings. It's uncomfortable for me to speak to a group and if I mess up, well, I ask your forgiveness ahead of time, because I knew before we got started tonight that I'd have to say something." Hartfield slumped his shoulders and seldom raised his head as he talked. "As you know, I've been known to walk in my sleep. It's awkward for me and for Sue, too. We'd just about decided to resign from everything and never come back, just to keep from embarrassing ourselves and from disrupting the services. I take medicine and it makes me drowsy, more so if I sit for long or get warm. Well, tonight, as you know," and with this his voice lowered, "I humiliated us again. I hope you'll accept my apology." He bowed his head even further.

Nev Wright broke in. "Yeah, Robert, we all saw it. We know. You're forgiven. Now let's get down to business."

But Robert Hartfield didn't sit down. He lifted his head and said, "Just a minute, Nev. I'm not through." His voice was strong and resolute. "Sue and I apologized to our new pastor, but instead of making us feel bad about it, he treated us with kindness and dignity and told us he wanted us to keep on coming. Unless you've been in my shoes you can't know what that did for Sue and me. Men, we ought to do everything we can to help a pastor like the Lord's given us, and I just wanted you to know I'm dedicating myself to do my best to do just that.

"Now, I've noticed we've not opened our meetings with prayer in a while," Hartfield raised his arm and pointed his finger at Nev to make his point. "I move that tonight and also from now on, we become the spiritual servants we ought to be and go before God in prayer to get His help for our church and our pastor. After all, if we don't have time to call on God to help us make the right decisions, we don't have time to conduct business, period."

Nev Wright stood with his mouth open for a few seconds, thrown off track by Hartfield's new boldness. When he recovered he said, "Of course, I meant to start the meeting with prayer. Of course. Yes, of course. Let's have a season of prayer." And with that at least a dozen men voiced their petitions. Since we were standing with heads bowed, I didn't know who prayed what, but one deacon asked the Lord to protect His church. Another requested, as a deacon body, God would help us never do anything that would hinder the Lord's work. Someone pleaded with God to help us never harm the Lord's church. Several men requested the Lord to help them appreciate their pastor and staff. My chest swelled with pride over these men.

When a good twenty minutes of praying concluded, Nev Wright said, "Now that that's over with, there are some matters concerning the pastor to deal with tonight. The officers now ask the pastor be excused from the meeting."

I continued to sit. No one said a word for at least twenty seconds. Nev broke the ice, "Pastor, I guess you didn't understand me. That means you leave now."

I continued to sit and with calm resolution said, "Mr. Chairman, I understood you but I also know I have a right, as pastor of Big Bottom Baptist Church, to attend the meetings. If this meeting concerns me, then I need to listen. If I've done something wrong, I'll be the first to admit it and learn from it. If something said here tonight is not right, however, I'll reserve the right to speak up about that, too."

S. A. stood up and began to clinch and unclench his fists. H. H. Smith stood also and tried to speak but no words would come. His jowls vibrated as if the words were boiling inside his mouth. About that time several men all spoke up at once so that no single voice was audible. After a few moments Early Washburn motioned for all to be seated. He said, "He's the first pastor we've had to stay in a situation like this. Just remember, though, the first mouse to the cheese gets his head caught in the trap." Several officers laughed and their tension subsided. S. A. and H. H. sat.

Nev read in a monotone as he lifted a prepared document close to his bifocals, "The officers of Big Bottom Baptist Church determined that when the search committee brought Brent Paulson to the church, they'd promised the church better communication than in past administrations. However, when the Reyes incident came up the officers had not been consulted before the personnel and mission committees were called in to deal with the situation."

Before he could continue, a new deacon, a young lawyer named Alex Reynolds who worked with Hancock Bank, spoke up. "Nev, I thought the personnel committee dealt with personnel, at least that's how it is with my company. We all know the mission committee deals with our mission. It seems to me that the committees acted with prayer and responsibility. Also, the Lord gave the church a good name in the community because we handled a bad situation with integrity." At least twenty men chimed in, each with a spirited, "Amen!"

At that point Nev Wright said, "Well, we shouldn't be talking without a motion on the floor, and so I recognize H. H. Smith, clerk of the deacons."

Smith stood and, with deliberate pace, read the motion with the solemnity of a jury foreman giving a guilty verdict. His bass voice and the roll of his jowls made me think of Alfred Hitchcock. "We, the deacon officers, move that Pastor Paulson be censured. We also recommend he meet with the deacon officers for an evaluation every month so the officers can give him appropriate guidance on how to proceed with leading the church."

There was a collective gasp from the deacons. Nev added, "Since the motion comes from a committee, it doesn't need a second and so the floor is open for discussion. Before we talk about this, though, we ought to recognize the officers have the best interests of the church at heart, and we ought to go along with the officers to show the church the deacons are united." I swallowed hard and wondered if I'd made the right decision by staying. I fumed inside. I feared I'd speak in anger.

No one said a word for at least thirty seconds, and you could've cut the air with a knife. By then I was having trouble catching my breath. Several men squirmed in their seats. Nev spoke up again and said, "Well, if there's no discussion, we should vote to make it unanimous." Before I could stand to keep them from railroading their ideas through, I noticed Sam begin to rise. Before he could speak, however, a farmer named John Anderson stood up, speaking as he rose. His face was red, and he gripped one arm of the chair for balance. With his other hand, he held a weathered cane.

"No you don't, confound your hides. You're not getting away with it this time! You've run off other pastors, and if I have anything to do with it you're not going to do it again. Why, in my day we'd have taken you boys out to the woodshed and taught you a little lesson you'd not soon forget," Anderson said. "I'm standing here against you if I have to stand by myself." I was afraid a fight would break out in the room. Sam later told me the fact that John Anderson, the most gentle and soft-spoken man on the deacon body, spoke out with such force compelled the other men to act.

One by one they stood. Man after man rose to his feet. Each one said something like, 'Not on my watch,' or, 'I'm standing with you,' or, 'You can count on me,' or, 'I'm with you, John,' or, 'It'll never happen again.' The fact that thirty-five of the thirty-nine deacons present were on their feet overpowered the officers, and they slunk down in their seats.

Anderson continued, "As a rule I don't speak up but this was more than I could take. I'm in my eighties but I can still smell a skunk. You officers been trying to run the show here at Big Bottom for a long time and now the rest of us are gonna have our say."

Nev interrupted and said, "It's not about that, now, let's stick to the . . ."

But Anderson wouldn't be denied. With a menacing wave of his wooden cane he cut off Nev and said, "You officers might think it's not about that but a bunch of us have seen what you been doing for years. You kept badgering the last two pastors till they had to leave and now you're not even giving the new man a chance. Why, if you had it your way he'd have to get your okay to turn over in bed. He'd have to get your vote to be with his wife. He'd even have to ask your permission to go to the bathroom. What you're doing is wrong and it's unbiblical." He continued to wave the crook of his cane as he spoke as if he'd hit Nev if Nev tried to interrupt again.

"I have a substitute motion to bring. I move the deacons censure our officers and vote to support our new pastor with our prayers and backing."

It shocked me soft-spoken John Anderson could be so forceful. It also surprised me that an aged farmer would know enough about Robert's Rules of Order to bring a substitute motion.

S. A. Tanner jumped up and said, "Oh, no, you can't do that. It's out of order."

"Sure is," Nev Wright added, "cause we got a motion on the floor."

"Well, I think it's in order and I appeal the decision of the chair," John Anderson said.

Again I was surprised at Anderson's use of parliamentary procedure. I didn't know Anderson well, but I'd thought of him as someone who knew farming but not the proper motions to use in a debate.

"Once in a while in my corn field," Anderson began again, "the one that runs along Black Creek, a group of wild hogs will find a hole in the fence. They'll get into the corn at night. If I don't repair the fence and stop them, they'll do more damage the next night and more still the next. Pretty soon they'll ruin the whole field. God's given us a church field to protect, and now's the time to repair the fence and reclaim the field from the hogs who want it all their way," he said while continuing to shake his cane toward the area where the deacon officers were seated. "It's time we deacons did some fence-mending and took back our church for the Lord and the people."

At least a dozen men shouted, "Amen."

I almost didn't believe what I'd heard. I couldn't have written that good a script. The scripture came to mind that the Lord can do, "exceedingly, abundantly, more than we ask or think."

Sam Jones rose from his chair and said, "Men, according to the rules of parliamentary procedure we now must vote to sustain the chair or overturn the chair." After further discussion to explain the vote, Nev's ruling was overturned by a sizable margin and the substitute motion was allowed.

At that point the officers saw they were defeated. Nev said, "Well, I can see you men are in no mood for proper business tonight and it's getting late, so we'll just dismiss and go home."

Anderson was quicker to his feet this time, as if the victory erased his arthritis. "Just a minute, buddy. What about my substitute motion to censure the officers and support the pastor?"

Nev's face tightened. "That's never been done in the history of Big Bottom Baptist Church."

"Well, it's high time we do it and if you keep on delaying my vote I'll amend it to have the officers report to a special committee of deacons each month so we can monitor your progress." The men began to howl with laughter. Several almost fell out of their chairs.

Nev opened the floor for further discussion and soon it was time for the vote. It passed, thirty-five for and four against. The four were the three officers, Nev Wright, S. A. Tanner, H. H. Smith, plus one former officer, Early Washburn. I heard him mutter something about "the worm's turned."

Even from the back of the room I could see S. A. Tanner's face redden and his hands clinch and unclench over and over again. The officers huddled to talk while at least five other groups of deacons talked among themselves. Although I couldn't hear all Tanner said, it seemed to be something like "lost this round but the fight's not over."

Nev Wright stated the meeting was dismissed. But at that point Sam Jones jumped up and said, "No, sir, we've not voted to dismiss yet. I still have a motion to bring."

DEACONS' MEETING IS NOT OVER

Nev Wright said, "Well now, the special meeting was called for a purpose and we've handled that purpose and it's time to go home."

Jones said, "Nev, you've just lost one appeal of the chair by a vote of thirty-five to four, do you want to take the time to lose another one and then handle my motion or shall I just go ahead and bring my motion now?" Several of the deacons snickered.

He exhaled with a heavy sigh, his shoulders sagged, and he said with disgust, "Alright, bring your lousy motion but remember it's getting late, so let's hurry things along, boy."

I wondered whether Sam, as Big Bottom's sole Black deacon, felt offended. When I asked him about it later, though, he said, "No, I didn't let it bother me. I knew he was trying to change the agenda. To tell you the truth, I was so overjoyed about the events of the night and that the other deacons at last had seen what the officers were trying to do, I just wanted to capitalize on our victories as soon as possible and extend them into the future."

Sam moved, "From now on, deacon officers are to be nominated by secret ballot with the person receiving the highest numbers of votes being considered chairman, the next highest as vice chairman, and the third highest as clerk. Also, the votes must be counted in front of the entire body of deacons." The nods of twenty or more heads told me the deacons grasped this would mean a shift in power. Several seconded the motion.

Before we could vote, however, Early Washburn said, "Haste makes waste when you get the cart before the horse." I didn't see how that applied but knowing Early it didn't surprise me.

Tanner then rose to say we couldn't vote for the motion because "the new officers have already been nominated."

Sam countered, "S. A., the new officers don't take office until October, and that's more than eight months away. Normal procedure is that the deacons vote on the new officers in September. Can you tell us who the new nominees are?"

S. A. replied, "Never mind that, they've already been nominated."

Sam asked, "S. A., how can this be? The new deacons rotating in haven't been elected for next year and won't be for at least six more months. Are you telling me the present officers already know who'll be the new officers?"

"Well, yeah," he replied, but just audible and with his head down like a boy whose mom had caught him with his hand in the cookie jar.

Sam said, "That kind of proves the need for a new system, doesn't it, men?"

With a chorus of "Amen," the vote totaled thirty-five for the motion and four against.

The meeting adjourned and the officers stomped out. The rest of us stayed and prayed for thirty more minutes. We laughed and joked, and I even saw some tears running down a cheek or two. Several of the men slapped me on the back and said to call on them if I needed them. Others said not to let the officers get me down because they were licked now. John Anderson said, "I've attended these deacon meetings for years, but tonight's the first time I felt like I had a real voice."

Darla looked so comfortable in her sleep when I got home that I decided to wait until the next morning to tell her the good news. I turned down the covers on my side of the bed, and crawled in beside her, and fell asleep soon after my head hit the pillow.

The next morning Sam woke me with a six o'clock call. "Pastor, you've got some good men behind you, but they're afraid you'll leave the church because you and Darla have been through so much in your first week. They asked me to phone you to ask you to stay and let them help you build Big Bottom Church. Will you stay with us?"

Pastors are not known for being at a loss for words, but I still hadn't processed the events of the previous night enough to answer. At last I tried but my voice kept cracking, "Sam, with your help and the deacons . . . it will be a joy to serve the Lord . . . at Big Bottom. I know there'll be some lean times ahead as we adjust, but with us all . . . working together . . . I believe we can honor our Lord and carry out the Great Commission. It'll be a joy to . . . serve alongside you."

Before getting off the phone Sam told me the group of twenty-five deacons who remained after I'd left had decided to use the church newsletter to publicize their support for me and the censure of the officers. Some hadn't wanted to have anything negative come out of the meeting and saw the publication of the censure as negative. This was the one point that divided the new deacon majority. The prevailing view, however, was that the people of the church would want to know what the meeting concerned and that it was an opportunity to show the church the deacon body stood with the pastor in the handling of the unfortunate incidents of the past week. It was also an opportunity to show the church the deacon officers do not represent the majority of the deacons or the church. Sam reasoned that the distribution of the results would discourage the officers from trying additional tomfoolery. He was wrong on that count.

The deacon officers had been defeated for the first time in at least fifteen years. Perhaps the cartel of selfish power would be no more.

Sam said that by the time the other deacons left, it was already past midnight. For Big Bottom Church, though, a new day had dawned.

I was ecstatic. Another flashback occurred as it had when I'd received the news of the reason for the deacons' meeting from Nev Wright. Once again I was outfitted in a football uniform. The ballgame was the same and the big fullback swept around the end, just as before. This time, though, I dodged the pulling guards as if they'd not seen me and planted my helmet into the stomach of the big fullback, just as the coaches used to teach us. The football popped back at least fifteen yards and our linebacker picked it up and ran with it more than fifty yards. The scene closed out as the referee signaled touchdown. I looked into the face of the linebacker who'd scored and saw Sam staring back with a big smile. No fog this time. It was Sam, and we were on the same team.

I shared the news from the meeting with Darla and she burst into tears. I held her in my arms. Her red hair shone as she looked up at me with big brown eyes. That hair and those eyes always melted me. She wanted to know the whole story, so I shared every detail I could remember. Breakfast was ready and we laughed and continued to talk through what had happened and its ramifications during an unhurried meal of smoked sausage, biscuits, and gravy, since discussion is always better served up with good fixings. This morning both the discussion and the food were delicious. I added my usual diet coke and Darla had coffee. Down South we believe God's marvelous grace tastes like biscuits, sausage, and gravy, shared with someone we love.

After breakfast Darla called her closest friend from our former church, one who'd promised to pray for Darla on the condition that Darla would keep her updated. I called in to the office and let the secretaries know I'd not be in until after lunch. And, as we say down South, I wet a hook. I also marveled, as I reeled in the lure at an unhurried pace, at the goodness of God. The deacon officers hadn't removed our joy at coming home; I'd just let them delay it a little.

The next day I went to see Jane Winfield. She confirmed the control battle had been an ongoing issue for years. I asked her how she knew so much about control issues. She answered, as I'd expected, "You learn a lot when you watch people, concentrate on what they do, and ask God to help you understand." And then she surprised me. "That and I once had a boyfriend who wanted me to marry him."

"Miss Winfield, what does a boyfriend wanting to marry you have to do with control issues?" I asked.

"He was a good man, I believe, but he'd been raised on a farm where his father had the one and only word about how things went. The young man used to quote his father's favorite saying, 'If I tell you a grasshopper can pull a wagon, don't say no, just hitch him up.'

"I was raised in Hattiesburg and I had a little more, shall we say, sophisticated view of the world. Long story short, I couldn't agree to spend my life with any man from whom I'd have to get permission to use the bathroom or his okay to turn over in bed," she said. "And those are the exact words I told him."

"Wait a minute; I heard words like those last night. Who was that man?" I asked.

"Oh, you don't want to know, preacher," she said and dipped her chin to the left. Her face turned red.

"Try me," I answered. "And I also want to know if you loved him and whatever became of him."

"Well, okay, but you've got to promise me you'll never whisper a word of it to a soul. You see, you might have met him already. He's a member of Big Bottom Church and he and Mary raised a fine family." Her face now glowed even redder.

"Okay, you've got my word. What's his name?" I asked.

"John Anderson," she said.

"You mean deacon John Anderson, the farmer?" I asked, astonished.

"I see you know him," she replied.

"No, but he saved my hide last night in the deacons' meeting. I look forward to meeting him. But anyway, what happened?" I asked.

"After I refused to marry him we went our separate ways. He married Mary, and they had four children and raised them all on his farm on Black Creek. I stayed single, and we both continued to work in Big Bottom Church. Mary and I were friends and talked pretty often, never about the time I dated John, of course, but about so many other things. I even taught their four children in Sunday school. Mary died about three years ago," Jane said. Her forehead gained a new wrinkle and her eyes narrowed.

"Wow, what a story. I guess we never know just how life is going to turn out. It's always interesting. God keeps it that way as we journey along," I said, but wished I hadn't. It was obvious she was the one with the longer journey and I should have let her explain more. My words must've sounded hollow. Why do I speak when it would be better to remain silent? She didn't take offense though, and continued as I whispered a prayer to the Lord to help me listen with my heart as well as with my ears.

"You're right about that one, because Mary died of cancer and just before she died she motioned to me to come near. She just could whisper and she wanted to tell me something."

"What'd she say?" I asked.

"She said, 'I've been praying for John. It'll be hard for him to give me up; we've been married so long. It'd be easier for me to live as a widow than for John to live as a widower, but God's not seen fit to work it out that way. I hope he'll marry again. A good woman would be such a help to him. And you're as good a woman as I know!"

18

After the deacon officers got their just deserts, things seemed to run without effort at Big Bottom Church. Darla and I worked hard to meet the people and find our distinct places in the flock. Both of us are people-people and enjoy the times of close camaraderie with Sunday school classes and the scores of high-touch events that come to pastors. The congregation appeared to progress, and the interest of Big Bottom members in spiritual matters seemed healthy. A number of people new to the area joined the church. Vibrant worship services buoyed all our spirits.

The Spanish mission elected Pastor Manual Castro as their new leader, and the mission seemed stronger than ever. It took a few minutes in business meeting to explain to the mother church that Manual Castro was no relation to Fidel Castro, but once that was settled and his background check proved impeccable, we hired him with enthusiasm. All seemed well in Gotham City.

For the next several months after the difficult beginning, we believed we would have a honeymoon with the church after all. Winter turned to spring, the air warmed, the grass turned green, and the flowers shot out of the ground. Dogwoods and azaleas bloomed. Scores of baseball teams sprouted up, too, and played on every available field.

The deacon officers stayed in the background, knowing they shouldn't get out of bounds again, lest they lose their positions and what power they had left. I wondered what the officers plotted in their meetings. As long as they didn't try to destroy what God was doing in the church, however, I didn't have to know.

The one sour thing in the church remained Wanda Washburn, who never failed to serve up a word of despair, disgust, or downright criticism. Time and again I was reminded by Wanda that, "Bro. Jackson didn't do it that way," or, "If you were smart, you'd call Bro. Jackson and let him advise you because he was good at _____" (fill-in-the-blank with visitation, preaching, meeting people, administration, counseling, listening to advice, involving the membership, getting along with all the people, or a host of other things.)

By and large I receive it well when church members esteem a previous pastor. It indicates I'll be appreciated one day, too, when I've earned my way with lots of weddings, funerals, and being with people at surgeries and other occasions that hold life's deepest meanings.

Pastor James Perkinson told me he was criticized a great deal by a lady in his church who said, "You can't preach." Of all the remarks made to a pastor, that one stings the most because it hits at the center of a pastor's call. Six months later that same woman called, but that time she was frantic. A serious car wreck had injured her daughter. Perkinson spent all night with the family in the emergency room. Afterward, she told him, "Since that night I never heard you preach a bad sermon."

Church members can help a pastor with criticism, if they give it with the right spirit. Some "words fitly spoken" have spurred me to improve. Also, I understand that church members have their favorites, and that's okay with me. I had trouble, though, with Wanda's constant harping. It got worse when she mentioned, "I told the Elite Ladies Sunday school class you'd do so much better if you'd call Bro. Jackson and get his advice." I could handle it when she told me, but now she delighted in spreading her poison to others in the church.

Bro. Jackson wasn't my immediate predecessor or even the one before that, but I thought it prudent to give him a call. Maybe he did have some insights on how to endure Wanda Washburn—the one area where she hadn't given advice.

After calling a number of folks who'd been at Big Bottom during his tenure, my assistant, Alice Evans, located his phone number. He'd retired in the pine country of east Texas, near Lufkin. After a few minutes of breaking the ice, Bro. Jackson asked about many of the members and, in particular, about Wanda Washburn. Thinking he must have enjoyed her, I asked how he'd gotten along with her when he'd been the pastor.

"Since you asked," he said, "she's the most objectionable woman I've ever met. 'Malcontent' must be her middle name because she never had a good word to say to anyone. At first I thought it was just me, because she constantly criticized me and compared me unfavorably to Bro. Rankin, her former pastor. I called him one day and he told me she'd treated him the same way.

"The one good thing I can say about her is that she never missed a service. The nominating committee thought maybe she wasn't using her spiritual gifts and that was why she was unhappy. So, they asked her to teach a new Sunday school class for ladies. Whew, was that ever a mistake! She gathered a group of malcontents around her and multiplied their unhappiness, kind of like a like a rotten apple does to the rest of the barrel. Last I heard she was still teaching that class and starting brush fires for the pastor to put out."

I wondered if my immediate predecessor had the same thoughts about Wanda. I hadn't talked with Ralph Perrine since soon before coming to the church in view of a call. I'd called him at that time to insure there weren't any hidden things of which I needed to be aware.

He'd told me of the church's potential and hadn't told me of any difficulties except, "the usual struggles for power, the kind you'd find in any church." Later I wished I'd asked him for more specifics, but

I hadn't. I assumed the problems weren't serious; therefore, I hadn't wanted to know so I wouldn't prejudge anyone. Now I needed to see if his thoughts about Wanda coincided with Bro. Jackson's and mine.

Perrine had moved to his native state of Louisiana to pastor a church in West Monroe. After several minutes of chitchatting he told me Wanda had been in prayer meeting on Wednesday night the last week of his pastorate at Big Bottom. His custom had been to call on a member for prayer to close the service. When the time had come, he'd said, "Shall we stand and Mrs. Washburn, would you lead us in a closing word of criticism, uh, I mean prayer?" He laughed for thirty seconds over the phone, not because it was that funny, but because it was sweet revenge.

Most of the folks there had picked up on his supposed slip of the tongue, and it had become a major topic of conversation at the church. Speculation had it that Wanda Washburn's sharp tongue had, "run off another preacher." That wasn't so, Perrine told me. He said, "What I did wasn't Christ-like and I've regretted it ever since."

Maybe, but he sure enjoyed telling me.

After talking with Jackson and Perrine, I made up my mind that Paul had his thorn in the flesh, and I had my Wanda W. Washburn, and I'd better not forget the W. I'd just have to grin and bear it. I asked the Lord about this, and I felt an instant reminder that Jesus had Pharisees and Sadducees who pass judgment on Him. I supposed if she wouldn't change then she must be God's sandpaper to smooth down my rough edges.

One Sunday afternoon as I drove into the parking lot of the church for the evening service, I noticed some guests pull into a designated visitor's spot. I went over to meet the couple and their children, a boy and a girl, both of whom appeared to be in their mid-teens. We chatted about their transfer to Hattiesburg from Arlington, Virginia, and his retirement from the Pentagon.

Then I saw Wanda emerge from a discipleship class in a nearby educational building and head our way. I lifted my thoughts to the

Lord to help us all. I should have been more specific and asked Him to keep her from noticing us.

Wanda interrupted my talking with the family in mid-sentence from a distance of thirty feet as she closed in on the newcomers. She said something about how she couldn't believe what the kids were wearing at Turtle Creek Mall these days. I tried to avoid introducing Wanda lest she turn the family away before they'd had a chance to enter the doors. I continued my conversation with them and thought I'd been successful in snubbing the introduction, but Wanda continued.

"Pastor, I don't mean to interrupt you," she blurted. It was a lie. "But we've just got to start a ministry for those poor kids down at Turtle Creek Mall. You can't believe what they're wearing these days. The boys are so poor they have to wear their daddy's blue jeans that hang down too low to be modest. And they're castaways—old and ragged jeans. Why, Salvation Army wouldn't even accept those trousers as donations. The denim has holes in it, pastor, do you hear me? Holes, pastor, holes, and not patched either. Why, you can see right through to the skin. I'm talking about seeing their skin! Their skin, I say. And not a single boy had on a belt. Poor kids, must be in desperate conditions and here we are worshipping God just two miles away and doing nothing to help these kids growing up in poverty right around us."

About that time, out of the corner of my eye, I caught the parents glancing at their son. He wore jeans, faded, comfortable ones with holes. At least he had on a belt. I felt for these folks.

But Wanda wasn't through. Before I could introduce the new people so she could hide her critical ways, she started on girls. "And the girls are even worse. They've all outgrown their clothes. Their shirts just came to mid-waist, their jeans were way too small—I don't even know how they got into those pants without breaking the zippers or popping the buttons—and the way they wore them. Pastor you wouldn't believe it; they just did rise above their hip bones. And without a momma to teach them where to put their earrings, they've got them all over their bodies. Their bodies, I'm telling you. Do you understand what I'm saying? Those poor things. And one of the girls even had her laced underwear on over her pants. Why, I never saw such a thing in all my life. But without a momma to teach them I guess that's the best they knew how to do."

Again, I glanced out of the corner of my eye and caught the parents looking at their daughter. She'd dressed with modesty and had no piercings I could detect other than some dainty earrings. I saw the mother breathe a sigh of relief.

"And pastor, it saddens me to say it but somebody has to," and with that Wanda's voice quivered and lowered two notches, "but all those girls had underwear showing because their jeans were so small. Pastor, if we don't help these poor kids, they'll grow up thinking this is normal. Next thing you know, they'll be wearing that kind of trash to church and we won't even be able to concentrate on the sermon. Maybe we'd better have a clothes drive next week. We've got to do something. I know if Bro. Jackson was here, we'd do something. What do you think we should do?"

"I'd like you to meet the Fredericksons," I said and cut her off. "They're new in town from Virginia and are looking for a good church. I told them they've come to the right place, wouldn't you agree?"

Wanda extended her hand with coolness. She said, "I'm Wanda W. Washburn from the old line of Washburns in Lamar County." She said it the same, matter-of-fact way she had when she'd first met me. She also accentuated the W the same way she had with me.

It struck me like lightning. About the time Wanda introduced herself and raised her voice to emphasize the W, I saw the sticker on the back window of the guest's SUV. It was visible above Wanda's right shoulder as she spoke, almost as if sitting on her shoulder or framed there in a picture. It read, "W, the President." And with a voice so loud I thought sure the others had heard it, came the thought, W, the Witch!

Visitors or not, I excused myself right away and said the service would soon be starting. I feared the voice indicating witchery had come from my own mouth, and I couldn't hide it any longer. I looked around as I neared the office door and saw Wanda still spouting off as the teens returned to the SUV followed by Jim and Carol Frederickson. Every step they'd take toward their SUV, Wanda would take another toward them, as if she were a sheepdog herding them in.

Soon I could see the taillights of their Chevy Tahoe exiting the lot. They'd come to Big Bottom to worship and hear a word from the Lord. They'd received a sermon, all right, but it was from the parking lot, not from the pulpit, and it was ghastly, not Gospel. I dropped to my knees and prayed the Fredericksons would hear so many good things from others about Big Bottom that they'd come back and give us another try.

I also remembered what a seminary professor said, "Some people are so obnoxious that your church would be better off without them. They'll cost your church far more people than they'll ever bring in." In more than thirty years of ministry, I'd seen few people whom I felt would qualify for his statement, but Wanda—well, she headed the list.

19

WITCH HUNT

The next afternoon after work, Mike came over to fish with me while the bass were feeding in their ferocious, pre-spawn stage. We went out on "Visitation," my fourteen-foot john boat powered by a battery-operated, Minn-Kota trolling motor. I'd named it so if I took off an afternoon and someone called in the church office, my assistant could speak the truth when she said, "He's not here, he's out on visitation." The boat was perfect for two wannabe fishermen on a small lake. We'd caught enough for a mess to feed Mike's family, and we talked about his plans at USM.

About that time he hooked into a big one, at least six pounds. It'd seen his topwater lure floating under the willow tree. It had rested there until all the ripples had faded and then, "Bam," with a powerful blast the bass inhaled it while coming all the way out of the water. The loud splash only fifteen feet away scared us both and we jerked, rocking the boat. Mike and I had to center ourselves in the boat to keep it from flipping. It shook side to side but righted itself. We found the bass had hooked himself on the treble hooks and was still on Mike's line.

Mike fought it through two more leaps from the water but the fourth time the big bass burst through the surface he spit the top-water lure out of his mouth with ease, as if saying, "I'm just playing with you." We were both breathless and our hearts were pounding. "Did you see that?" Mike said. "I'd have taken him to the taxidermist and hung him on my wall."

With all the excitement going on, Mike lowered his barriers and began to talk with ease. He shared about several things—his doubts about going into business as a major, his struggles with his girlfriend, Sandy, and even some questions about whether his Mom and Dad would remain married, since they argued so much.

I listened, and from time to time threw in a question or two to help him clarify his decisions. It seemed to mean a lot to him that I'd listen. I recalled how much a mature believer had meant to me in the confusing years of late high school and my freshman year of college. After a while, Mike asked me point blank, "What do you think about Wanda W. Washburn?" He swelled the W. as a way of making fun of her.

"I think she's hurting down deep inside. What do you think?" I asked.

"But why in the world does she always have to take it out on everybody else?" he asked.

"Good question, Mike. I don't know the answer. But then again, I don't know why I do everything I do, either. Maybe she doesn't like herself and that's why she can't like anyone else."

"Did you hear what happened to Hunter?" he asked.

I groaned in secret, thinking she'd run off someone else. "No, tell me," I answered.

"Wanda got on to Hunter Davis at church last Wednesday night," he said.

"Got on to?" I asked.

"Yeah, you know, complained to him, criticized him. Come on, pastor, you been gone from Mississippi so long that you don't even know what a good 'getting on to' is all about?"

"To tell the truth, I'd almost forgotten that phrase," I said.

"Well, just stay around Wanda a while and it'll come back to you."

We both laughed.

"Wanda heard Hunter was dipping tobacco, listening to loud music, and displaying other red neck habits like throwing an empty beer can or two into the back of his pickup. She told him, 'Hunter, you ought to be ashamed of yourself.'

"I don't know if you know Hunter, but he don't take no flack off nobody," Mike said. "He just threw it right back at her and said, 'Mrs. Washburn, why should I be ashamed of myself when you're ashamed enough for both of us?'

"It didn't seem to faze her, though, she just kept right on getting on to him like she'd taken him to raise," Mike said as he cast his top-water bait underneath some overhanging willow branches. "Mrs. Washburn told him, 'All that gallivanting around and playing that loud music in your truck. Why, when you stopped beside me on Highway 98 the other day, I thought there was a construction crew nearby. Bah Boom, Bah Boom, Bah Boom, Bah Boom! With that bass turned up so loud, it's a wonder your pickup windows stay in place because my car windows were sure rattling.'"

"What happened then?" I asked while steering the boat into position for another cast.

"Well, Hunter was polite in his answer. He said, 'Mrs. Washburn, it's a free world and my generation, well, we like our music. Weren't you ever young? Didn't you like music back then?'

"'Young man,' Wanda said, 'I'll have you know I love music, if it's real music, but that trash you listen to is about as close to real music as etch-a-sketch is to real art.'

"Now that hurt. If she'd stopped there Hunter would've let it slide, but she wouldn't stop. It's like when that woman gets on a tear, she won't let up. I heard her go on and on with Early one time and he muttered something like, 'Wanda, you'll keep pushing till the cows come home.'"

We laughed again and that made me miss a bass that had inhaled my plastic worm into his mouth for a brief moment. At least that's the excuse I gave for not setting the hook in time.

"She told Hunter, 'And not only that, but it's the way you dress. Hunter Davis, I never thought I'd see you in church wearing faded blue jeans and a shirt with no collar,'" Mike said.

"You know she's run off a lot of college students with her sharp tongue and judgmental attitude. It's got to where we warn high school and college students to just ignore it if a thin, Pentecostal-looking woman starts criticizing you, because the problem is hers, not yours.

"One honors student from Southern Miss told me that she couldn't believe in a Christ whose followers were so harsh in judging other people's clothing or looks or music. She quit coming. I hated it, too, because she was good lookin'. Man, she was cool. I was just about to ask her to go to the movies with a bunch of us, but she quit attending. So I called her and found out what'd happened.

"Anyway, Wanda kept pushing Hunter. She said, 'That stuff I saw you put under your lip the other day. I never thought I'd see the day when you'd dishonor your body—the temple of God—like you're doing. What does your poor momma think about you?'"

"And that's when Hunter gave it to her. 'I inherited it from my mom.'

"'Inherited it?' Mrs. Washburn said. 'Why Hunter Davis, I'll have you know your momma is one of the most cultured women of God I know. Her mother is in the Elite Ladies Sunday School Class. I've known your grandmamma for years and your momma ever since she was born. No, you didn't inherit those sleazy, red-neck ways from her, young man.'"

"'Oh yes, I did, Mrs. Washburn.'"

"'Well now, how do you figure that?'"

"'Haven't you noticed she has red hair? When the genes came down to me, my hair turned out brown but the red just settled on the back of my neck,' Hunter answered." With that we both laughed so hard it shook the boat and little ripples formed, as if the lake were laughing with us.

"Yeah, Hunter said he had to cover his mouth to keep from laughing out loud. He didn't want to dishonor Mrs. Washburn, but at the same time he couldn't help but think how his friends would react when they heard ole lady Washburn had been put in her place."

"Well what did ole . . ., I mean Wanda say?" I asked.

"All she said was, 'Well, I never.'"

The lake laughed again.

"How'd Hunter ever think that one up?" I asked.

"That's the same question I had," Mike answered. "He told me he'd known she'd come after him one day, just like she did with all the students his age. He said, 'I figured for weeks and weeks about how to draw her out a little more and a little more until, bam! The trap door flew shut.

"Hunter told me, 'It's a little like deer hunting. You just can't rush right into it or you'll scare the deer off. But if you'll bide your time and don't reveal yourself too soon, the right moment will come and bam, you'll bag her—Mrs. Washburn, I mean. Just like deer can't stay away from corn, Wanda Washburn can't stay away from criticism. You might say she hunted me til I caught her.'"

I'll have to get to know Hunter, I decided. He sounds like a sensible young man. I didn't choose his Skoal or his booming music, but I liked the way he processed things deeper than the surface level. Wanda didn't stop criticizing him, but he didn't stop coming to church because of her. He realized an oak is bigger than its acorns, and Christ is bigger than His followers.

CHRIST AND CULTURE

"Can you hold a conversation in confidence?" I asked Jane Winfield.

"Do you need to ask?" she replied.

"No, but I guess I needed to hear it from you again because this one is sensitive."

"If God's led you to share, He's led me to listen. If I can remember it until tomorrow, I promise not to share it. So, shoot or put your gun back on safety."

"What's your opinion of Wanda W. Washburn?" I asked.

To my surprise, Jane began to talk about some of the first missionaries on the plains of Kenya. When these missionaries shared Christ, they expected the native men to wear suits and ties and the women to wear long dresses. Furthermore, they expected the converts to build brick church buildings in an area where mud huts with thatched roofs abounded.

"That's interesting, but what about Wanda Washburn?" I asked.

She adjusted her walker, took a sip of tea, and continued as if I'd not spoken, "The tribesmen couldn't afford suits and ties and long dresses, nor could they afford brick buildings, so most of them didn't convert to Christianity. Those that did had to seek the help of English or American Christians to build their brick buildings and became dependant on outsiders for support and advancement. And even when the churches did grow, the Kenyans said the structures looked strange and the people who attended didn't look normal, all dressed up in foreign clothes like that."

Again I spoke, "Okay," drawing out the "k" sound so as to help Miss Jane get to the point. The thought crossed my mind that she was in her eighties now and I should expect some slippage. "But how does that apply to Wanda?"

Jane raised her hand with her palm outward like a school teacher does to an interrupting child and pressed on. "Not all the missionaries were like that. Most of them helped the people build with the materials they were accustomed to. Those missionaries encouraged modest clothing, but dress that was native to the people. And they taught the people music accompanied with their native drums. Those Kenyan churches grew because they hadn't formed artificial barriers."

With that Jane stopped speaking. I hated to do it as I didn't want to show disrespect, but I had a meeting scheduled to start in a few minutes. With a slight movement of my head forward and a circular motion of my hands indicating the pulling out of something slow to emerge, I said, "And . . ."

Jane inched up her left eyebrow and said, "Don't they teach you guys anything at seminary? What I'm saying is that folks like Wanda mistake their culture for their Christianity. They think Christianity means wearing suits and ties and long dresses and having a long face and sitting without a word in a pew. They sit on their antique oak pews and sing seventeenth century hymns written by white European men and sung out of hymnals to the accompaniment of an organ. At the same time they criticize to no end those who don't practice religion like they do."

"Wait a minute. Are you telling me that you don't like Handel's Messiah or the hymns in the old Baptist hymnals?"

"No, no, no. You've got it all wrong. That's the kind of music I do like. And there's nothing wrong with worshiping the Lord that way. In fact, there's a whole lot right with it, but it's just that no one should expect the natives in our land today to worship like people did a hundred years ago. To expect it would be as strange to them as the brick buildings were to the villagers on the Serengeti Plains.

"Well-intentioned as they might be, folks like Wanda are erecting barriers to the Gospel. The truth be told, Jesus didn't wear what we wear in the Deep South. He also didn't wear the Sunday-go-to-meetin' clothes of a generation ago. He didn't worship every week in a brick building or wear his hair short or sing to the accompaniment of piano or organ music. He looked like and worshipped like the people of His time."

Stunned by her wisdom, I didn't speak for a few seconds. It dawned on me that of the two of us in the room, Jane wasn't the one slipping. "Miss Winfield, I think you've got something there. You're saying Wanda's not turning people away on purpose, it's just that she is trying to make people conform to traditions she identifies with Christianity?"

"That's what I think," she replied, and then added with a twinkle in her eyes, "but many Kenyans came to Christ despite some of the folks who brought it there. That's the kind of God we have."

"Amen to that," I said. "I can think of lots of times He's done something good not because of me, but in spite of me. Two questions, though: one, how can we help her separate what she thinks is Christianity from the real thing? And two, I wonder if I also have some blind spots where I've substituted my own traditions for service to Christ?" I asked.

"Good questions, Brent," she said with a nod of her head and a quick point of her finger towards me like a teacher gives when her student gets it at last. "And I'll leave them with you," she said. She had a satisfied look on her face, one I'll bet she had many times after teaching four-year-olds in Sunday school. It made me happy that she'd called me

Brent, though. I felt we'd passed into a new phase of friendship. She's a wise woman and I felt honored she's willing to share with me.

As I pondered the words of Jane Winfield, the story of E. Stanley Jones came to mind. The evangelist had been a Methodist missionary to India some seventy years ago, before and during the nationalist movement that led to India's independence. He knew Mahatma Gandhi and counted him as a friend.

Gandhi admitted to Jones that he'd read the Bible and it fascinated him. Gandhi also learned some of his pacifist ideas from the Bible. So Jones asked Gandhi why he didn't become a Christian.

Gandhi answered, "I think I should become a Christian if I should ever see one." The answer shocked the evangelist, but he realized the Indian people had observed so much English colonialism masquerading as Christianity that it had turned off many to the idea of receiving Christ and living for Him.

As I considered these things over the next few weeks, it occurred to me that if Wanda could get out of her culture and experience another, she'd be able to read the Bible with fresh eyes. She'd stop trying to push her old style of practicing Christianity and begin giving witness to a genuine relationship with the Lord, one that transcends culture and time. I can't say for sure the idea came from the Lord, but it did come from somewhere—that I should invite Wanda W. Washburn on an overseas missions trip. And I knew just the trip.

Big Bottom had a retired minister, Robert Stringer, who served part-time on the staff as minister of missions. Pastor Stringer had already invited me to lead a mission trip to Tanzania in the summer. Since Darla and I had served as missionaries to South Korea, we had missions in our blood. Pastor Stringer had said if I led a trip it would encourage the people of Big Bottom to deepen their focus on and commitment to missions. A trip guided by their pastor could be just the thing to help people who believed in and supported missions to personalize their beliefs with action. If I could get Wanda to go on the trip, it would be enough of a culture shock to awaken her to the difference between her traditions and the claims of Christ that rise above the customs of any people.

Darla serves as a sounding board for me on many ideas, including harebrained ones. She helped me think through all sides of a matter as we discussed it. This time, however, she nixed the idea before I'd had an opportunity to explain the reasoning. She said, "You're asking for trouble."

When I countered with, "Darla, are you saying that Wanda's beyond the power of God to change?" I knew I had an argument she couldn't overcome.

Darla still wasn't for asking Wanda to go with us to Tanzania and remained forceful in saying she'd ruin the trip. I asked my wife to pray about it and concluded that I should ask Wanda to pray about going. If Wanda agreed, then we'd receive that as God's will. On the other hand, if He didn't want her to go, then He could give her plenty of reasons not to and we'd take that as His will.

My friend Sam didn't think much of the idea, either. He asked, "Pastor, do you like yourself?"

I told him, "Sam, it's not about me; it's about the Lord. It's also about helping Wanda experience His grace in another culture so she'll stop trying to spread her narrow version of Christianity to the exclusion of most everyone else."

Sam then asked me, "Do you know the meaning of the word, masochist?"

Pastor Stringer also thought it a bad suggestion, not due to her age but, for the most part, due to her crankiness. Stringer said, "Do you think Wanda has the disposition to be a good team player? She could ruin it for everyone else. You've been a missionary. You know how frustrating it is to have to change plans in mid-stream. Yet, that's what we have to do on almost every mission trip. I question Wanda's flexibility to adjust to the changes that always accompany mission trips to remote places like rural Tanzania."

I could tell he'd pondered the matter before discussing it with me and that it hurt him even to mention that someone from the church shouldn't make the trip. So, I told him I'd pray about it before asking her. God didn't stop me, though, and since I'm an incurable Don Quixote—at least that's what Darla says—I still thought a mission trip might be just the thing to change Wanda's life.

If her life changed for the better, mine and dozens more at Big Bottom Church would also change for the better. That was reason enough to invite her.

21

VISITING THE WASHBURNS

I called Early and Wanda and asked if I could come over for a chat. Even though Early was one of the former deacon officers who'd lost the pivotal vote in the deacons' meeting, I believed he was a follower, not a leader, and could be won over with some attention and care. I intended to do all in my power to provide it. After all, the Bible tells us, "Be at peace with all men." The Washburns agreed to meet me that afternoon at five o'clock.

I drove out Oak Grove Road until I reached the black, dented mailbox with fading numbers indicating the Washburn's address and turned up their lane. The path was bordered on both sides by live oaks and sycamores, but not paved and not well kept. Broken branches littered the ground. The grass needed mowing. Old leaves molded where they had fallen months earlier.

I'd never before laid eyes on the home and it surprised me. I don't know what I was expecting, but from the teacher of the Elite Ladies Class who married into the "old line of Washburns in Lamar County,"

I had thought more in terms of a mansion like the one owned by the Maddens.

Instead I saw a small bungalow built at least sixty years ago. The house was deteriorating. The white paint peeled at places along the outside walls and fascia. Many shingles had upturned corners, the sign of a roof that should have been replaced a year or more earlier. A blackish mildew claimed half of the ceiling over the front-porch swing.

The contrast with the J. Redford Maddens and the Early Washburns struck me. The big-hearted Maddens had wealth, but no airs about them. They used their possessions and influence to encourage others. Though they could drive any vehicle they wanted, J. Redford drove an old pick-up and Mrs. Madden a twelve-year-old Olds 88.

The Washburns, at least from what I'd observed and heard, had little, but could strut while sitting. Their home was in strong need of repair and paint, yet Wanda drove a new Cadillac and Early drove an expensive SUV. Their influence seemed be geared toward clinging to a type of negative Christianity in which status played an important role and people knew their places.

Early sat on a porch swing supported by rusty chains hung from eyelets in the ceiling. He looked at his watch when I pulled up. I arrived fifteen minutes ahead of schedule, an unusual thing for me. Darla says my internal clock runs five minutes behind. I'd left in plenty of time to find the Washburn place, though, because I'd never been there before. I didn't want the wrath that might descend due to my being late. Fury could erupt like a volcano from Wanda. That should have been enough to raise red flags about asking her on the mission trip. I could kick myself for not seeing it; but, many of us pastors are savior types who always try to help people move from where they are to where we think they can be. I suppose the possibilities blinded me. That's my excuse and I'm sticking with it.

Early's first words to me that day? "The early bird slits the worm," and with that juicy tidbit I entered a home sixty yards off a busy road and sixty years back in time.

I thought I detected a sour smell as I passed Early and his nose looked redder than it had the last time we'd talked. He wore an old pair of overhauls that had a hole in the right knee and showed stains. Whether the stains were from work or from several days' wear, I didn't know. I thought it inconsistent that he had tucked a white, button-down dress shirt into the overhauls.

"Early, your overhauls make you look a lot more relaxed than the night we met at the funeral home." He'd worn a suit and tie that day. He'd also worn one to the deacons' meeting but I didn't want to go there.

"Yeah," he mumbled, "daylight sand slark."

He ushered me up some creaking steps, over a threshold needing a new coat of varnish, and into the living room. He showed me to a seat on an antique sofa. The thing that grabbed me was the contrast of the home's interior with its exterior. The two were incongruent, like they belonged to different houses. Although the house was small, Wanda had arranged everything in orderly fashion, giving attention to detail. The house was tidy and the rooms full of light.

On a central wall, where no one could miss it, hung a framed, crocheted piece with fine craftsmanship. I estimated it stretched four feet high and five feet wide. Gold leaf formed its borders and a medium blue its background. It had been placed as the focal point for a reason. Inside the walnut frame hung St. Francis of Assisi's words in tan stitching, the work of skillful hands:

O Divine Master, grant that I may not so much seek
To be consoled as to console,
To be understood as to understand,
To be loved as to love;
For it is in giving that we receive;
It is in pardoning that we are pardoned;
It is in dying that we are born to eternal life!

Early had left me to notify Wanda, so I rose to examine the piece. It stunned me that Wanda would choose this as her centerpiece. I was still examining the delicate details when Wanda entered. "Do you like it?"

"Like it? I love it," I replied. "Someone very talented did this beautiful work. And the colors—wow, they bring such light to your room." Although I'd been careful to comment on the piece itself and not its meaning, Wanda moved to the main point.

"The colors and the framing are nice, but I had it hung over thirty years ago because of the words. Not a day goes by without my reading those words and asking my Lord to help me live them out."

Just when I thought I had Wanda W. Washburn figured out, she came out with that, and I realized there was still hope for her recovery a life of harsh judgment of others. I'll have to admit that a question occurred to me. If she hadn't read those words each day, how much more of a troublemaker would she be? But I put the thought aside and concentrated on the purpose of my visit—to ask Wanda to pray about going on a mission trip. The centerpiece of her living room removed my doubts about the decision.

The Wanda in front of me stood tall and thin and with her hair in a bun. She looked, and her voice sounded, like the old Wanda W. Washburn. But I saw a new Wanda, one that showed vulnerability, one that was trying to grow. The Lord reminded me of something that day. All Christians are on a journey towards the heavenly city, and I'm not to judge where they are on the journey, just to help them along the way.

After Wanda and I talked for a while, I noticed that Early sat motionless to the side without joining in. I looked over from time to time to see if he'd fallen asleep. Twice I asked him a question to pull him into the conversation. Both times he answered with a slurred voice. Clichés delivered with a thick tongue don't sound right.

Wanda proceeded like all was well, so I avoided the subject of Early and got to the reason for the visit. "Mrs. Washburn," I said, "I've decided to lead a mission trip to Tanzania this summer and felt it right to ask you to pray about coming on the trip. Would you pray about it?"

"Pray about it? I'll tell you right now; I'd love to go." And with that her face lit up and the pace of her voice quickened and raised half an octave. "I've wanted to be a missionary since I was a little girl when a couple from the jungles of Brazil came to the church to show slides. I've been fascinated with the thought of missions; but when Early and I married, he didn't feel any leadership from the Lord, and I knew my mission support would have to be giving and praying and promoting missions in my Sunday school class and in the Women's Missionary Union. Please, please tell me all about the trip."

"Well, I'd like you to pray about this specific trip because it is not like most mission trips. Darla and I and a team of ten from the church are going to Tanzania to help with the annual mission meeting. All the missionaries from each country meet once a year for a week in the summer to worship and pray and formulate strategies. They need a team from the United States to teach their children Vacation Bible School. Most of the team will be doing this, and I'll be preaching for the missionaries each morning and leading a Bible study each night. Then, after the meeting is over, we'll spend one or two days working with the national Christians on some specific mission project and one or two days sightseeing. Does this sound like something you'd like to do for the Lord and our missionaries?"

Before she could answer, Early said something unintelligible. His face had turned red and he was huffing. He growled and discharged several words, but the first one audible, "Bitch," was followed by something incomprehensible. Then he slurred, "Can't tweach an old dod new ticks, Wander. What makes you thinking bout such a crazy idea?"

"Early Washburn," she said with dismay and irritation, "are you calling me a female dog? You've never used such language around me."

I couldn't comprehend the exact words Early said next, but it was something like, "the smeller's the feller."

"Now just what does that mean, Early?" she asked.

"Means, le leeping hogs lie," he slurred with a tone of finality.

"Early, I won't go if you forbid it because the Bible says for wives to be submissive to their husbands. Are you telling me not to go?"

"Timin' has lots to do with the outcome of a rain dance, Wander," Early replied.

Wanda threw up her hands, "Honest to goodness, Early, sometimes I wish you'd speak plain words," echoing a sentiment I'd often had. At that point I noticed a tear flowing down the side of Wanda's cheek, and her hurt brought a tear down my own. How sad it would be if a husband held his wife back when she felt God's leadership to go on a mission trip.

"If at firsh ya don't succeed, cry, cry agin," he replied as he rose from his chair and stomped outside, bumping into a chair along the way. Moments later I heard the rhythmical squeak of the porch swing.

I'd felt out of place during the discussion and tried to ease my way out. "Listen, I'm not here to make trouble. If the Lord wants you to go on this trip, He can convince Early, too. I'd hate for you to go if it would cause difficulty at home. Why don't you and Early pray about it, come to a decision together, and let me know in a week or two? If the timing's not right this summer, there'll be several more trips next year," I added, to give Wanda an easy out without losing face.

The next day my assistant, Alice Evans, asked if I could take a call from Wanda Washburn. I did. She spoke for fifteen minutes about going on the mission trip with the same high-pitched voice she'd had when she first heard of the trip. "Just think, I'll get to be a missionary and fulfill the Great Commission like William Carey and Lottie Moon and Adoniram and Ann Judson and Albert Switzer and Bill Wallace. I always wanted to be a missionary, but Early said he didn't feel the calling. Now, I'll get to go."

We talked about passports, inoculations, air travel, the ticketing process, appropriate clothing, the exact dates of the trip, who was going, when the preparation meetings would be held, and the costs involved. Then I eased into asking Wanda how Early felt about her going.

She said, "That's the strangest thing of all. I prayed and prayed last night about his supporting me on the mission trip. All told, I'll bet I didn't get three hours of sleep. I'd wake up and then pray for an hour or more before I could go to sleep again.

"The Lord gave it to me to cook Early's favorite breakfast. When he awoke I wanted him to smell the grits and eggs and bacon and the coffee. I topped that off with biscuits and tomato gravy, cooked just like he likes it in the old iron skillet. When he seemed to be enjoying his breakfast, I asked him about your visit, and would you believe it? He didn't even remember you'd come. Can you believe that? The Lord just took it from his mind.

"So I talked about the possibility of my going on the mission trip. I even told him I'd be gone for close to two weeks this summer. All of a sudden he lit up with a smile and said, 'Sounds like the greatest thing since sliced bread.' It's a miracle, and now I know God wants me on that mission trip."

"That's wonderful, but I'm a little concerned about Early. Does he often forget the things from the previous day?" I asked.

"No, not too often. I'd say he's like that about one morning every two or three weeks. He'll get grumpy late in the day and slur his words and that's how I know he's not feeling well. But after a good night's sleep, he feels fine. I think it's just old age, but don't breathe a word of it, pastor. You wouldn't know it from talking to him, but Early's a proud man. He's sensitive about that kind of thing. He doesn't want anyone to know.

"I can tell he's slipping, though. Just like the house. All our marriage I've taken care of the inside of the house and he's taken care of our land and the outside of the house, but you might have noticed that the outside needs some work. Never, and I do mean never, would it have been like that five years ago. I know he doesn't have the energy or mind he used to have, so I just do the best I can."

"Has Early seen a doctor in the last few months?" I asked.

"No, and he'd never hear of it. He's so tight he'd never volunteer to go to a doctor. He wouldn't want to part with the dollars. He uses his wallet so seldom that it squeaks just like our porch swing," she said. "Oh, please forgive me; I know I'm not supposed to talk about my husband like that. You'll promise not to tell anyone, won't you?"

"Without your permission, I am bound by pastoral confidentiality. If anyone hears it, it won't be from me, barring a life-and-death situation, of course."

"I guarantee you, if you tell, it'll be my life and your death!" she said.

For the first time, I could have sworn I heard a chuckle in her voice.

We talked some more about the mission trip and then I transferred her to Pastor Stringer for more details. Later, it came to mind that Wanda and I'd talked for twenty minutes, and she'd never complained about me or the church a single time. I thanked the Lord and then thought to myself that the mission trip may be just the answer, after all.

22
TWICE CAUTIOUS

There are few things a pastor entering a worship service hates more than a person giving him a torn sheet of paper with words on it. Even worse are those thrust into his hands just before the time to preach. "Announce this," usually accompanies the scraggly piece of paper. Sometimes an usher will deliver the note and with it say, "Someone handed me this for you to announce. Said it couldn't wait."

I'd learned early on that I shouldn't announce everything people thought I should. I pastored a small, country church while in seminary. Every community event, being an item of interest in the church, was routinely announced. I hated this part of the job because some of the items announced didn't rise to the caliber of things to which Christians should give their time. I was still trying to learn the right things to do and say, so I cooperated as best I knew how.

Still, when a crumpled scrap of paper came my way just before I stood to preach, it knotted my stomach and scrambled my thinking. More often than not the scribbled memo had something to do with a widow's toe surgery or praying for a person to get a job he sought. I don't mean to make light of these concerns, because a job is important to the one seeking it and a surgery of utmost importance to a lady whose sore toe had kept her from her activities.

The difference between a major and a minor surgery is simple. Minor surgery is one someone else is having and major surgery is one you're having. I made announcements as I'd been asked. That's the way it is in a small, country church with a new pastor. That is, until the pivotal day when three scraps of paper came my way.

They'd come all at once, during the time the congregation participated in the morning welcome, and at a time my mind was on the sermon. Truth be told, I didn't know from whom any of the three notes had come. Out of the blue three scraps of paper lay on my Bible, placed there by a succession of people during a whir of "Good to see you," and "How are you?" and "Glad you're here," and other greetings.

I rose to continue the worship service and told the folks I'd been requested to read some announcements to them. I unfolded the first and read, "Mrs. Glenda Matthews is having a hysterectomy in the morning at Methodist Hospital, and we should pray for her." Several in the church giggled because Mrs. Matthews came across as more proper than many ladies and didn't seem the kind of person who would want the world to know the type of gynecological surgery she'd be having.

The announcement frustrated me, especially when I saw the look of disgust on Mrs. Matthews' face, but I pressed on, trying to please the folks. The second piece of paper unfolded and I read, "Bob Odom passed away last night and visitation hours are from four to six tomorrow afternoon with the funeral service on Tuesday, out of state. Please pray for the family." I heard some quick gasps.

Before I could open the third piece of paper, a tall man with a gruff voice stood up and said with a slow drawl, "Pastor, I know you're new here and don't know everybody yet, but I just wanted to let the church know that I'm kinda like that Mark Twain feller. He said, 'The news of my death has been greatly exaggerated.' I think what you meant to say is that my granddad, Robert, passed away in Florida and his funeral will be on Tuesday in Orlando. The missus and I'll be traveling after lunch and we'd appreciate the prayers."

With that, a rush of laughter ensued. Some even slapped their legs, as country people sometimes do with a robust laugh. They enjoyed the events more because they got to laugh at the expense of their new pastor. I didn't suspect that anyone had made this mistake on purpose. People don't see each other every day and when they do, they often get bits of news mixed up. The rush not to leave anyone out of our prayers and concern does leave something else, however—lots of room for error. I was new and trying my best to get it right, but that announcement even made me laugh.

I apologized and explained that all I did was read what I'd been given. I hadn't meant to get it wrong, but someone must have been mistaken. I promised to pause for prayer for the Odoms and the other people on the announcements after I read the third one. I reiterated, "Folks, I hope you'll forgive me, because this is the first time I'm seeing these words so I'm just assuming their accuracy; all I can do is read to you what comes to me. With that I unfurled the third piece and read, "Your fly is open. Zip it." The reality of what I'd read in public sunk in. Horrified, I looked down and verified the accuracy of the announcement.

Some of the men rolled on the floor with laughter, as I hid behind the pulpit and zipped. Of all times, why did this have to be the one my shirt tail got caught in the zipper? The effort took several tries, but soon I accomplished the job and breathed a sigh of relief. And then I looked up at the congregation.

There was not a straight face in the building. Most were laughing out loud. Mrs. Matthews even joined in. I sat down to compose myself and let the congregation regain respectability. It took ten minutes before order could be restored. Twice I tried to get up to continue the service; but before I could announce the scripture, guffaws would break out again and we'd be in for another round of merriment.

At last our deacon chairman stood to move that "In the future, before any announcement is read, the deacons will help our new pastor verify the contents for accuracy and respectability."

The motion passed, but by a slim majority. One of the young men said he wasn't in a habit of coming to church every Sunday but that morning was the most fun he'd had in months and he'd be back again.

Darla and I were still new at the marriage thing and didn't know one another's habits well. I knew something had hurt her when she didn't say a word on the drive home after the morning service. When we arrived, she broke the news that she'd been the one to write the zipper note.

"I thought you were smart enough to read notes before you announced them. I realize I did the wrong thing now, but what did you want me to do, leave you hanging out to dry?"

She knew she had to get word to me because she might not get another chance before I stood before the people to preach. Since I didn't want to get into the topic of my intelligence, or lack thereof, I let the matter drop after thanking her for her concern and assuring her it was no big deal.

In truth, the day turned out well. Country people love a good laugh and they forgive with no trouble. The young man who'd spoken up about having fun? He received the Lord and joined the church that day. It seems that seeing the church wasn't a stuffy place, but a real one where people could make mistakes and even laugh at themselves, had been just what he needed to remove an obstacle to his coming to Christ.

I never again read an announcement to the church before reading it for myself. I also talked with a number of other seminary students and confirmed all of us had had similar problems. A few dealt with conflict in their church, and one had been given an announcement with the intention to mislead the congregation about a member, he felt.

One student reminded us that a famous evangelist, Dwight L. Moody, had been given an unsigned scrap of paper to read just before he preached at a crusade. He opened the folded paper and read the word "fool." Moody read it to the congregation and said, "I've often been given notes by people who'd forgotten to sign their names. This is the first time, however, that I've been given a note by someone who signed his name but forgot to write the note!"

We formed a focus group of seminarians and drew up a policy for making announcements, one I've stuck by until this day. It included three major items. The first was not reading an announcement about a death or surgery before verifying it, except in emergencies. The second? Not announcing a death or other event of non-church members, since the church was a worship center, not a newspaper. The third was not announcing deaths or other events of information in public that could be distributed better in other ways, such as through a Sunday school class or on rolling announcements played on the screen before the services began.

All these things came back to me at Big Bottom when, in mid spring, I was handed a slip of paper from an usher during the offering time. I glanced at it and saw the words, "Announce the surgery of deacon Red Broome in the morning at Forrest General Hospital. I couldn't verify that deacon Broome was having surgery. I didn't know for a fact it was in the morning. I wasn't positive the surgery was at Forrest General Hospital. And, I didn't know whether Red wanted his surgery announced. Before the usher walked off the pulpit area, I called his name and asked him to give the slip to my administrative assistant, Alice Evans, in the welcome area and request she call Mr. Broome's Sunday school teacher to get the word to his class.

Because the announcement policy entered new territory for Big Bottom Church, I made it a point to visit Carolyn and Red Broome that afternoon and have prayer with them. Red Broome's given name was Walter but everyone called him Red, even though his hair was brown, since in the first grade another child had seen him sweeping with a red broom.

These gracious people were astonished I'd come so soon when I'd found out just that morning. "Yeah, I'm having hernia repair," Red said. "I didn't want everyone in the world to know about it. Somebody told me they gave you a note to announce my surgery to the church. Thanks for not doing it." I left praising the Lord for delivering me one more time. Once unzipped, twice cautious.

23
PLEASE ANNOUNCE THIS

•

The next Sunday I felt a sudden chill. When I glanced up I saw S. A. Tanner approaching my seat in the worship center. He stood over me with his hands on his hips, like an employer giving instructions. He handed me a crumpled piece of paper with his handwriting on it. It said, "Announce a death that occurred last night, my sister-in-law's mother. Many of the people will know her." Suspecting the deacon officers had heard of the previous weeks' omission and searched for a way to get at me; I grabbed his hand as if shaking it and held on while opening the note with my other hand.

After I read the contents, I asked S. A. if his sister-in-law's mother lived nearby. He said, "No, she's over in Arkansas, but I know I can find ten people here who know her well." I asked him if the deceased lady had once lived in the area or had been a member of Big Bottom.

"No, can't say that, but they'll know her, alright."

"S. A., I'm not going to announce this. I'm not going to take the time of twelve hundred people when just ten might know her. I'll pass it along to a Sunday school class, though, if you'll tell me the most appropriate one to contact her family," I said, looking straight into his eyes with my jaw set and my voice unwavering.

S. A. had accomplished his mission. He knew he'd caught me in an area where my policy differed from previous pastors. He'd found a ground of complaint some would feel was legitimate. He'd done what he'd intended.

I had to pray before delivering the sermon from the text where Jesus said, "Forgive them, Lord, for they know not what they do." I believed S. A. knew precisely what he was doing. The chill I'd felt had added to the effect. The coolness left as soon as I heard the peculiar squeak his shoes made as they exited up the aisle. I wondered whether I'd heard the squeak as he came, but below the level of consciousness, and that'd been the warning that had made me feel colder. Or could it have been that God cautioned me to beware? I didn't know. I just knew he gave me the heebie-jeebies, and I trusted a rattler more than I did him.

That was Palm Sunday. On the next Sunday, Easter, I received another note and another one the next week and for twelve weeks in a row after that. In my estimation, not a single one of them merited a public announcement. The notes came from present and former deacon officers, from S. A. Tanner one week, from Nev Wright the next, from H. H. Smith the next, and from Early Washburn the following week. Then the group would begin again, as if this had been plotted out and assigned by rotation.

The time came when I would take the note, smile and whisper a prayer for the one who delivered it while looking in their eyes, fold it, and place it in my pocket. After several weeks of this, it shocked me that one note said, "Will you even read this slip of paper?" Reading them ruined many a Sunday afternoon, but usually by the evening service I'd forgiven all and had had a good time talking with the Lord. Their notes were forcing me to pray. I was thankful for that.

I also thanked the Lord that in thirty years of ministry, I'd never known a vindictive group before this one. I'd heard of other pastors who had them, but I'd never had any come my way before. I thanked Him that the majority of Christians desired a close walk with the Lord and would never plot subversion. I thanked Him for the hundreds of wonderful church members over the years who'd done all in their power to build up and not to tear down their pastor. I also thanked Him that, though I was the one being maligned—and I knew that because I'd heard it from several sources—that I wasn't the one maligning others.

And then, I thanked the Lord that these men were driving me to my knees. It produced a deeper humility than I'd known. For the first time, I felt I understood the words of James in the first chapter of his Book, verses two through four, "Count it all joy brethren, when you encounter various trials, knowing that the testing of your faith produces endurance. And let endurance have its perfect result, that you may be mature and complete, lacking in nothing."

I began to hear people give compliments I'd never heard before as we shook hands after the services or when coming in for counseling. They were saying things like, "I feel you know the hurt I'm going through." Or, "I couldn't share this problem with anyone before, but somehow I felt you'd understand."

The officers didn't know it, but they were making me more empathetic with the people. I've always loved people. God made me that way, but now I felt the pain of others and somehow they intuited it. For the first time I could even thank God for announcements.

That changed, at least for a while, when I received a note from Wanda W. Washburn the third Sunday of June. Four weeks remained until the mission trip, and Wanda had been acting like a different person ever since I'd asked her to consider going. She'd become much more cheerful and much less critical. Even Darla, Sam Jones, and our minister of missions, Robert Stringer, had noticed. All three had remarked that it looked like I had been right about asking her on the mission trip. On that Sunday morning, a deacon officer had slipped by to hand me the usual note but soon Wanda followed with another note.

Since she'd reformed her act, I took it to be a genuine note of concern when she handed me the paper and, with a wrinkle of concern in her forehead and narrowed, pleading eyes, said with a soft voice,

"Pastor, I know you prefer not to make announcements at the last minute like this; but I've just found out my neighbor, Mr. Bullington, passed away and will be buried tomorrow afternoon. Since we have no newspaper on Mondays, many people will miss the funeral if they don't hear it from you. Will you please announce this?"

I looked at Wanda and prayed for the words to say and the approach to take. Maybe the Lord did want me to announce this one. To gain clarity about the situation, I asked, "Mrs. Washburn, I'm so sorry you've lost a good neighbor. How long was Mr. Bullington a member of Big Bottom?"

"Oh, he wasn't a member here," she said. "He was a good Nazarene, though, and most everyone in the area knows him."

"Wanda," I said with tenderness, "I can't announce his demise without announcing the departure of every person in this area and beyond who go to their eternal reward on a Saturday or on a Sunday morning after the paper has run. But if you'll take the note to the sound booth and let them know I authorized you, they'll scroll it through the announcements when the services are over."

"Well, I never," she said, with a voice that'd turned harsh. "Bro. Jackson would've announced it right away. And furthermore, young man," and by now her voice had risen to a level several rows of people behind us could hear, "don't you call me Wanda again. That's disrespectful. You call me Wanda W. Washburn. S. A. gave me this note. He told me you'd never announce it. But we'll get that policy changed, young man, you just wait and see." As she stomped off I saw several ladies nearby put their hands over their mouths while their husbands exhibited soft smiles of understanding.

What went through my head were the words of Hunter, "Like a deer comes to corn, Wanda W. Washburn comes to criticism." I'd also noticed through the months as her pastor that Wanda, "Well-I-never-ed" a lot when she got upset.

In addition, it came to me that I must not have graduated from the school of hard knocks. God must have some more sanding to do on my life to make me look more like Jesus. I knew this issue wasn't going away any time soon. No, it was far from over and I'd have some more suffering to do.

Oswald Chamber's words, "He whom God would use greatly He must first wound deeply," came to mind. I don't know if God will ever use me greatly. I used to plan and dream of that. But no more. Not since I've matured a little. Now family and friends, with a few quiet moments of writing or fishing thrown in, mean far more than the fleeting applause of men. I feel a lot freer than I did in those days when I was knocking myself out trying to achieve greatness in the eyes of others.

To hold my three-year-old granddaughter, Claire, to feel the softness of her skin, and to hear her giggle with delight when she flicks a ladybug off the porch screen—to learn from her to take joy in the simple things of life—that's greatness enough for me. To enjoy an evening watching a good movie with Darla, that's greatness to me. To know my boys and my daughter-in-laws are growing in the Lord and maturing as responsible adults, that's greatness to me. To counsel a man and see him turn from drink or drugs and back to his family, that's greatness, too. To see a child brought to Sunday school by a neighbor and grow up learning more and more about the Lord and then one day to come to the awareness that the Lord of the universe wants him to respond to His love by receiving the gift of His Son, what could be greater?

I'm content to serve God the best I know how and leave the recognition with Him and those to whom He chooses to give it. I am positive that a great many pastors and other Christians deserve it far, far more than I, above all some who serve overseas or in inner cities in much more difficult circumstances. And since I've learned God has given me a Barnabas gift of encouragement, I find as much joy in helping others achieve their goals as in achieving my own.

The thing is, I didn't want announcements that meant something to ten people to go out to more than a thousand. When someone would tell me, "You've got to announce this one. Everybody knows him." It would always come to me that they meant the fifty people in their circle know him, but that also meant more than a thousand in the worship service didn't. When those would sit through an announcement about Homer Hessian's hard-of-hearing surgery, it would leave hundreds feeling like outsiders because they didn't know Homer. They were more concerned with their own hearing from God that day than about Homer's ear surgery the next. I saw I had some teaching to do to bring the policies of the church to the level where the worship service was viewed as just that, a service to worship God. It's not a time to draw lines between insiders who know information and could have their announcements made and outsiders who didn't know what was going on and felt estranged by the process.

There were a few exceptions, of course. One Sunday a man had a heart attack near the back of the church just as the worship service began. Some doctors in the congregation stretched him out on the floor near a back door and began to work with him. The cry of his wife was heard all over the building. When I became aware of what was happening, I paused to announce it and to ask the congregants to form a hundred small prayer cells all over the auditorium for him, his wife and family, and for the medical professionals called in to work with him.

I didn't change the policy, though. The staff loved the new policy, despite the criticism, and cited a litany of errors that the old policies had caused. Associate Pastor Carter Ross recalled that the members, as a matter of course, timed a former pastor each week as he read numerous announcements and then had prayer. One Sunday the routine had taken seventeen minutes. The staff voted, without opposition, to keep the new policy. It often fell to them to make announcements, and they didn't like the old way any more than I did.

The new policy meant the music minister could plan with more precision the time of worship. It meant another hymn or chorus each service. It meant God-centered worship. It meant an increased emphasis on the Sunday school class or the small group as the primary care-givers in the church. It meant a more uplifting time of praise and worship. The crowd in Sunday school and worship continued to grow, and the enthusiasm in the worship services made them more worshipful. With the staff and most of the people behind me, I stayed the course.

On Sunday afternoon I received a call from S. A. Tanner. I knew it was serious when he didn't take time to tell me of meeting someone in a store or barbershop or airplane terminal. He cut straight to the chase. "Pastor, some men would like to meet with you to express their concerns."

"Hi, S. A., It's always good to hear your voice," I said, reversing roles. "So nice of you to call. I'd been meaning to talk with you ever since I met a lady at Kroger's last week. When I invited her to church she said she was a distant relative or yours. Said her name was Scarlet Tanner. You know her?"

"Yeah, I know her; she's my third cousin once removed, but I didn't call you about that. Some men want to talk with you. When can you meet with us?"

"Well, Scarlet said she'd been thinking about coming to Big Bottom but said something about a family squabble and didn't know if you'd want her to come," I said.

"Confound it, Brent; we can talk about Scarlet later. I called you about a meeting and I intend to get a meeting scheduled," S. A. stated firmly.

"You know me, S. A. I'm a people person. I love meeting with people and do so whenever I get the opportunity. Who wants to meet and what's it about?" I asked.

"It's six deacon officers who've been involved with Big Bottom Church for many years. We've got the good of the church at heart, but we've got some concerns and we want to express them to you to see if we can get the church on the right path again."

"S. A., I'm always ready to meet with people who want to help our church go forward, deacons or anyone else. Tell you what. I'm up to my armpits in alligators getting ready for this mission trip next month and then Darla and I are on vacation to see our kids and granddaughter. With something that sounds this serious, maybe I'd better wait until I can give it some thought and action. Do you have your calendar with you?"

"Now come on, pastor. You know you can spare an afternoon to meet with us. Most of us are retired and we can meet with you most any time. You'd better listen now rather than get hurt later," he said.

Laying aside the power play, I replied, "S. A., I meant it when I said I'd be glad to meet with you. I know it takes all of us serving together to make the church effective. I don't have all the ideas. You men can help me and I'm willing to listen to what you say, just like I'm willing to listen to what any person in Big Bottom says. It takes us all working together, wouldn't you agree?"

"Yeah," he said in a softer voice indicating he believed he'd been heard, "so when can you meet with us?"

"I've got my calendar with me, and you can't believe how full it is with the normal schedule plus the extra meetings preparing for the mission trip. A time after my mission trip and vacation would allow me to consider your concerns with the attention they deserve. How about the afternoon of August tenth at two?"

"Don't you have anything this month?" he asked.

"Let's be honest, S. A. You guys may ask me to make some changes. If I'm to have time to pray about and consider your concerns, don't you think I might need some time? With my attention being given to missions and family in the next two months in addition to the normal church program, looks like August is the earliest time."

"Alright then," he shouted. "Have it your way. August tenth it'll be." He slammed the receiver so hard it hurt my ear.

It didn't escape me that the officers had been meeting without me every month and could have asked me in to any of these meetings. It also didn't escape me that these officers would be replaced, in all probability, by some more in line with the church as a whole, on October first. The delay until August would help me by giving a few more months to establish policies that could ensure a better future for Big Bottom and by enabling me to earn the love and support of more members.

Earlier I could have kicked myself for scheduling a mission trip in my busy first year of pastoring Big Bottom, but now I thanked the Lord over and over for filling my schedule until August. The proper priorities of missions and worship solve a lot of church problems. When the main things become the main things, the other things have a way of taking care of themselves.

24
THE CHURCH IS ALL ABUZZ

Almost every pastor who's been around a while has received anonymous letters. Nameless letters are negative, because if a person wants to send a positive one, he or she will take ownership and sign. I usually read the unsigned ones, as I want to know what people are thinking, but if they begin to get numerous or to disturb me, I toss them in file thirteen. If a person cannot stand behind what he or she says, that person shouldn't send a note.

In late spring I began receiving mail without signatures, more often than not one or two a week, but sometimes three or four. They had to do with cell phones going off, disturbing the worship services. My hearing is poor and I don't always hear the phones, but they were doing some damage to the spirit of worship at Big Bottom.

When I talked it over with the staff at our regular meeting on Tuesday afternoon, they confirmed that cell phones had been upsetting the worship services. We decided to put up small signs at every door requesting that all cell phones be turned off, "so as not to disturb the worship." The next Sunday a cell phone rang. I heard this one, as it was loud enough that no one in the church missed it. The Yellow Rose of Texas was the ring tone and it blared away during the most important part of the sermon, the invitation. Providentially, the Lord gave me words to share, "Can't you hear God calling you right now?" The people laughed. Some responded by joining that day, saying the Lord had, indeed, been calling them.

The next Sunday two more phones went off. The one during the prayer time was not too disruptive as the ring tone was a classical piece. The second one, during an important announcement, however, was a different story. "Who Let the Dogs out . . .Who, Who, Who Who," could be heard from front to back, from wall to wall. So, I took the issue back to the staff, and we decided to place an announcement in the bulletin each week, "Please do not disturb the other worshipers. Silence your cell phone during worship services." The following Sunday three more cell phones went off, all three during the sermon.

At the Wednesday night deacons' meeting, one man brought up the problem of the cell phones. H. H. Smith jumped into the conversation, jowls shaking like former President Nixon's. Every matter was a serious one to him. He said he understood the pastor had received several notes about the matter and wanted to know what I was going to do about it. How he knew I'd received notes, I do not know, but his words left me on the spot before the deacons.

I shared with the men the actions the staff and I had taken, the notices in the bulletins and beside each door. I told them that we could also scroll announcements on the screen to remind people as they came in. The men, and in particular the officers, didn't seem to be satisfied, so I asked them to help me come up with some fresh approaches.

A number of ideas surfaced. One man recommended X-ray machines at the doors, like they had at military hospitals. No, that wouldn't work, some said, because it would cause a significant delay for people entering the building, would cause worship to run over the time allotted to it, and would cause some to be late for lunch.

Another suggested we word the announcement in a different way, something like, "A fine of fifty dollars will be assessed for anyone whose cell phone rings in the worship service." That suggestion garnered a significant debate, but in the end failed because of the difficulty in making the fines stick, especially when it "wouldn't be fair because some would pay it and some wouldn't."

Vigorous discussion followed the next proposal, that the ushers to pat people down at the doors to ensure no cell phone got through. Early Washburn volunteered to be an usher. Nev Wright and H. H. Smith volunteered the deacon officers to cover the worship center doors. Then they realized the suggestion to pat people at the doors was tongue-in-cheek. Some phones belong to women, it was noted, and they'd not put up with a man patting them down.

"Why not?" Nev asked. "If it was done to everyone, no one could claim discrimination."

Reason took over, though, and the majority of the men took the suggestion as a joke. I wasn't so sure, but I knew the idea had turned the men's attention from mission—reaching people with the Gospel—to maintenance. The deacons of the New Testament did not serve as a decision-making body, they served tables and witnessed. It's been my experience when deacons move from a service body to an administrative board, trouble soon follows. Deacons need to be involved in ministries to people, not in running the church.

In churches of ten people, everyone can vote on everything, paper versus plastic plates, for instance. In churches of three hundred, everyone can vote on some issues, like a paved or gravel parking lot. In churches of one thousand, in theory every member in a Baptist church can still have a voice on everything, but if everyone did, business meetings would last until Jesus came again. For the most part, large churches realize this and let committees or a business manager and the staff handle the everyday decisions of running the church.

In the end, the motion that won the day? "The deacons respectfully request the pastor and staff to announce each Sunday, until the problem gets under control, that cell phones be turned off or rendered silent until the worship service is over." I appreciated that approach and would abide by it. I thought about doing the announcement like Joel Osteen begins his services at his Houston megachurch.

Osteen has the folks hold up their Bibles and say something like, "This is my Bible. I am who it says I am. . . I have what it says I have. . . I can do what it says I can do. . ." I'd ask all people present to hold up their cell phones and say, "This is my cell phone. I talk with people through it. I am alerted by its ring. I can do without it for one hour so I can listen to God. I will now turn off my cell phone. I will turn off the world's calls and tune into God's call."

The next Sunday associate pastor, Carter Ross, requested all phones and paging devices be rendered silent for the hour of worship. When I got up to preach, I made a similar announcement. That Sunday, however, two cell phones went off, and it seemed to take two minutes for one and three minutes for the other to become silent. After the service I discovered that both phones had belonged to senior adults who'd been given the phones by their children. Mrs. Gwaltney had had her phone for a year and Mrs. Cuevas for two months, but neither had learned how to silence the phones or put them on vibrate mode. They'd forgotten the cellular phones were in their purses and neither had thought it was her phone ringing.

Mrs. Gwaltney said, "I'm so sorry about my cell phone this morning. I heard a phone ring and ring and I thought that person whose phone is ringing is disturbing the service this morning. Then, a lady looked at me and said, 'Are you going to turn that thing off or answer it?' It embarrassed me so much. I'll bet I'm still red in the face." She was.

I said, "Mrs. Gwaltney, don't think another second about it. It could happen to anybody."

Her smile spread the width of her face, she lifted her shoulders and said, "Yes, it could. To anybody. It's kind of like that mulligan I give my partners at Canebreak Golf Course. Anybody can make one mistake. I'll just learn how to turn it off. Thanks for the mulligan."

I got word while shaking hands that the deacon officers had called a special meeting to precede the evening worship service by an hour. It didn't surprise me. The officers had been looking for an opportunity to stir up the church about something in an effort to regain their control.

A restless afternoon passed and I attended the called deacons' meeting. Nev Wright and H. H. Smith were fighting mad. It's not a good thing to be angry on a Sunday, just before hearing the Word of God. It quenches God's Spirit and isn't much good for digestion, either.

The deacons seemed to hold me responsible for the cell phones ringing that morning. Nev said I hadn't made a strong enough announcement. Others expressed a similar sentiment. Why the issue had to be resolved then and there was beyond me.

I said, "Nev, could you help me out? Explain how you would've made the announcement about cell phones. Maybe I can learn from you."

"Why, I'd hold up a cell phone," he said while holding his in the air for all the deacons to see, and say, 'If any phone rings this morning, I'm going to stomp on it and that'll be the last time that phone'd ring.' Then I'd do it. That'd take care of the problem."

S. A. Tanner said, "Amen to that, brother. That'd stop it right there. We wouldn't have this problem if our pastor would show some gumption."

At that moment, Nev's cell phone rang. His face turned red. It took him at least thirty seconds to get the things turned off. He started to talk and stopped; started and stopped; and at last he stammered, "I planned that to show how much one of these blasted things can disturb a meeting. This shows us we ought to confiscate any phone that goes off in a service."

Sam Jones spoke up, "Wait a minute, brothers. Remember, we are servants of the church, not masters of it. We can't control anybody's life here. We can't just take their property. The services may seem a little confusing with all the phones ringing and all, but let's not get dictatorial here. Remember, people come to Big Bottom of their own free accord. If we get too pushy with them, they'll just go elsewhere."

Tanner wasn't finished. "Well, maybe that's what they need to do."

Sam didn't stop. "You mean, let all the newer people go so you can run the church again?"

Tanner replied, "You know that's not what I said."

Sam was masterful in pointing a group to the important issues. He continued, "No, but isn't that what you meant?"

S. A. Tanner's face grew red and then rigid. He clinched and unclenched his fists, and I wondered if he would swing at Sam. Some of the other deacons caught on to the power play going on, though. They began to calm down about the cell phones, and picked up the real issue involved: Who's going to call the shots in the church?

About that time, John Anderson spoke up. "Men," he said, "I've been a farmer for a long time, and God has taught me some things on the farm. Take that new man I hired to help me out when I was taking care of Mary. I found I could give him a job to do and tell him in every detail how to do it. He'd get the job done alright, but I could tell he wasn't happy.

"Well, Mary saw how I was breaking him in and made a suggestion to me. She said, 'John, if you'll show him one time and then let him make his own mistakes, he'll start taking initiative. You'll get more done, and he'll take a lot more interest in the work if you don't crowd him so much.'

"I didn't much like her advice because it was my farm and I knew best how to run it, but I loved Mary so much and it hurt me to see her going down like she was." Anderson stopped, took out his handkerchief and wiped his eyes. The men gave him time. He was well-respected and his words brought calm to the situation. After a while he regained his composure and continued.

"Do you know she was right? In no time at all the feller was taking a real interest in the farm. Before long, I didn't have to tell him what to do at all, just encourage him when he did the job well.

"Now some things still went wrong once in a while, like the time the fertilizer got wet in the hopper on the tractor and we had to shovel it out by hand. But you know what? Things went wrong with me once in a while, too, and that was before I'd hired the man.

"It seems to me we've hired a fine pastor and he's helping us bring people into this church right and left. We better leave him alone and just encourage him when things go well." A chorus of "Amen" went up.

One deacon noticed it was almost time for the evening service and moved to dismiss the deacons' meeting. And with that we left. The last thing I remembered from the meeting was the squeak of S. A. Tanner's shoes as he walked away. It seemed louder that afternoon. The screech of his steps made the hair on my arms stand up.

What a fertilizer hopper had to do with a cell phone, I didn't know, but I was thankful for the homespun wisdom of John Anderson and his ability to use it at the most appropriate time. I decided I'd have to get to know him and to see if there was yet a future for him and Jane Winfield.

The next Sunday, a couple needing marital counseling caught me about fifteen minutes before the morning worship service. They had to—had to—speak to me right then. It didn't matter that, as we talked, they shared about their major problem being one that had existed for twelve years. I understood, though. Sometimes things go wrong in a relationship and there comes a definite time when we want it fixed, right now.

After fifteen minutes I rescheduled an appointment with them three days later when we could meet for an uninterrupted hour, led them in a quick prayer, and ran to the sanctuary. It hit me, just as I passed the organ, that I had my cell phone and keys in my pocket. I took them out, turned off the phone in a hurry, and left it and the contents of my pockets on the organ. I hooked up the earpiece for the wireless microphone and opened the service with prayer and a warm welcome to all.

Halfway through the sermon I heard what sounded like bees. Sometimes the buzz was louder and sometimes quieter but it continued all the way through the sermon. At one point in the sermon, it distracted me so much that I asked, "Does anyone hear what sounds like bees in the sound system?" The choir laughed, a few of them non stop, but no one moved. My hearing isn't good, so I just ignored the sound. I thought it must be some aberration we'd have to work out with the sound system technicians later. At least it's not another cell phone disturbing us, I thought.

After the service, the whole congregation was abuzz wondering where the bees were. No one had seen them, but many had heard them. At last choir member Betta Lovett exited the door where Darla and I had chosen to shake hands.

"Pastor, I think I know the source of your bee problem this morning." Another choir member behind her snickered and a small group gathered around to hear. It was obvious she'd been laughing. "You couldn't see it from your angle, but half of the choir could. I saw you fiddle with your cell phone before placing it on the organ, but you must've turned it to vibrate instead of turning it off. It traveled the length and breadth of the organ several times, quivering away. We weren't laughing at you, it was the cell phone. Who'd have ever thought a cell phone could have a mind of its own and run back and forth over the organ top without bouncing off?"

I was as embarrassed as I'd been in a long time, and my face felt flushed. Most of the people left, chuckling. Mrs. Gwaltney came through the line next and said, "Have you played golf in the last few weeks?"

I said, "No, ma'm, I haven't."

She said, "Well, the look you have on your face right now, I've seen it before. More often than not it's on the first hole when one of my playing partners plans to shoot a low score but then slices her first drive into the lake. We let her start over. What you need is a mulligan!"

Soon S. A. Tanner passed through the line. He had some words, too, direct, curt ones, "Brent, I don't know who caused that buzz in the church today. Whoever it was disturbed us all. They may have thought it was funny but we'll find out who it was. That's right, we'll find out and when we do we'll see who gets stung."

Mrs. Gwaltney was right. I needed a mulligan. I'm glad God gives second chances. And thirds. And five hundredths. I'm thankful my salvation is not dependant on my living life without flaws. I've tried it. I need mulligans every day. Life's all abuzz without them.

25
A HOUSE NEVER VISITED

Associate Pastor Carter Ross served as my right-hand man at Big Bottom Church. I liked him. He thought ahead. He kept the staff on track in the day-to-day work and kept the church up-to-date on whatever was needed. When I learned how gifted an administrator he was, I handed more and more details to him, and that freed me to spend additional time in study and with people.

Because Ross had been a pastor himself and knew the pastoral role, I could count on him to do things to lend a hand. Some folks think a senior pastor should be on call all the time. By taking some on-call hours, Carter helped me beyond words to explain. Despite people's saying that pastors have a great job because "you just work one day a week," the truth is most pastors work long hours. We have the usual office routine and then work most nights of the week in church activities, fellowships, visits, or committee meetings.

I work about seventy hours a week. They aren't hours of hard labor, if you don't count the hours working with the present deacon officers, but they are long hours. It's crushing when some project comes up that will take twenty or thirty hours in the next couple of weeks, as projects around the church inevitably do, because I have to crunch the numbers to see from where those hours will come. Sometimes the tyranny of the urgent wins out and the important takes a back seat to the pressing.

Leading someone to Christ is important. Counseling a family in marital crises is important. Ministering to a family whose loved one has just died is important. Studying for Sunday morning's message is important. Dealing with an upset mother whose daughter was not chosen for the lead role in the children's musical is just pressing. Dealing with cell phones going off during worship is pressing. Because Carter Ross understood the demands and searched for ways to take an hour here and one there from my bucket, he served an invaluable role.

Ross reflected a spiritual walk with God that went far beyond the usual. I'd heard of several growing churches he'd pastored over a twenty-year ministry before he'd come to Big Bottom. When June rolled around, I asked him to go to Mac's Fish Camp with me for a working supper in order to talk over duties while I would be on the mission trip. Carter stands over six feet tall, and at 270 pounds he could put a serious dent into a platter of fish when he sat for a meal.

We entered the newest of the chain of catfish houses, this one opened just before Christmas in 2005. I can still remember when the original Mac's opened near Pep's Point on the Bouie River a few miles north of Hattiesburg when I was a boy. For some time they served all the catfish you could eat for seventy-five cents. Later it went up to a dollar, then to a dollar and a quarter. Over the years they've served South Mississippians hundreds of thousands of tons of delta-raised catfish and enough tea to float a battleship.

Mac's built their West Fish Camp on Highway 98, ten miles west of Hattiesburg and about a mile and a quarter east of the home of USM's most famous graduate, quarterback Brett Farve. Mac's West offered a larger variety than I'd remembered as a boy. The menu now included a seafood buffet, a bargain at a price of $15.95.

We walked up the steps, crossed the porch of the huge, cabin-like structure, and into the dining room where more than four hundred people could be served at a time. Stained concrete served as the floor and antlered deer heads, a gigantic steer with horns that stretched ten feet from point to point, stuffed fish, and assorted other animals covered the walls. I loved looking at the collection of wild life, in particular since one of them, an albino raccoon, was taken by my father and me when I was a boy. Dad allowed the owner of Mac's to display him.

The delicious smell of catfish cooked in peanut oil rose into our nostrils and made our mouths water. Keisha, a slim, dark-haired lady who could have been just out of college but greeted and seated us with the kind of professionalism that told us she'd been at this a while. Keisha informed us she'd be our server tonight, as one of the normal waitresses was out.

She helped us to a table by the wall and, in a snap, took our orders. Our mouths were set on the catfish, and we both ordered an all-you-can-eat plate. Carter and I substituted baked potatoes with low-fat sour cream in place of the French fries, however, as it's always good to be health conscious before eating too much fried fish. Hushpuppies and slaw rounded out our meal and our stomachs.

After Keisa left with our orders, I asked Carter about his years as a senior pastor. He took off his brown-rimmed glasses, placed them on the table, and hung his head. His face turned red. "You've heard, haven't you?"

"No, I guess not," I replied, "is there something I should hear?"

"It happened during my third church," he spoke with a low voice. "I'd pastored a church in North Carolina right out of seminary that showed rapid growth. Candice and I stayed there six years and the church almost doubled in size during that time," he said. "Two of our kids were born there, and we loved the people and what God was doing in the church."

"It doesn't surprise me at all, Carter. I knew you had strong abilities," I said.

"Then we went to a county seat town in north Alabama and pastored their First Baptist Church. It was a different kind of ministry than the open country church I'd pastored but the variety was good for us. Candice and I grew, we had our other two children there and things were looking up. After we'd lived in north Alabama for eight years, a large church where I'd led a conference on Sunday school growth contacted me to request a resume. Our church was going well and we didn't want to move, but having them phone me out of the blue like that made us think maybe God had orchestrated this, so we told them we'd pray about it."

By then a huge plate of catfish fillets arrived, along with all the side dishes, and we had no trouble thanking God for the bounty He'd bestowed. Carter continued between bites.

"That third church was a suburban congregation. You'd know the church if I told you the name, but I'd just as soon not because our experience there didn't turn out like the other ones. It wasn't the people or the situation. That church prospered just like the others when we applied church growth principles, preached the Gospel, loved the people, and evangelized the community. I was the problem."

"You? A problem? I can't imagine that," I replied. "You're the most complete associate pastor I've ever worked with. You make so many things easy for me. I'll tell you right now, I love your work, and you're a team player. I can't imagine your being a problem."

Carter finished his third catfish fillet and summoned Keisha to order some additional napkins and ketchup and a refill on the tea before continuing. "It's not the kind of problem you think. You sure you've never heard of this?"

"This is the first I've heard of it. I knew you came as an associate to Big Bottom more than ten years ago, but I just figured you felt your talents would work better in an associate role or maybe it would give you more time with your family," I said.

"All of that is true, but there's more to the story."

I finished my bite of cold slaw and said, "Let's hear it."

"You promise it'll be confidential?"

"Carter, you know me by now. I'm an encourager. I don't do things behind the scenes to hurt folks; I'm always on the lookout for ways to help people. And besides, the people at Big Bottom appreciate your talents. Almost every day I hear someone brag on you."

"Okay," he said, "but I hope you won't think worse of me because of this." And with that he paused and even pushed back his plate for a few moments. "You know that I have trouble at times saying the words I want to say. Spoonerisms for the most part; you know, like saying to a groom, 'It's kisstomary to cuss the bride,' instead of the other way around. Or, when I preached from Psalm 23 one time, I kept on saying, 'Our Lord is a shoving leopard.'" Carter's head jerked to the right.

"Now that you mention it, I've heard you misplace a word or two, but it's nothing serious," I said.

"I didn't used to mix up my words. But right after we moved to the suburban church, I had a serious car wreck and my head hit the windshield. I was in a coma for about a week. It was touch and go there for a while. When I came out of it the people all thought it was a miracle. And so did I. I soon recovered most all my abilities, and now I seldom think of the wreck any more. The one lasting effect seems to be that I sometimes get my words mixed up.

"It must hurt you to mix up words you didn't used to jumble but I don't see why that caused you a problem at the church," I said while reaching for another hot fillet and the ketchup.

"The difficulty happened about a year after the wreck. My problem of confusing words was no longer as pronounced, and I'd been back in the pulpit for eight months. The church needed to grow in giving, so I'd instituted a stewardship program. I still remember that Sunday morning like it was yesterday. I preached from Malachi 3:10; you know, the passage that says to bring all your tithes into the storehouse?

"I preached that the tithe is a biblical principle for us. In order to explain it, though, I needed to define the storehouse." Every time he said "storehouse" he slowed down and spoke it with deliberation, pronouncing the word as if it had four syllables.

"What happened was. . ." and with this he looked side to side to ensure no one could overhear us and spoke in a much lower voice. "I had to say the word, 'storehouse' again and again in the message, but every time I said it, it came out, 'whorehouse.' What I told the people to do was to bring all their wives into the whorehouse." He had an odd grimace on his face as he whispered it, almost as if his face contorted.

"Yeah," I said, "That's going to leave a mark. But the people must have known your difficulties stemmed from your wreck. They cut you some slack, didn't they?"

"The men all understood," he said. "They wanted to take it easy on me. The women, however, thought I would never have said it if I hadn't been thinking it in my subconscious. They supposed it was one of those Sleudian frips," he said blinking and snapping his head to the right. "They said they could never permit their children to attend a sermon delivered by a minister who was thinking about a brothel while preaching. Some even said they wondered what was in my mind when I looked at them."

"Wow, that's serious. Didn't they give you an opportunity to get a doctor's opinion to see whether you'd improve?"

"The personnel committee suggested it," he said as he looked around once more to assure he could not be overheard. "And I went, but the specialists could find only a few cases like mine in their textbooks, and they couldn't give a definitive answer that I'd improve. They said the area of my brain that processed limitations showed less activity than a normal brain, and they didn't know if it would get better.

"My wife and I came to the conclusion that the women were right—oh, not in the sense that I think of sexual things more than most men, but it was just that I didn't know if I'd ever say something like that again. I sure didn't want kids to hear that kind of language in church." With this a tear rolled down his cheek. I dabbed at my own eyes with the napkin.

"I'd hate ever to do anything to put a barrier in the way of one of the little ones." A wave of sadness flooded over me for Carter and his tragic situation. I also felt his love for people.

"We thought our ministry had ended, but about that time Big Bottom Church was exploding in growth and needed a new associate. One of the men in the Ministerial Relations Department of the

Mississippi Baptist Convention talked with Pastor Vernon Leigh and the rest is history. It seems my problem is better now and I've preached a few times over the years at Big Bottom, but I toose my chexts with care," he said as he blinked and snapped his head again.

"I hurt for you, Carter. You were doing what you loved and bam, all of a sudden you had to change roles."

"Oh, don't worry about us, pastor. The truth is that we believe Paul when the Spirit led him to say, 'All things work together for good to those who love God, who are called according to His purposes.' We were down about it for a year or two, but we love Hattiesburg, and we believe we're right where the Lord placed us. We can even laugh about it now, if no one's around to hear us."

Carter paused to look around the room a third time to ensure no one else could hear him. He lowered his voice and continued, "I mean, just think about it—I'm the only man you know who lost his job over a whorehouse he never visited!"

26
DIRTY PANTS

"And speaking of losing a job," Carter said while salting his baked potato, "have you heard about the difficulty our preschool director is having?"

"You mean Lorna McWhorter?"

"Yes"

"Well, Alice Evans did mention something to me about touching base with you on a preschool policy matter, but I had no idea it had to do with someone's losing their job."

"It could come to that," he said, "and it's a pity, too, because Lorna is excellent and the incident never should've happened."

"Is this something I should know?" I asked.

"Yes, I think so, because you are sure to hear of it in the next deacons' meeting," he replied.

"Just what we need," I said, "another issue for the officers to rope and ride like a wild horse."

"Well, this one's wild, alright," he said.

"Then wait just a minute and let me get a refill on my tea and some fresh fillets. Sounds like this may go down better with some hot fish." When I lifted my hand, Keisha appeared, refilled our drinks, and rushed off to complete the meal for us.

"Here's the tall and short of it," Carter said while spearing a short fillet. "Lorna instituted a policy change across all the childcare departments last year. The policy came into place due to the proliferation of lawsuits against childcare agencies all over the country. She brought the new policy to the staff and deacons, and both bodies liked the new policy. The biggest difference from the old policy is that now teachers are not permitted to touch preschoolers to help clean them after they go to the bathroom."

"And how would that help?"

"The idea was that if a teacher never touched a child when they were undressed and using the bathroom, then the teacher could not be accused of improper conduct and this would protect both the church and the teacher," he replied.

"Ah, the whole litigious society thing," I said.

"You've got it," he answered while piling his plate with some hot catfish fillets Keisha brought and reaching for the ketchup. He began attacking the meal as if he'd just begun.

"Well, what's the problem?"

"Last year when the new policy took effect our preschool kept children three-years-old and up. The new procedures worked out fine. Beginning in January, though, we began to receive two-year-old children also," he answered.

"So?" I asked.

"It seems that some two-year-old children can take care of cleaning their behinds with verbal encouragement from the teacher, but other two-year-olds need the physical touch to make certain of cleanliness."

With those words the catfish lost all appeal. The smell turned abhorrent and caught in my nostrils. I was through with my meal and shoved my platter to the center of the table but Carter kept putting the fish away as if he'd done this every week for years and wanted his money's worth, despite the topic of conversation. No alteration in the dialogue was going to get in the way of this week's appointed round.

"It happened a month ago. Little Alex Reynolds, III, a two-year-old in our church daycare, came home with poopy pants and his mom went berserk. The teacher had followed the letter of the policy, but young Alex wasn't able to clean himself, so he went home with dirty pants.

"His dad is a young lawyer and a deacon in our church and this is their first child. It may be a first child syndrome, you know, where the parents get upset over every little thing that happens to their first one, but by the time the second one comes along they just roll with the punches."

"Yeah," I said, "like the first child drops his pacifier and the parents boil it five minutes, but by the second child the parents yell 'fetch, Spot, fetch?'" We laughed because we both knew from personal experience about raising children.

"Something like that, but the Reynolds threatened to bring the matter of Lorna's employment to the deacons. If they don't get action there, they say they'll bring it to the church business meeting," Carter said and reached in rhythm for another fillet. "If they do that the foopy pants may hit the pan." His head yanked to the right as if pulled by an invisible rope, but the fork, full of fried catfish dipped in ketchup, altered its flight and found its way into his mouth.

"What's your take on this, Carter?"

"What do you mean?"

"I mean, what do you think is the solution and how should we approach this?" I asked.

"I think the policy was a good one for three-year-old children and above, but not such a good one for two-year-old children. I'd recommend the preschool committee meet and revise the policy before the Reynolds can meet with others and stir this up. If the committee can come up with a new policy, it'll save Lorna's job and also the trouble an open discussion of poopy pants can have on the floor of the church," he said.

"Are you saying poopy pants on the floor of the church are not a good thing?" I asked with a smile.

"I'm saying we should go ahead and get the scoop and not poopenly discuss open pants on the floor," Carter said as his head took a quick turn to the right.

"Let me try that again," he said. This time he spoke more slowly. "I'm saying if we find a way to handle it before deacons' meeting it'll keep the Reynolds from staising a rink," he said, his head jerking to the right again. "Oh, forget it," Carter said, as he dropped both hands by his side and slumped back against his chair. "You know what I mean."

"The deacons meet this coming Wednesday night, and the business meeting is the following Wednesday. Can you call a special meeting of the preschool committee and get this changed before then?"

"I can if Lorna will go along, but," and with this he paused, "she has some ownership in the previous policy and still thinks it's a good one."

"Carter, back in seminary did you have a class in Church Administration?"

"Of course. Had to. Required," Carter mumbled through a mouth filled with hushpuppies.

"Do you remember a discussion about picking your battles and how not every issue is so important that we should take our last stand on it?"

"Yeah, I remember that class," he answered.

"At the seminary I attended they called it, 'A hill on which to die,'" I said.

"I get your drift," Carter said. "In the total picture of Big Bottom Church, a dunghill is not one on which to die."

"You've got it, my friend. With the deacon officers going out of office in a few months and looking for any issue the church can buy into to keep their power, this issue can be that lightning rod. Why not ask Lorna to take one for the team, decide to recommend to the preschool committee that her policy be applied for three-year-olds and up, and that a new policy for two-year-olds be adopted by the end of the month?"

"I can do that if it's what you want," he said.

"Isn't it what you think best, too?"

"It sure is," he said as he finished his last fillet and sat back in the booth with a contented sigh as if he'd just completed painting a masterpiece.

"If Lorna wants this to work out, since we both know she has a good heart and cares for the children and their parents, ask her to call the Reynolds to apologize for their trouble and to make things right with them. You know, the scriptural principle, 'love covers a multitude of sins.'"

"I'll do it. That's a good idea. Humble pie on her part could spare the church a stink, so to speak, and set things right with the family."

I drove Carter back to the church where he'd parked his pickup. Before leaving we decided to have prayer together. I thanked God for a good working relationship and for giving us second chances in ministry.

Then Carter asked God to understand our dilemma about the poopy pants. I laughed without a sound as he continued to pray. "Lord, You've told us to call on You. You've promised to be an ever-present help in time of need. And we come to you needy, Lord. Help us to find a way out of these poopy pants." I looked up just in time to see his head twist to the right before he concluded, "In Jesus' Name, Amen."

I'll swear to it. That's just how he prayed it. And what's more, I believe God answered his prayer. Before the deacons' meeting, the preschool committee met and revised their policy for two-year-olds. The Reynolds, somewhat embarrassed by the whole thing, quieted down and said they loved the preschool and the personnel in charge. The policy change was all they'd wanted.

When the deacons' meeting rolled around, Nev Wright asked me, in a harsh tone and in front of the other men, "Brent, you aware of a problem with the preschool policy?"

Before I could answer, Alex Reynolds, Jr. spoke up and said he no longer had a problem with the policy. He said the pastor had helped facilitate a slight change that made the parents of two-year-olds happy.

Seeing the matter was a non-issue, Nev Wright moved on to the other business at hand. I went to bed that night, content in the thought that the God who created the whole world and knew best how it could operate, still loves and cares for us. He hears what we meant to say, not what we say, and sees what we meant to do, not what we did. I'm amazed that a matter as normal as stinking pants in a young child could stir up people. By the same token I'm amazed that people can calm down again when treated with respect and given a quiet answer, with love.

Lorna took one for the team. The church was better for it. The Reynolds were better for it. The policy was better for it. And Lorna was better for it, as she'd restored her relationship with the Reynolds. And the two-year-olds? They were cleaner for it.

27

HIT ME AGAIN

S. A. Tanner dropped by the office in late May with a proposal. He'd done this before with off-the-wall ideas. One time he'd suggested a mass visitation of our area, giving each home a roll of toilet paper with the wrapper being replaced with the words, "Wipe away your sins—come see how at Big Bottom Baptist Church." He even had a salesman buddy who'd already donated a crate of five thousand rolls of toilet paper.

The staff talked over S. A.'s idea. None of us liked it. We believed there are some things a person should do alone. Choosing one's personal toilet paper would be one of those things. We liked the mass visitation plan, but instead of toilet paper we'd distributed AA batteries wrapped with the words, "Need some energy in your life? Jesus can help. Find Him at Big Bottom Baptist Church."

People had appreciated this act of servanthood. A family named Haire began attending the church and joined us. Tanner, not satisfied with the staff's alteration of his plans nicknamed the Haires, the "energizer bunny family." Nevertheless, our church budget for supplies stayed in great shape since we didn't have to buy toilet paper for several years.

S. A.'s thoughts were strange to me, and often selfish, but he seemed to have the greater interests of the church at heart, too. At least he cared enough to think about better ways to do things. His latest suggestion resonated with me. A visiting evangelist, a personal friend of the Tanners, would be staying in their home on the second Sunday night in June. Tanner wanted me to let the man preach at Big Bottom that Sunday night.

His suggestion attracted my attention because I thought it would be good to perk up the folks a bit. Also, I'd be getting back from the Southern Baptist Convention in San Antonio late in the week previous to that Sunday and wouldn't have as much time to devote to developing two new sermons.

Tanner's idea might be just the thing to put me in his good graces at a time when I was about to be away from the church on a mission trip. During a ten-day mission trip, I wanted S. A. to think good thoughts of me and not to stir things up. His proposal seemed a winner for him, for the evangelist, for me, and for the church.

I'd heard the name of the evangelist and, although I didn't know him, I'd never heard anything bad about Rob Patrickson. Almost every evangelist had some distinction that set him apart from the pack. Scottish roots proved Rob's claim to fame. He even wore kilts with his clan's tartan when he preached. The kilts made people sit up and take notice, in particular when he kicked his legs to make a point. If he'd come from Scotland, though, it must've been a generation or more ago because his name card and advertisements gave an Albany, Georgia, address and his twang sounded just like other people I'd known from south Georgia.

After a busy first half of the week with convention business and meeting with old friends in San Antonio, Darla and I meandered along the River Walk and enjoyed each other's company. It was thrilling to get away and focus on one another for a while. Just five months earlier we had moved to Big Bottom Church and the transition turned into the most difficult of our lives. We took one last stroll by the River, stopped under the shade of an oak, and prayed for Big Bottom Church before we returned home. We had super services on Sunday morning, and I anticipated a joyful, revival-type atmosphere that night.

When Sunday afternoon came, I rushed to the office to meet with Rob an hour before the service. He didn't arrive at the agreed time. Fifteen minutes later he still hadn't shown, so I busied myself reviewing a message I'd preached elsewhere, just in case he didn't make it. Ten minutes before the six o'clock evening service, into the office strode S. A. Tanner and Rob Patrickson.

"I told Rob not to worry about getting here so soon. He needed to stay at the house and look over his message so God could use him tonight," said S. A., winking as he spoke. Of course they hadn't bothered to share that information with me.

After the briefest of introductions, the time showed five minutes before the start of the evening service, so I began wiring Patrickson with the microphone. I emphasized, since the evening service was live on the radio, he must limit his message to twenty-five minutes.

Finding a place to put the wireless transmitter proved difficult because his green-and-black-checkered kilts had no pocket. I'll admit I felt funny when my administrative assistant entered my office to rush us onto the platform. Alice found me on my knees beside a man and fiddling with his skirt. "Ahmff," she said, clearing her throat to catch my attention.

She had a look I'd seen before. She always turned to the side a bit, lowered her chin, and peered over the top of her glasses when she was puzzled.

"Mrs. Evans, I'm so glad you're here. Can you help me get this wireless microphone attached to the evangelist's kilts?"

"Oh," she said, lifting her shoulders and resuming a normal gaze through her glasses, "is that what you're doing?"

"What'd you think?" I asked, and then followed up with, "never mind, we don't have time; we've got to get to the platform now." She clipped the base of the wireless microphone onto his waistband as I hooked up my own lavaliere microphone and grabbed my Bible. Alice Evans emphasized again the importance of staying within twenty-five minutes for the message part of the worship. The station manager had already threatened to pull our evening service if we couldn't abide by the one-hour time slot for the entire service.

To say Patrickson understood and assured me with all his heart he'd stay within the time constraints would be stretching it, but he did agree. It surprised me that a visiting evangelist, since he'd preached in dozens of churches, would be so reluctant to understand our situation. I accentuated the importance a third time. He agreed again. I prayed for him, and we entered the sanctuary one minute after the hour.

A super crowd awaited us in the sanctuary. The staff and I had pumped up the congregation to expect a terrific service. I'd told the people, "We can't make the wind of the Spirit blow, but we can set our sails and be ready to catch it." They understood and bought into it. Two even wore sailor hats to the evening service. For my part, I tired of putting out brush fires every time I turned around and wanted to concentrate on loving and serving God. I needed reviving, above all because the mission trip would come next month and I needed to be strong in spirit. I looked forward to a fresh word God might speak to me through Patrickson's preaching.

The deer hunters, fishermen, and football players of the congregation pointed and snickered when the evangelist walked down the aisle wearing a skirt. But hey, that's the way he wanted it, and I didn't know of any biblical prohibition. I've found that a little different approach sometimes helps people pay attention. I will say that Patrickson's high-pitched voice fit with his kilts, but didn't win him any friends among the deer-hunting crowd.

I'd taken the precaution to ask the minister of music to shorten the singing part of the service by two songs, "Just in case he gets long-winded." We turned the service over to the evangelist at twenty-six minutes after the hour, a full five minutes before the average time I stepped into the pulpit on Sunday evening. I felt it a major victory, since S. A.'s glowing introduction had lasted four minutes.

S. A. had stated, "Our church is in dire need and God has sent this man to help us." A strange introduction, I thought, but dismissed it in favor of seeking the Lord and hoping God might do something through the evangelist.

Patrickson strutted in his kilts to the Big Bottom pulpit and proceeded to take fourteen minutes telling the results of his latest revivals. We could hear about them, too, if we just bought the tapes and booklets he'd brought. He rolled his r's like a true Scotsman when he first began, but soon lost the trait as he became excited about his tape sales. He made it clear that they could be had for a price—but that the fifteen dollars for a CD or cassette tape or thirty dollars for a book would be helping his worldwide evangelistic efforts. S. A. had set up the sales table in the foyer and would be waiting after the service to fill all orders, he said. I wanted to throw up.

When I thought of what Jesus would do, His overturning the table of the moneychangers in the Temple came to mind. While Patrickson overworked the crowd with his sales pitch I daydreamed of stepping into the foyer and turning over the table and watching S. A. scurry for the coins.

At last, Patrickson asked the congregation to stand for the reading of the Word of God, and we turned to the passage about Zaccheus who climbed a tree to see Jesus. He preached fifteen minutes. When added to the fourteen minute sales job, it took him beyond the twenty-five minutes we'd permitted. I still had high hopes we'd close the services within the allotted hour, however, because of the extra time we'd allowed. But he didn't stop. He whined on and on about Zaccheus. He'd gotten him up the tree, but couldn't get him down.

My mind went in all sorts of directions while the man continued his high-pitched prattle. As I considered Zaccheus up the tree, I reflected on a news story of the local fire department called to get a cat down out of a tree. Since the Hattiesburg fire chief often attended Big Bottom Church, I'd asked him about the story. He said the firemen made a mistake by trying to get the cat down. He said children cry and some firemen think they are doing a good deed by trying to get their pet down. However, he said, "Across the United States an average of four fireman die each year from falls while trying to get cats out of trees."

Then he asked me a question. "You grew up hunting, didn't you?"

"Sure did."

"Would you say you've covered hundreds of miles of woods in your lifetime?"

"Yeah, if you include hunting and walking in the woods. Several hundred miles, at least."

"How many cat skeletons have you ever seen up a tree?"

"None."

"Right, and I've asked over a thousand other hunters and they've never seen one, either. Truth is, when a cat wants to come down, he'll come down, so why risk a man's life to force him down before his time?"

I understood his point, but realized it appeared I'd have to force this visiting evangelist's illustration out of the tree. Patrickson asked over and over again, "How did Zaccheus get down from the tree?" Every third or fourth time he'd ask it, some brave soul would say, "Uh, he fell out?" Or, "He slipped?" Or, "His friends helped him down?" Each time the evangelist would say, "You've not got it yet, I'll explain a little more."

Forty-eight minutes into the message, when the man asked the question again, my brave friend Sam Jones said in a loud voice, "He listened to some preacher babble on and on, dropped off to sleep, and fell out of the tree." The people laughed for two minutes without a break. Wanda Washburn gave her usual, "Well, I never." But the reality was most people had never heard a preacher draw out his sermon so long. They needed a good laugh and it was a solid reminder to Patrickson that working folks can get tired. Still, the evangelist didn't get the point.

When they quit laughing he screeched, "I'm serious now, how did he get down?"

At this point, Tell Connie said, "Well, if you don't know, how do you expect us to know?"

Patrickson said, "Well, let me explain a little closer." By the time he'd preached thirty minutes, each time he said those words one or two people left. But when he'd preached fifty minutes, ten or fifteen people exited the building each time he stated his desire to explain a little further.

I sat without a word and fumed as I thought of how I'd have to apologize to the congregation, to the nursery workers, to the manager of the radio station, to the parking attendants and to the watchmen. Our preschool director, Lorna McWhorter, stood at the back door of the church and made wide motions with her hands until I saw her. Then she pointed at her watch and made the 'kill it' sign with her thumb across her throat.

I knew she didn't indicate a child had died in the preschool. Nor did she signify for me to slash Patrickson's throat. She meant that the lay people who'd volunteered for a one-hour hitch in the nursery were now well into their second hour with no end in sight. They were fomenting rebellion. I'd had enough. He'd already preached fifty-four minutes. I determined he'd not go an hour.

Patrickson had ruined our service. A third of the people had already left. I couldn't blame them. I'd have left, too, if I hadn't been the pastor. I felt my integrity was on the line because I'd made a big deal in promoting the service that morning. The man was self-serving and he'd also broken his word to me.

Darla, from her usual spot on the front row, made the motion she makes to me once or twice a year when I threaten to overburden the people. She brought her hand up to her shoulder, held it perpendicular to the ground, and little by little glided it down to her waist. I know she meant, "Quit circling the field, land that plane, and let's go home." She gave me the encouragement I needed to insure Patrickson didn't speak a full hour in addition to his sales hype.

At precisely fifty-nine minutes I pulled off my dress boot, the right one from the pair I'd bought the week before at the Western shop in San Antonio. I'd try to hit his back and, when he turned around, point to my watch. That'd do the trick, I felt sure.

I waited until Patrickson settled in front of the pulpit, grabbed the boot by the top and hurled the heavy heal towards his back. About the same time, to make a point, the evangelist stepped to the side and the boot flew beyond him, off the six-foot platform, and down into the second row where it hit Mrs. Grace Clinton just above the left ear. It knocked her out cold.

A nurse practitioner in the congregation, happy to have a diversion from the constant droning, rushed over to attend to the lady while Patrickson continued to preach. Mrs. Clinton soon awoke. I later learned the first thing she said was, "Is Zaccheus still up the tree?" Assured he was, she said, "Well either help me out of here or hit me again!"

I felt horrible. I'd let my anger get the best of me and had harmed a member. In addition to that, but I'd have to hobble now, since I lacked one of my dress boots. I'd seen it in Mrs. Clinton's hand as the nurse assisted her out the door.

An hour and eight minutes into the evangelist's sermon, with several people motioning for me to shut it down, I stood by the visiting cleric's side and said, "We'll sing our invitation hymn now while our brother finishes his message." The half of the congregation who'd stayed jumped to their feet, applauded, and burst into the hymn with such enthusiasm that it drowned out Patrickson's words. That is, all stood except H. H. and June Smith, S. A. and Tina Tanner, Nev and Missy Wright, and Wanda and Early Washburn. On cue, Wanda mouthed her perfunctory, "Well I never." By the time the hymn finished, the visiting preacher had completed his thoughts, sat with his head in his hands, and bent down almost to his green-and-black-checkered kilts.

The trouble was not that it wasn't a good sermon—the first time around. It was a fair-to-middlin' message on Zaccheus up a tree and Jesus coming by to call him. He did have one factual error. He said ole Zach had climbed a sweet gum tree when, in truth, he'd crawled up a sycamore. The trouble was that the man never could get Zaccheus down. Although he preached all around the subject, it seemed he forgot Jesus called him down to share a meal in Zaccheus' home. The evangelist had Jesus doing everything but going to Home Depot to buy a ladder for Zaccheus.

I once asked a man how he liked his new pastor's preaching. He replied, "The first time he preaches a sermon it's super." Aware that his pastor had served the church for a mere three months, I asked him, "You're not saying your pastor repeats his sermons, are you?"

"Yes," the man replied. "He preaches a good message and then preaches it again, and then repeats it a third time, all in the same morning. It's a wonderful fifteen minute sermon but a terrible forty-five minute one."

Patrickson followed me to the office. "Pastor, I hate to say it but your people are just dumb."

I'd had about all his putdowns I could take for a night, so I said, "About half of them weren't so dumb as to stay for the entire message. And while I'm at it, let me get this straight. You gave me your word you'd preach for no more than twenty-five minutes, but you went for well over an hour. Even then I had to stop you, and you've got the nerve to tell me the people of Big Bottom are dumb?"

"Well, yeah. Everywhere else I preached that sermon, when I looked for the answer of how Zaccheus got down, someone would say that Jesus called him to come out of the tree. When they came up with that, I'd close the message with, "Yes, and Jesus calls you out of your troubles, too." But when no one came up with the answer, I just went on. I felt sure they'd get it if I just explained a little closer."

I suggested to him that he come up with a plan in case he ever preaches that message to another congregation, a plan of what to do if they don't answer to his satisfaction. I once more asked about his promise to stay within twenty-five minutes. He said, "Yes, but if the Spirit's leading, you can't quench the Spirit."

I didn't like his theology any more than I liked his preaching or the way he kept his word. I've seen powerful moves of God in several countries; times when both the people and the speaker knew it wasn't time to stop. Patrickson's preaching didn't qualify. I felt he'd quenched the Spirit by lying to me and by imposing on the people of Big Bottom

Church. Furthermore, I believed he'd never planned to stay within the twenty-five minute time limit.

Then Patrickson had the gall to say, "You've got to forgive me, you know. The Bible says we have to forgive one another, so you have to forgive me; you don't have a choice. You will obey the Word of God and forgive me, won't you?"

I asked him, "Just which verse in the Bible says we have to forgive one another?" It's there, plain as day in Ephesians 4:32, Colossians 3:13, and several other places, but I figured he didn't know. He didn't. So I suggested, "You may find it near the verse about the sweet gum tree."

I told him I'd forgive him but it might take me a day or two. I gave him his honorarium check plus a roll of S. A.'s donated toilet paper. I told him the roll had a special meaning to Big Bottom because it had come from a valuable member. I suggested he always keep it as a symbol of being at Big Bottom unless, of course, he needed an extra roll after one of his sermons.

Patrickson spoke back, rolling his r's like he did when we first met. "I've never received a gift like this before. I don't know whether to take it as a kindness or a slap."

"Do you remember when Joshua led the children of Israel across the Jordan River and then built a statue of stones to remind the people?" I asked.

"Of course," he said.

"They built the memorial out of something common, from the rocks in the bed of the river. Fact is, with five thousand rolls of toilet paper donated to Big Bottom Church, there is nothing more common around here than rolls of paper. Just consider this roll as something like that memorial. It'll be a reminder to you of being at Big Bottom Baptist Church. And you can be assured that I'll never again look at our church's toilet paper without thinking of you."

With that explanation, Patrickson's countenance picked up and he was enthusiastic in his thanks.

S. A. finished hawking the man's goods and came by the office to take Patrickson home for the night. His first words to me were, "Now that's good preaching. Don't you think so, pastor? Good, solid preaching. He cleared off the pulpit and pitched a fit. Good preaching. The man had something to say. We can sit an hour if a man has something to say and says it with conviction. The one thing wrong with the whole night was when you threw that water stand and hindered the Holy Spirit's leading."

"S. A.," I said, "it was my boot. I'd never throw a wooden stand at someone." Before I could explain what I'd tried to do, he interrupted.

"If you hadn't cut the man short, no telling how many would've been saved tonight. I can't believe you did that. And just think, you're supposed to be our spiritual leader. You . . . you . . . you." His face turned red, his eyes bulged until I thought they'd leave their sockets, his nostrils flared, and his fists clenched.

He's about to hit me, I thought. S. A. wanted to say more, but his jaws puffed up and contorted, and he lost words and wind. He waved with a big sweep of his right hand for Patrickson to follow and stomped out the door, shoes squeaking.

28
GRACE

I'd had all night to think about it. I'd stayed up praying. May as well have, I couldn't sleep. They say if you can't count sheep, talk with the Shepherd. I did. I first erred by not praying before I'd invited Patrickson to speak. And then I wronged the congregation by not stopping the visiting evangelist earlier than I did. It hurt me and went against my principles to stop anyone from speaking, but he broke his word to me and overstepped his authority by droning on and on.

My third error? I hadn't handled the matter well. I should have just stepped up to the podium and said something about the lateness of the hour, had the invitation hymn, called on someone to lead us in prayer and dismissed the folks. Why in the world did I throw my boot at the man? I gave in to Satan's temptation and the result, a knockout, proved disastrous.

At four a.m., the thought came to me if I hadn't cut the man short, he might still be preaching now. The rest of the people would've left, and I'd have felt like punching him. In fact, the more I thought about it, the more I felt a little like giving S. A. a cross, a right cross swung with all my might. He was the one who was so all-fired hopped up on bringing in this evangelist. Now, however, it wouldn't be the skirt-wearing man who'd get the blame for the happenings; no, that would be me.

At seven I couldn't wait any longer. I called Mrs. Clinton and asked if I could come over. Like many senior saints she'd already been up an hour and said, "I've been expecting your call. Come right on over."

On my way out the driveway I picked up the *Hattiesburg Advocate*. I didn't have time to read it but glanced at the front page as I laid it on the passenger seat. It surprised me to see a column on the bottom right side of the front page with the headline, "Other shoe drops at Big Bottom Church." Of course, after seeing the headline, I read the brief article that purported to be from "reliable sources" that Pastor Brent Paulson of Big Bottom Baptist Church had thrown either a piece of furniture or a large boot at a guest speaker. The article went on to say this was one of several mishaps at Big Bottom, including a moral indiscretion by a staff member several months ago. The reporter added that anyone who accepted an invitation to speak at Big Bottom might want to think about wearing headgear.

It hurt me but didn't surprise me that the *Advocate* had the story wrong. They hadn't bothered to contact me before running the piece. I believed some of their reporters had had it in for me since a star reporter lost his job over misrepresenting the facts during the scandal over the mission pastor.

The *Advocate* had continued losing circulation the more they ran ridiculous headlines like some I'd seen the past few months: "Man found dead in cemetery;" "Researcher links obesity with too much food;" "For sale: vacant casket, probably unused;" "Health study shows men and women are different;" "Dead man's brain removed without consent;" "Headline goes here;" "President Bush increases intelligence;" "Plane too close to ground, crash probe told;" "Man steals clock, faces time;" "If strike isn't settled, it may last a while;" and "50,000 loose screws on Mississippi roads." If you asked me, I'd say someone at the

Advocate had a screw loose. Fact is, though, there would be no story if I hadn't blundered by throwing the boot.

Grace Clinton taught me in the second grade. I remembered her from years ago as a kind, sweet-spirited lady with worlds of patience. It thrilled me to find, one month after assuming the pastorate at Big Bottom, that my second grade teacher was a member. I hoped and prayed—all five miles and eleven traffic lights from my house to hers I prayed—that she'd still be the sweet-spirited, patient lady I'd remembered. I arrived at her home on Thirty-Eighth Avenue and noted almost no grass grew in the front yard because of the shades of a live oak and two of the largest magnolia trees I'd ever seen.

The house was a white-frame building, perhaps fifty years old and with a large front porch. A swing occupied the center of the porch. It appeared that it got plenty of use because the finish on the porch's floor had worn beneath the swing. Before I could ring the doorbell, Mrs. Clinton met me at the screen door with my boot in her hand and the words, "Lost something?" We laughed and I felt indebted for her sense of humor. It put me at ease. If she could laugh about the incident, maybe there was a chance for forgiveness.

I sat on the porch swing and rocked with leisure back and forth while she sat in the glider. The porch with the ancient glider reminded me of my grandparents' porch on what is now North Black Creek Road. I'd sat on their porch or under their live oak trees for hours on end as a boy growing up. My granddaddy Paulson and I shelled beans or peas and talked. Grandparents seemed to be the ones who had time for us children. From him I learned the stories of how things used to be, or we planned the day, or we talked about dogs or cows or hunting or his garden. Best of all, we anticipated going fishing in his pond late in the afternoon. For pure excitement, the anticipation often surpassed the fishing.

After I apologized, Mrs. Clinton said, "I've been thinking about the whole scenario. Have you ever seen a football game where the running back faked a tackler off his feet?"

"Yes, ma'am," I replied.

"The way I've got it figured is that screeching, kilt-wearing evangelist preached so hard, he preached you right out of your boots and one of them found its way to my row." We laughed. She looked so pretty when she laughed with her silver hair, upturned eyebrows, crow's' feet around her eyes, and a radiance I could feel from halfway across the porch. Now eighty years old, Grace Clinton reminded me of my mother.

I told her what my thinking had been and why I'd thrown the boot. I hung my head and once again asked her forgiveness. I felt so ashamed. Like any good teacher, she asked if I'd learned a lesson from the previous night.

"I sure have," I said, "In fact, I learned two lessons. First, I've never worn dress boots to church before going to the convention in San Antonio and seeing all those Texans in their boots. I bought a pair and they've been the ruin of me. I learned to wear my dress shoes to church and leave the boots for Texans."

She smiled.

"But more than that, I've learned to talk with The Lord when things aren't going right and seek His input on what to do."

"You always were a quick learner," Mrs. Clinton said, "even in the second grade. I can't believe I had the privilege of teaching my pastor some of the basics of education. Let me say here and now for you or anyone else to hear. I'm glad you're my pastor, even if you did knock me out. I'm glad you're my pastor and I don't care who knows it. And as far as the incident last night, if you never mention it again, I sure won't. You tried to do what was right; it just didn't work out that way. But it did bring you over to see me and for that, I'm glad."

"You mean you forgive me? Just like that, you forgive me?"

"Well, what'd you want, for me to make you walk over a pile of hot coals or lay on a bed of nails? Of course I forgive you. Let me tell you something, young man. Fifty-nine years ago, I remember it just like yesterday because I'd just started teaching; anyway, fifty-nine years ago I gave my life to the Lord. He forgave me, just like that. He forgave me and I've been free ever since. It's not hard to forgive you. You meant well. The hard to forgive times are when people don't mean well. But God helps even with that."

With those words the telephone rang. "That blamed phone has rung all morning," she said. "Pastor, you won't believe how many phone calls I've gotten. I'll bet fifty people have called."

"People checking on you?" I asked.

"Yes. And the papers and television stations wanting interviews. Someone named Matt Drudge even picked it up and wants some words from me on what he calls the Drudge Report. And some members want me to file charges to have you arrested."

I swallowed hard. "You can't mean it?"

"Oh, yes, I mean it. But it's inspired by S. A. and the other deacon officers. And the whole church knows their days are numbered. It's a good thing your boot didn't hit Tina Tanner or Wanda Washburn or you'd have spent the night in the Lamar County jail. Least that's what they told me.

But you know what I did? Every time someone wanted to say something bad about you I just told them I taught you in school and what you are now is a reflection on me. Pretty soon they'd start saying good things about you. And the few who didn't, well, I wouldn't let them continue. I told them if they wanted to say anything bad about you, they'd have to call someone else because I wasn't going to listen to people raise their voices against God's anointed. And now, I have to go inside a minute. Will you excuse me?"

"Oh, of course," I said. I'd heard the telephone ringing again and figured she'd gone in to take the call. While she was inside, I thought of grace, not the lady but the gift from God. Wonderful grace. Unmerited. Undeserved. Pure and clean and refreshing. I'd come to Big Bottom to model the grace of God to others but found people like Mrs. Clinton modeling it to me.

I sat on her porch, rocking back and forth on the swing. I heard the methodical chrumph, churmph of its chains and closed my eyes to revel in what it means to be forgiven. I don't know how much time passed, but all at once I was aware of Mrs. Clinton at the screened door just outside her front door.

"It's ready," she said.

"What's ready?" I asked.

"Why, breakfast, of course. You didn't think I'd let you come before eight in the morning and not have breakfast, did you?" And with that I entered a home small in size but large in the love of its lone inhabitant, Grace Clinton. We sat at her antique, walnut table and ate grits and omelets with "cat-head" biscuits cooked in a cast iron skillet, molasses made from sugar cane pressed and boiled down the old-fashioned way by a man on West Black Creek Road, link sausages, and coffee. I can never remember better—food or grace.

I also don't remember when the tears began to flow, and I'm not sure why, either. I do know that I had to dab my eyes halfway through the meal. Maybe it was catching up with a second-grade teacher who'd poured her life into mine and continued to do so. Maybe it was Grace Clinton's reminding me God had returned me to my roots. Maybe it was the complete forgiveness by one who, by all rights, should have held a grudge. Maybe it was transference because of the fine breakfast delivered with such tenderness and care by a lady who was about the same age and demeanor as my mother. Maybe it was the fact that one who could have cost me my job instead decided to encourage me. Maybe it was an overwhelming feeling that God still cared despite all the troubles. Maybe it was a combination. I don't know. The more we talked and ate, the more tears flowed.

Soon the napkin wasn't enough and I was crying without restraint, more than any time since my first son was born years earlier. Mrs. Clinton did what any compassionate second-grade teacher would do. She rose from her chair, walked over to me, held my head in her hands, ran her fingers through my hair, and cried with me.

Maybe it was the situation at Big Bottom not turning out the way I'd hoped. Maybe it was the hurt flowing throughout the world. Maybe it was the accumulated heartaches of a thousand parishioners

I'd counseled through the years and still carried down deep within. I didn't know then and still don't, but the tears wouldn't stop.

After a few minutes, Mrs. Clinton said, "Sausage too hot, huh?"

We laughed and then the tears stopped.

"Could be the onions in the omelets. You know onions can make us cry but there's never been a vegetable invented to make us laugh."

I chuckled at her homespun wisdom. In the middle of the laughter I saw her eyes and read them deep within. Grace Clinton also knew what it is to hurt. She empathized with me over the fact some wanted to hang my head and stretch my hide as their trophies over the entrance way of Big Bottom Baptist Church. But she had her own hurt, deep down inside. She couldn't have done what she did for me that morning if she hadn't. Yes, she knew pain and disillusionment herself, but she'd worked through it somehow, else she couldn't have forgiven and loved like she did.

On the way to the office I stopped by the Salvation Army store and gave away a pair of Texas dress boots, worn just once. They were glad to get them and I was glad to be rid of them. It's strange the memories some actions evoke. Giving away the boots made me think of what deacon Louis Atkins told me when he'd sold his boat. He said, "Preacher, do you know the two happiest days of my life?"

"No, I don't guess I do. Why don't you tell me?" I said.

"The day I bought a boat and the day I sold it!"

I was bootless once again. And happy. As I drove to the office the words to an old hymn came:

Grace, grace, God's grace,
Grace that will pardon and cleanse within;
Grace, grace, God's grace,
Grace that is greater than all our sin.

Forty-nine years after I'd left her classroom, I'd tasted His grace through a second-grade teacher.

29

PREACHING

"Why would S. A. treat me like that?" I asked Darla. "It hurts that the chairman of the pastor search committee, the man most responsible for my coming to Big Bottom, has turned on me."

"It's a control thing, Brent. He feels threatened. He's going to lose his job as a deacon officer, and he's trying to cause problems for you so he can keep power."

I recognized it was his problem but he'd made it my problem, too. In over thirty years of ministry I'd never had a chairman of a search committee remove support from me, but this one had, soon after I'd arrived. The hurt deepened because Tanner had now resorted to attacking my preaching.

He'd bought several copies of the first series I'd preached at Big Bottom to give as gifts. The church media center makes sermons available for the price of the materials and labor, about two dollars per compact disk. I'd felt honored when the media assistant told me Tanner had purchased twenty copies of The Ten Commandments series.

Although we'd had the difficulty over Pastor Reyes, when I heard Tanner bought so many copies of the series, I'd hoped he'd moved beyond our troubles. Recently, however, my neighbor, Dr. Ben Dover, took some items to the Salvation Army thrift store. While there he found sixteen copies of my sermon series, all inscribed with the name S. A. Tanner with indelible ink on the vinyl cover. Tanner had given them to the thrift store under the condition they be advertised for sale at twenty-five cents each.

Sam Jones heard from three people that S. A. was calling me, "the two-bit preacher." When Sam confronted him with his accusation, S. A. had countered that my latest sermon series was bringing a quarter at the Salvation Army resale shop; "that is, when people will buy them."

Two Sundays after the Patrickson episode, S. A. called me to a room off the front of the sanctuary, just before the sermon, to chide me about my use of humor. Because he'd made a public spectacle, motioning to me to follow him with great waves of his hand in front of the whole congregation during the worship service, I hurried after him from my seat beside Darla on the front row. I thought someone had died or some emergency had occurred, so I met him at the side room door. I found Nev Wright, Early Washburn, and H. H. Smith already waiting there. Early greeted me, "You make everybody happy—some when you enter the room and some when you leave it."

All four jumped me with their accusations, in large part over my use of humor. I thought it inappropriate, even more since they did it just before the message. I told them humor was part of who I am and that taking it away from me was like taking a hammer from a carpenter or a stethoscope from a doctor. The carpenter or doctor could still practice, but not as well. Early said, "What you say works in practice but will it work in theory?" I ignored him.

Smith said, "Why can't you just do like that Scotsman we had here on Sunday night and get people excited about things without making them laugh?"

Patrickson had made such a poor showing that Smith's statement also didn't deserve a response. I gave one, though, "Men, you've got to let the humor thing go. If a person never laughs, it gets bottled up inside and makes his stomach bulge and his hips wider. In fact, I'm not sure it hasn't already begun." I noticed Nev Wright, the slimmest of the officers, cover his mouth to keep from laughing.

"That's what I mean," said H. H. His overgrown eyebrows, like Andy Rooney's, bounced up and down as he spoke. "Right here in the Lord's house and you're cracking jokes. Are you ever serious?"

"Tell you what," I said as I directed my gaze towards H. H. "I'll tell you a time when I'm serious if you'll tell me a time when you laugh." H. H. threw up his hands, though his jowls began to work up and down as if he were still speaking.

S. A. jumped in the conversation, "Now let me tell you. If we lose our positions," he said as he looked around the room at the other officers, "you're going to lose yours, too. It may take us three months, six months, or a year, but it'll happen."

"Yeah," said Early, "and you can take that to the bank and smoke it."

"But Early, don't you know every barrel's got to stand on its own bottom?" I asked.

"Good one, Brent, good one," he said with a smile.

As soon as possible I left, saying, "Gentlemen, please excuse me, I have a message to deliver to God's people."

When I opened the door to leave, it surprised me that all four of them fell in line behind me. Darla later told me it looked as if they'd just disciplined a recalcitrant child and were now making him face the people who knew he'd taken a whipping. I recognized their actions as a calculated ploy to upset me just before the sermon and prayed with intensity that God would help me overlook them and concentrate on delivering His message of grace.

It didn't help their feelings when I began the message with a joke. It offended them again when the congregation laughed and laughed. I felt the congregation's being moved by levity helped gain the people's attention, and opened them to the Gospel. I knew my motives for humor more than anyone else and determined I'd continue to use it when I felt it appropriate.

After the service on Sunday night, Darla and I got a quick bite at home and then drove six miles west on Highway 98 to North Black Creek Road, turned right, followed the winding road a mile-and-a-half, crossed the creek, drove up the hill, and turned right into my parents' driveway. I wanted to know Dad's take on the day's happenings.

Mom hadn't felt well for a couple of weeks and looked yellowish to Darla and me. I suggested she call a doctor. The whites of her eyes didn't look clear, either. Mom had been complaining about itching for several days; and her doctor, thinking it was an allergic reaction, had written a prescription that hadn't helped. I sensed this might be a liver problem and secured her promise to call her doctor the first thing in the morning. I knew she'd begun several new medicines, and I thought one of them might be affecting her liver.

Darla makes fun of my diagnosing, calling me a medical doctor when I give her my take on someone's condition. I'm no medical doctor, but I've visited hospitals about twice a week for thirty years and couldn't help but soak in some medical knowledge. Besides, I sometimes sleep in a Holiday Inn Express.

Even though Mom didn't feel good, she insisted on serving us a slice of sweet potato pie. Her sweet potato pie is the best I've ever had, so Darla and I succumbed to one piece and soon followed it by splitting another. Delicious, as always. It thrilled Mom that we thought so.

Dad is a Baptist deacon and I got my love of humor from him, so I thought he could comprehend both sides of the difficulty at Big Bottom and help me understand the contrary actions of these men. He listened and told me he'd pray for me. Then he asked, "Brent, do you know how a Baptist deacon is different from a newborn puppy?"

"Pardon?" I asked.

"A puppy. How a deacon is different from a newborn puppy? Do you know?"

"No, sir, I guess I don't," I said, falling for the line like I always did with Dad. "Wait a minute; let me guess. Is it that the puppy opens his eyes at last?"

"No, that's not it, but you're close," he said.

"Then tell me how a deacon differs from a newborn puppy," I asked.

"A new puppy quits whining after about six weeks!" he said, and we both roared. I'd never tell that one in church, though. I respect the majority of deacons far too much to demean them or their office. Some deacons, like the aforementioned officers, however, do a remarkable job of demeaning themselves.

Since Darla and I had often discussed these matters, she suggested I visit "Wise Jane," as she called her, to get her take on my preaching and the actions of these deacons.

I called Jane Winfield to discuss the matter and she invited me over the next afternoon. I brought a slice of Mom's sweet potato pie to her and she appreciated it, but she set it aside for a later time so she could concentrate on our conversation.

"Now what's this I hear about the deacon officers not liking your preaching?"

"Yes, they seem to like a more rambunctious approach, but one without humor," I replied.

"Well, every man to his own taste, but one of the things I liked about you right off the bat was the conversational tone you use. Brent, when you preach like you do, people can't separate Sunday from the rest of the week."

"What do you mean?"

"Too often, people come to church and want the preacher to yell at them. They get a verbal whipping to assuage their guilt, and they can go home feeling better about themselves, since they've taken their punishment. Then they go right back to their old actions until they get whipped again the next week. A sermon to them is like a B-12 shot. It boosts them for a day or two, and then they're right back into the same old shape.

"To me a good sermon ought to have a little of three elements: it ought to warm your heart, it ought to inspire your mind, and, yes, once in a while, it ought to tan your hide!

"But, beware of those preachers whose sole purpose is to tan your hide. I think they're angry and don't know it. You just keep up the good work. Your value with the people will increase as time goes on. People will see your integrity and they'll listen. Words have power. You remember what Paul said, 'I didn't come to you with cleverly devised words but with power.' God can bless a preacher who'll just preach the Word."

"Thanks, I needed that today."

"And about that humor thing. You don't have humor, it has you. The officers don't have humor and, being jealous, they're trying to remove it from everyone else. But imagine how colorless the world would be without laughter. Humor is your rubber sword. It helps you make a point without drawing blood.

"It's your funny way to be serious. And no telling how many folks are coming to Big Bottom in part to leave a drab existence outside. We all love your use of humor. Well, okay, a few of the jokes are old ones, but we love most of your humor. And have you noticed I've attended the morning services? My health hasn't improved since last year when I couldn't come, but now I do. You know why? You and the people of Big Bottom make me feel good, that's why."

"You sure it's not to bump into John Anderson?" I asked.

"You rascal. I never should have told you about John. No, I make myself come because you encourage me. Be danged if I'll exert extra effort, take Tylenol, fiddle with this walker, and come to be whipped, though. Please don't stop using your humor."

"I won't," I said. "Tot ell the truth, I can't. It's part of who I am."

"Another thing while we're on the subject. I think you're doing right by preaching just twenty to twenty-five minutes. I get nervous about these showboats who keep you an hour but don't say any more than people who keep you twenty-five minutes. I don't have much money, but at my age my time is worth more than money. If someone steals my time, I also watch my pocketbook when I'm around them.

"But you're doing right. The mind can only absorb what the seat can endure. One thing, though. I wouldn't throw any more shoes if I were you."

"No, ma'am. I won't. The Lord's already dealt with me about that," I said.

"Did you read the Drudge Report this morning?" she asked.

"You mean you read Matt Drudge?" I asked. My face must have registered my surprise.

"Sure thing. I've got to keep up with the world, you know. But did you read it today?"

"No, not today."

"He's got an interesting link to the *Hattiesburg Advocate* and he named his link, 'Slain in the Spirit or Crowned by a Clodhopper?'"

"Great, that's all I need, to have my shortcomings exposed to the world," I said.

"Whatever got into you to do such a thing?" she asked.

"As Flip Wilson used to say, 'The Devil made me do it.'" We both laughed.

"That shoe-throwing episode would've gotten you in a heap of trouble if the folks didn't love you already."

"I know; it's one of the dumbest things I ever did."

About that time Jane Winfield raised her left eyebrow and sat a little taller. I knew some wisdom was about to come, so I paid attention. "Brent, I've found through the years that some of Satan's biggest temptations come when I'm under pressure. That night you were under pressure because the service had lasted so long, and also because the man preaching seemed a brick shy of a load. Am I right?"

"Right on target," I said.

"What were you afraid would happen if he continued another half hour?" she asked.

"I noticed people were leaving. In my mind, they'd had a bad experience. More and more left. I had to think about the preschool workers, the watchmen, the greeters, and the radio service, not to mention that Patrickson's self-serving approach was contrary to what Jesus would do. I wanted that character out of our church and out of my life."

"What would have happened if he'd preached on and on another half hour?"

"I suppose most of the rest of the people would have left, and maybe he'd have closed out with the remaining few," I replied.

"Then who would've gotten the bad rap for it?"

"He would have. Maybe S. A. would've for hosting him. And I would've for allowing it to continue. But I couldn't let it continue. One of the primary requirements of a leader is to lead. When I saw the service dragging on and on, I had to do something."

"Ah," she replied, "did you now? And that's one of the main times temptation comes, when we feel the pressure to do something but haven't prayed about what to do."

"How'd you know I hadn't prayed?"

"Easy, because you threw your boot. God often tells us to do something extraordinary, but He doesn't tell us to do things that hurt others in the process," she answered.

"Now let me ask you something. How are your times of prayer and Bible reading each day?" she asked.

My stomach tightened. I felt a little offended by the question because I did my doctoral project on prayer and often asked others similar questions. However, true to form, Jane Winfield's wisdom rang true. I hesitated a minute, then lowered my head a bit and said, "Miss Jane, I'm still reading the Word every day, but some days it just seems so rote. I pray every morning, but sometimes God seems far away. I wish you'd pray for me to draw closer to the Lord." I'd never made such a confession to anyone but God.

"I will, pastor; you can be assured I will. And I'll not tell a soul about our conversation, either. Let me ask you another question, though. When your boys were growing up, did they get everything they wanted?"

"Of course not. No good parent would give children everything they wanted. I tried to give them everything they needed, though," I said. "Why do you ask?"

She bumped her walker and it fell with a twang, but she ignored it and my question and continued, "And when they didn't get what they wanted, were they still pleased with you?"

"No. A parent has to continue parenting whether or not his children like him," I said. "I remember a time when our boys wanted money to go on an outing Darla and I thought was questionable. They didn't get the dough, so they didn't get to go. They weren't happy campers for a while."

"Do they love you now?" Jane asked.

"Yes, we have a wonderful relationship with both boys and their families."

"But back then they didn't like being around you for a while, is that right?" she asked.

"Yes, that's right."

"Since you've come to Big Bottom, you've had the disappointment of a fallen staff member. You've had the heartache of deacon officers who want to control you and the church even though they aren't spiritual men. You've had some bad publicity. A huge number of people have joined, but overall things haven't been as you'd hoped at the church. You acted up and threw your boot. Do you think you might be behaving like your boys were tempted to do when they didn't get what they wanted?"

I couldn't move. Her remarks stunned me. No, more like paralyzed me. I couldn't speak. She'd told the truth, and my chest now hurt as if pierced by a knife. I was angry at God for not getting what I wanted, and she'd helped me realize it.

"I'll go get us some cookies and tea now while you think about it," she said as she picked up her walker and began a slow trek toward the kitchen.

Before she came back with the cookies and tea, I walked into the kitchen and said, "You've done me a great service today. You've shown me some things I hadn't seen. Why is it we can see sin in others, but not in ourselves? Thank you for the offer of cookies and tea, but right now I have to go. I think fasting is a more appropriate response than eating right now."

With that she hugged me. It was the kind of tight hug that felt warm on my skin minutes after it was over, the kind a mother gives when she's proud her son has faced up to his wrongdoing. It was the kind of hug that let me know I was still loved even when I'd done wrong.

I phoned the office and asked that all my calls be held except for emergencies. I drove home, picked up my Bible, and walked down to the dock. I apologized to God for behaving like a spoiled child who had to have his own way. He met me with mercy as I studied His Word. It became alive and His Spirit taught me lesson after lesson on the example, the meekness, and the humility of Jesus.

When the sun went down Darla brought me a diet coke, and we talked and laughed together. In the background the bugs, attracted to the light, in turn attracted the bream. They popped at the top of the water with the peculiar sucking sound a sunfish makes when he tries to pull in a gnat, a fly, or a mosquito.

Darla had known. The Lord had shown her about her own recalcitrance just two days before. But she'd also known I'd be more apt to hear about mine from "Wise Jane" than from her because Darla and I had kayaked the Big Bottom rapids together.

I now knew my biggest problem wasn't how others treated me but how I reacted. More to the point, would I allow God to mold and shape me when hours of difficulty arose? Would I become more like Jesus?

Someone asked a stone mason why he was chipping a piece of limestone. He pointed to the top of the almost completed wall of the church building behind him. He said, "I'm shaping it down here so it'll fit in up there."

30
SUPPER WITH THE OFFICERS

Within a week the boot incident became a non-story due to the refusal of both Grace Clinton and me to comment to reporters or take part in any interviews. Rob Patrickson had stirred the waters at first by telling a journalist, "I was just finding my groove with the message and folks were beginning to respond when, out of the blue, this boot flew by my head. I didn't know what to think, but it ruined the spiritual atmosphere I'd worked so hard to achieve."

When a reporter from WMAD read Patrickson's comment to me, it was all I could do to keep from saying, "Patrickson's right. The response of the folks was overwhelming. They were leaving the building in droves due to his droning on and on." I didn't counter, however. I'd messed up one time, and I didn't want to add to the problem, since the mission trip lay at hand.

We'd fly to Tanzania in a week, the mission volunteers, Darla, and I. We looked forward to the trip. For the last two months we'd met after the morning worship, after the evening worship, and before the

Wednesday night activities to pray and to make sure we'd completed all the details. God did a marvelous job of pulling the team together.

Most leaders have known the joy of a group that jelled like this one. Even Wanda Washburn vocalized her prayers for each member of the team and appeared to find her place. Wanda had artistic gifts and surprised the group three weeks before the trip with excellent Vacation Bible School displays for the entire group, not just for the class she'd be teaching. She'd even been mindful enough we'd be flying that she'd had Early cut the six-foot displays and put hinges at several points so that all of them would break down to fit into a single overseas suitcase.

The group, for their part, rationalized Wanda's occasional snide remark as, "just Wanda." Their acceptance of her as a full team member paid dividends in the feelings of the entire group. Each one had been growing in the Lord as part of the preparation for the journey, knowing that if we weren't yielded to Him, the trip would come to nothing. I'd divulged how God humbled me after the incident with the boot. It'd been hard to share, but I'd done so to request additional prayer to be the leader I should be. My openness about the need to grow had had the affect of enabling transparency in the other members.

Denise Jones, wife of deacon Sam Jones and a mission participant, shared she'd allowed the deacon officers' quest for power to embitter her. I thought it a bold move on her part since Wanda's husband, Early, was one of those officers. Denise requested prayer to forgive the officers.

Darla and Denise were emerging as deep friends. Others going on the mission trip were developing strong bonds, too, the kind joint service for the Lord always produces.

Four days before our trip, Early Washburn surprised me by phoning. When my assistant told me Early was on the line, I spilled the diet cola I was drinking.

"Hello, Early. How are you?" I asked while I fumbled with a napkin to clean up the mess.

"Like I been playing drums again," he replied. His voice sounded sedated.

"I give up; what do you mean?"

"Can't you guess?"

"Do you mean you feel like someone has been beating you?"

"Noooo," he said. "Don't you understand anything? Re-percussions, man, re-percussions."

Even though I didn't understand Early half of the time, I was elated by his call. The thought crossed my mind that healing might come between us since Wanda and I, plus the group, had unified over the mission trip.

My initial clue that something might be amiss was his wanting to meet me in a side room of the church and to cater in food from the Crescent City Diner, "so we can have privacy." However, since it was his idea and his invitation, I accepted and ordered a shrimp po boy. In the back of my mind I also thought he might want to extract from me a promise to watch over Wanda during the trip. Maybe his term, "repercussions," meant he felt contrite over his dependence on alcohol. Perhaps he would request prayer or a referral for counseling. It could be he wanted to meet at Big Bottom Church so we could kneel before the altar while he confessed his sins and rededicated his life.

When I arrived I saw Early standing at the door of the educational building, waiting for me. When I stepped out of the car, I thought I caught a whiff of Old Spice, but soon the distinct smell of moth balls overpowered all others. The building superintendent must've taken on a project to fumigate the building, I speculated.

I'd looked forward to seeing Early due to the surprise factor. I didn't know what mood or condition he'd be in and his first words never failed to interest me; yes, and sometimes to shock me. This time his buoyant walk toward the car and his broad smile indicated joviality, but his first words were, "You're going out of country and when the cat's away the mice will play." I didn't bother to ask him what he meant because it would just cause issuance of another cliché. As Sam Jones, a true wordsmith, once said of one of Early's utterances, "An idiom initiated by an idiot."

I followed him into the room and received a further surprise. In addition to Early, H. H. Smith, S. A. Tanner, Nev Wright, Altus Rawls, and Tony Powell sat around the table. It didn't take a genius to size up the situation. Each was a present or former officer of the deacons. It appeared the officer meeting with me would take place on their timing, not mine, and before the mission trip, not after. Since God had showed me to look to Him, I lifted a silent prayer. I felt the prompting of the Holy Spirit say to my heart, "You'll not have to lift a hand. The battle is the Lord's. Stand aside and see the Power of God." Again without words I thanked God for whatever victory He'd win through this meeting.

After cordial greetings which belied the kiss of Judas, S. A. opened the meeting by saying, "I'll bet you're wondering why we're all here."

I decided to play coy. "It doesn't surprise me that the deacon officers would want to gather for prayer before their pastor and some of the people go on a mission trip. After all, I've been asking the people to pray for us; and I figured you men, being spiritual leaders, would want to lead the way."

"Don't get smart with me, young man," S. A. retorted, nostrils flaring. "You know good and well we've had some complaints with you, and tonight you're going to sit there while we spell them out!"

I felt like leaving due to his disrespect. Who'd blame me? If this had happened before the boot incident and my humbling before the Lord, I'd have done just that. That night, though, something inside kept compelling me to stay. I took it as the Holy Spirit's guidance. After all, John tells us the "Spirit will guide you in all things," and I'd been trying to live more in step with the Lord.

"We're going to go around the table and tell you what's on our hearts. If you want to take notes, you can and it might be helpful because we've got a lot to say and you need to remember it." With that S. A. shoved a legal pad and a pen across the table to me.

"Your predecessor used to call us the Council of Elders when we met with him. He was good about taking our advice. I figured he'd have told you we've led this church for a long time and you'd better listen to us. Did he?" S. A. asked.

I spoke with firmness. "No, he didn't and neither did the pastor search committee. But it wouldn't have mattered if anyone had because

I work for the Lord, not for any man or group of men. However, I'm willing to hear your suggestions, just like I'd hear the suggestions of any member of the church."

"Well alright, then," S. A. said. "Let's get started. Early, why don't you go first?" And with that the men went around the table voicing their concerns.

Early said, "We decided that which must be done eventually is best done immediately." Then he just sat there, as if he'd forgotten the next lines he'd memorized. The other men stared at him wondering what else he'd say, but he stayed silent.

So I jumped in with, "Early, that's about the most sensible thing I've ever heard you say."

Early countered with, "Every tub sits on its own bottom and we're about to kick yours."

"Pardon?" I asked.

"Yeah, Big Bottom officers, we're going to kick the bottom out from under your comfortable seat. All's not well till it ends well, and it hasn't ended well with you; your bottom, that is."

Nothing was said for a few moments but I noticed several of the officers scrunched their eyebrows while others scratched their heads.

"Nev, let's see if you can remember what you wanted to say," S. A. said as he continued the moderator role.

Nev was careful to begin, "The situation's not yet gone too far to be redeemed, but it's gone pretty far." I interpreted that to mean I'd better shape up to his expectations soon, or to mean I'd be better off beginning to look for other employment. The Lord enabled me to hold my tongue, however. I just wrote down what the men said and from time to time noted a powerful emotive clue, like H. H.'s jowls continuing to bounce after completing his words about humor in the pulpit. I also noted S. A.'s clenching and unclenching his fists while talking about the "frightful way you treated Rob Patrickson, even giving him a roll of toilet paper as a memorial to Big Bottom after you'd thrown a desk at him. You shamed the whole church—even made us look bad in the national news."

I didn't have to correct S. A. as Nev said, "I think it was a boot, S. A." If S. A. kept exaggerating, he'd soon have me throwing the back wall at the evangelist.

On and on went the litany of complaints. I began to feel nauseous, but kept writing down their comments. When they finished the first round, the six each took another turn, voicing various "problems" that went unsaid in the first round or underscoring already mentioned ones. There were so many that my eyes must've glazed over. I knew I'd entered the zone where words no longer penetrated, but just bounced off me like rounds fired at bullet-proof glass.

Some of the so-called difficulties amazed me, like S. A.'s criticism of my buying a "foreign" car. Darla's Camry had more than a hundred and fifty thousand miles on it, and we'd sold it before our move rather than pay another large tax when we transferred the title in Mississippi. Soon after arriving we'd bought her an Avalon. Even though the car was built in Georgetown, Kentucky and was sold by a Hattiesburg dealer, S. A. must have believed the purchase of a Toyota showed a lack of patriotism at a time, "when our nation is at war." He referred to post 9/11. I didn't tell him I planned to trade in my Buick Rendezvous for a Honda Pilot.

I thought the matter of our car purchase was none of his business. God had warned me to be still and let Him work, though, so I just wrote his comment on my legal pad with the word "bigot" beside it. I put a space between the "g" and the "o" and scribbled the "t" in bigot to look like I'd written, "big one," but I knew what I'd written and I knew what S. A. was.

Nev surprised me with a grievance about my wearing a blue shirt every third or fourth Sunday, as opposed to the traditional white shirt. What that had to do with Christianity, I didn't know but it seemed worth mentioning to Nev. I glanced around at the six men and noted all six wore white dress shirts while I dressed in my favorite color, blue. Mine was a sports shirt fitting for what I'd believed was an informal meal with Early.

On and on the complaints came: not announcing deaths from pulpit; not keeping deacon officers appraised of the goings on in the church; too many choruses and not enough hymns; complaints about the day care causing problems with young families; mishandling the mission situation; causing bad publicity for the church; not supporting fund raisers for the youth trips; the change in the way the deacon officers are elected; and phones going off in the sanctuary. S. A.'s face turned red about that one, as he'd vowed to get to the bottom of the buzzing one Sunday and later found my phone had caused it.

H. H. even wondered aloud if I were a Democrat. I'm not. I served as an officer of the young Republicans in college, but I didn't answer his concern as it was none of his business and, after all, I had voted for Jimmy Carter for President when he revealed he was born-again and made decisions informed by biblical principles. I was also sensitive to any form of voter intimidation because there's a history of that in my state. I don't consider myself tied to a donkey or an elephant, but lashed to a cross.

Each deacon promised if he lost his position, he'd work to see I lost my job. More than once it was said, "If we fail to get your job this time, we'll keep trying until we succeed." H. H. said, "It may take us three months or six months, maybe even a year, but we'll make it happen. We've got clout, boy, and you'd better be listening to what we say. One way or another, we know how to get things done."

I thought about the strong-armed tactics and the unfairness of all this criticism. Attendance had grown quite a bit since I'd come to Big Bottom. Almost two hundred people had joined since I'd begun pastoring the church five months earlier. God helped us initiate the work the pastor search committee envisioned, reaching a broader spectrum of the community. Worship services were joyful and filled with anticipation each Sunday. Youth and college groups were strong and growing.

The steady finances of the church and sweet spirits of most of the people told a far different story than what I was hearing from this self-proclaimed Council of Elders. Yet, I heard not a word about the good things. When I could take it no longer, I asked the men, "I've heard a lot of disapproval; isn't anything going right? What about all the people who've joined?"

Early pounced on this, "Even a blind hog will find a few acorns."

"Sure," S. A. added, "a few things are going well, but with so many things going all wrong, we knew the good things couldn't last. For the sake of the church, we knew we'd have to bring these items we've shared tonight to your attention."

After all the men had completed their denigrations, Nev dropped the bomb designed to devastate me. The deacon officers had decided to begin a new web site: bringingbackyourbigbottom.com. The six men determined to withhold their tithe money for the next six months and pool the funds to ensure the best webmaster and site money could buy.

"We've noticed," Nev said, "some people have moved their membership to other churches. Others stopped coming to Big Bottom. We couldn't afford to let the church go down any further without doing something. So we thought we'd feature the stories of those who left and throw in some things we've seen going wrong, too. Of course, if the things we've been talking with you about this evening change, we can always stop the web site, but we thought this approach would ensure we'd help the church move forward."

"Yeah," Early said. "It'll be a site for sore eyes."

Nev covered his mouth to keep from laughing. Early was right, I thought. Sore eyes and soreheads. So, that's the way it was, a web site designed to bring down their new pastor and stir contention in the church.

I knew they were wrong about people leaving Big Bottom Church. Twenty-four people had moved their membership from Big Bottom since I'd become pastor. Because I conduct exit interviews on a regular basis in order to improve procedures and ministries, I knew that twelve of these had moved to other areas of the state or country. Three were college students who'd met friends in other churches. Of the nine remaining, five had attended other churches long before I came but had delayed switching their membership. The other family of four who'd changed churches told me it was due to the deacon officers trying to run everything. But I knew the officers would put their negative spin on everything they sent out over the web.

Before I could respond, a knock came at the door. Our food had arrived. The waitress forgot the catsup for my po boy and for the French fries others had ordered with their meals. Altus Rawls said he had a key to the storeroom since he was on the kitchen committee, and I saw him leave with the waitress.

It took several minutes, long minutes of painful small talk, but after a while the two returned to the small dining room. Rawls said we were lucky because they'd thought we were out of ketchup but at last he had located the one remaining bottle. It was out of sight on the back of the top shelf, but Altus had stood in a chair to search the shelf and found it.

Try as I might, I couldn't budge the cap. I rapped the cap with the handle of a knife but it still wouldn't turn. S. A. said, "For heaven's sakes, are you going to be all day with that bottle? Can't you take criticism like a man without fiddling with your food?" I was frustrated, but remembered the lesson of the boot and breathed a prayer for him.

"Let me have that, I'll show you how a man opens a bottle," he said. I passed it down to him because I didn't want to get into a discussion about the making of a man. The bottle gave him some trouble, too, and an animated discussion ensued about who was man enough to open the bottle.

After thirty seconds or so S. A. smacked the cap on the table with a POW! He'd brought the bottle down with such force I thought it would break. By now all six deacon officers had heard the call to true manhood, a call revealed in the ability to open a bottle. The six circled around and bent over the bottle, each wanting a turn to prove their strength. The pounding of the catsup bottle top on the table apparently did the trick because this time when S. A. turned the cap, it burst open with a shower of red dots.

The bottle, pushed to the back of the shelf in the hot storeroom and left there no telling how long, had fermented; and the pressure had built inside. It exploded when the seal broke open. I looked up at six white shirts of S. A., H. H., Nev, Early, Altus and Tony, each peppered with hundreds of red dots,.

The thought came to me, "Be still and know that I am God." I'd not had to do a thing. This council had spewed poison from their mouths, and God had spewed back poison back onto their shirts. Catsup covered the walls, the table, the men, the carpet, the food, and everything else in the room, except me. I'd been at the other end of the table and the hulking bodies of the officers had blocked any of the red splotches that would've come my way.

H. H. began to curse, but all of a sudden showed a remorseful look when he looked at his shirt and said no more. I'd not seen him like this and it concerned me. Nev didn't stop his cursing, though, saying he'd planned an outing with his grandkids and now he'd have to go home first. Early said, "Thar she blows," and laughed it off. Tony and Altus said not a word but looked disgusted as they began to wipe away the red spots. Each speck smeared and left a small stain.

S. A. showed the most anger of the group. "Pastor, you knew that bottle would blow up like that, didn't you? You planned this to get back at us. I'll bet you even planted it on the shelf. Well, this'll come down on your head, you hear me, boy? You've got it coming now and nothing'll save your job. When we get through with you, you'll be begging us to let you go without any further damage to your life or reputation. You. . . you." With that he lost wind, his face took on the same weird distortion I'd noted after the Patrickson incident, and he stomped out.

This time I noticed something I now remembered after the Patrickson incident, something that must've lain just under the realm of my conscious thought. When S. A. lost his voice due to anger, a hiss emerged, like a snake about to strike. Also, why I always hear his shoes squeak when he's angry, I don't know. I shouldn't be able to hear it because my hearing isn't good, but this time I heard the shrill noise all the way down the hall and to the door leading to the parking lot. The combination of the redness of his face, the clinching of his fists, the squeaking of his shoes, and the hiss of his throat formed a powerful warning, equivalent to a rattlesnake's rattling.

I helped clean the room, ate my po boy, and left, legal pad and pen in hand. I had a surprising calm I attributed to shock. It would take a while to process all the barbs thrown my way. I felt like I'd had a spirited game of darts and I was the board. If I'd written "Hit me," across my face and walked down the street in a bad neighborhood, I don't think I'd have encountered a more disastrous beating. And I wondered why.

I asked God about it. "Why, God? It's just not fair. And all this just before going on a mission trip to serve You. Why'd you let it happen?" I intuited a calm reply. No verbal answer came, but I knew the response in my spirit, "Like Jesus, Brent, like Jesus. Besides, how'd you ever identify with the hurts of so many in My world unless you walk, as they have, through the valley of the shadows?"

MORNING BEFORE THE MISSION TRIP

June Smith phoned me on Friday morning, the day before the mission volunteers flew out, with a request she and H. H. drop by to see me. I figured this was another trick of the deacon officers. I hated being so suspicious, but their actions demanded it. And so I refused her. "June, I've got more than I can handle, what with the mission volunteers leaving early in the morning. I've got to finalize the packing of my bags and get ready for that mission trip."

June persisted. "We've got to see you before you go on the mission trip."

"But June, I have to finish these details. Besides, my Mom has been sick, she may need a gall bladder surgery, and I need to spend an hour or two with her. I'm sorry but there aren't enough hours in the day. I know you'll understand."

"Alright, pastor," she said as her voice became pleading, "but this is one visit you'll be glad you accepted. It's wonderful news, and I think it'll help you as you go on the trip."

I'm a sucker for a crying woman, and the way her voice trailed off, it seemed June was about to do just that. "Tell you what. I have to run over to the church in a few minutes to pick up some forms, some Larium a doctor dropped off to prevent our catching malaria, and my Bible. If you can meet me there in thirty minutes, I'll clear a few minutes for you and H. H."

"Pastor, we won't take long, I promise; but you'll be glad you gave the time, I guarantee it," she said. Her voice had resumed its original cheerfulness.

June Smith didn't fit the role the other officer wives played. It's not that she wasn't supportive of her husband, but unlike the others, her worship on Sundays was authentic. The way she poured herself into the choruses and hymns and the way she took in the sermons spoke volumes about her heart-felt faith. I'd heard June participated in most of the Beth Moore and Kay Arthur discipleship courses our church offered for women. She'd even led a few. She had to have some depth to do that.

I saw the kind way June treated a lady who came by the church sanctuary looking for the place the Hispanic mission meets. She greeted the woman with a smile and kind words, took her by the hand, and walked with her to the chapel. June stayed for the Hispanic service so she could sit with the lady.

H. H.'s personality obstructed the way for anyone attempting to enter his or June's space, so I'd not gotten to know her. If Tina Tanner had asked for an appointment, I wouldn't have accepted the invitation, given the time pressures. But I figured, what's the difference between four hours of sleep and three and a half? I'd be sleep deprived anyway. Maybe the Lord would give grace by allowing me to sleep on the plane.

I asked Alice Evans to buzz me when the Smiths arrived. She just shook her head and muttered something about how, "You're such a people person you just can't bring yourself to say no to meeting with anyone, even H. H. Smith." She agreed, however, rather than try to change my habits on a busy day. I had just enough time to place the supplies in my car and return to the office for a last-minute check on my emails when Alice's voice came over the intercom. "The Smiths are here for their appointment."

June Smith led the way into the office, but who was the man accompanying her? H. H. looked like a different man. For one thing, he was bald. Despite the remaining tufts in both ears and the bushy eyebrows, the top of his head was slick as glass. For another, he smiled. I knew this was either a major change or I was in for big trouble.

I hadn't finished my greeting when H. H. interrupted. "I done you wrong. That's why I had to see you today. I've come to apologize. Maybe that plane would get underway and who knows what'd happen and I'd never . . . get to see you again. I had to tell you before you flew that I'm sorry and to ask you to forgive me." By now H. H. had tears running down his cheeks.

I couldn't believe what I'd heard. "H. H., your talking is so unlike you. And the way you look. What happened?"

"You didn't know I wore a hairpiece, did you?" H. H. asked with a smile. He ran his right hand over his bald head. "Yeah, the waves are gone and only the beach remains."

This was too much for me. H. H. had cracked a joke. His whole persona was dissimilar from anything I'd known. Despite the lack of hair and the contrition, his smile and pleasant personality made him look ten years younger.

"Tell him what happened," June said.

"Don't know if I can," H. H. replied. "Every time I tell it I break down. If I can't finish, will . . ."

"You know I will, honey. It's the best thing that's ever happened to us," June answered.

"Alright then," H. H. replied. "Pastor, I got saved."

"What?" I asked in astonishment.

"Saved, I got. . ." and with that he hesitated and the tears began to flow again. "I was born again last night."

"H. H. was it one of my sermons that got through to you or something God showed you out of the Bible?" I asked.

"Nope, neither one," he replied. Not that your preaching is bad. I haven't given you a chance. Ever since you told a joke on the Sunday you came in view of a call, I haven't listened. You didn't know it, but I had a portable radio in my pocket. I've been tuning in to Main Street Church on the radio every Sunday while sitting in our sanctuary judging you. I was one of the few who voted against you. But I was wrong. I've been wrong on so many things. I've made a list of more than twenty people I've got to ask to forgive me and you're the first one on the list."

"Well, H. H., I forgive you, but tell me how it happened."

"Well, two things. That evangelist, what's his name? Patrickson or something like that. Anyway, he got Zaccheus up a tree and couldn't preach him down. While that evangelist was speaking the Holy Spirit said to my heart, 'H. H., you're just like Zaccheus. You've been up a tree a long time, and you've gotten used to people looking up to you. Isn't it time you come down to be with Jesus?'"

The tears began to flow again. "Imagine. I've been so mean and conniving but God hadn't given up on me." He began to sob with great heaves of his chest. His hands rose to cover his eyes. Even this wasn't enough, though, as the tears began to overflow his fingers and drop to the floor with a peck, peck, peck on the carpet.

"But I shrugged off what God was saying to me until the officers met with you three nights ago. We'd agreed to shake you up by each of us piling on the criticism. We thought the cumulative effect would devastate you. We also knew that it's human nature to respond to criticism by getting defensive or fighting back. We wanted to get you to say something out of anger so we could take it to the deacon body and to the church, but you didn't say anything except to ask if everything was bad at the church. Then when the ketchup shot out and peppered everyone but you, I saw you'd not done a thing. God had fought for you and had warned us about our sins by covering us with red splotches.

"I'm . . ." H. H. began crying again. "I'm so sorry. We did wrong. We set a trap for you, but God sprung it on us." H. H. paused to dab at his eyes with his handkerchief. "The Holy Spirit spoke to me again that night. He said, 'H. H. this is your last chance. If you don't repent now I'll never urge you again. I've done my part by showing you your life is spotted with ten thousand sins; however, "though your sins be as scarlet they can be as white as snow."'" With those words H. H. sobbed like a baby and laid his head on June's shoulder.

"See what I told you," June said. I knew you'd want to hear it before your mission trip. We serve a powerful God who is able to help anyone who'll turn to Him. It doesn't matter the age or the wrongdoing. If someone will turn, He'll forgive. I thought H. H. might be too far gone, but I never stopped praying. God is so good."

H. H. raised his head. "Ever since that happened I couldn't stop thinking about it. For the last three days what the Holy Spirit spoke to me blocked everything else in my head. Over and over the words pounded like a nail gun tacking shingles on a roof. 'Up a tree, scarlet, last chance . . . Up a tree, scarlet, last chance . . . Up a tree, scarlet, last chance . . .'"

"Last night I came in from a committee meeting at the church but I don't know a single thing said at the meeting. All I could think was, 'Up a tree, scarlet, last chance.' I prayed God would help me make it home so I could talk with June about all this. She didn't know I'd come in. When I heard talking in the back of the house, I went to see what it was. I found June on her knees beside our bed pouring out her heart to God.

She was saying, 'Lord, please don't let those officers hurt our pastor. Protect him for the mission trip and guide the group to be strong helpers for our missionaries in Tanzania. And Lord, save those officers if they aren't saved. Above all, save H. H., Lord. He's been under such conviction. Help him. Please don't give up on him. Give one more chance, Lord.'" With this H. H. pulled out his handkerchief and wiped the tears. He sniffed several times and then cleared his nose.

"She prayed with such fervor she didn't even know I was standing right beside her. The next thing I knew, I couldn't stand. It was the most natural thing in the world. My knees buckled, I was kneeling beside her, and I began to pray. 'Lord, save me. Don't let me die a sinner and go to hell unforgiven. I'm a great sinner and I've brought pain to people around me all my life. But if you'll have me, I'm here to say I'm sorry for all that. Save me and help me be a good husband and a good man and live out the rest of my years bringing some joy to my wife and my kids and my grandkids. Help me make it up to those I've wronged and do some good for You and Your people. Get me out of that tree, Lord. Take my spots away, Lord. Save me.'

"I can't explain what happened. We must have stayed on our knees for another half hour but it seemed like a minute. All at once the weight I'd carried on my shoulders lifted and I felt love flow into my heart. It was like someone had taken a funnel, opened the windows of heaven, and poured God's love in. I felt twenty years old again. Something happened to me, something I've never experienced before. I felt clean. I felt happy. And I still am. Before, I never wanted anyone around me to smile or laugh because I didn't feel like it; but now I'm laughing and I want everyone else to laugh, too. Pastor, am I saved now? Have I been born again?"

"It sounds like it to me, H. H. Let me ask you a couple of questions. Do you believe when Jesus died on the cross He died for your sins?"

"I sure do. There's no way I could make it to heaven based on my life. It has to be based on what He did for me or I couldn't go at all," he replied.

"And are you willing to live your life for Him, obeying His leadership and doing what He asks of you?"

"I sure am. I've tried it my way all these years and I know that doesn't work."

"Then get ready for the ride of your life, H. H., because the Lord said He came to bring life more abundantly. You're about to experience life in abundance. You've already started your new life as a Christian in the right way by telling others. Jesus said, 'If you confess Me before men, I'll confess you before My Father in heaven.' Have you told anyone other than June and me?"

"Told anyone? I can't keep quiet about it. I'm telling everyone I meet. I told the secretaries on the way in your office. And I'm coming to the front of the church on Sunday to let the church know. I'll get baptized, too, because when I was baptized as a child, I just did it to join in with the other kids. I didn't have Jesus in my heart. Now I do, though, so it'll be a real baptism this time."

"I think you're doing right, H. H. The Bible says a Christian is a 'new creation in Christ.' Your old sins are gone and now your new life has come and the best way to show that is to begin with public baptism. I think you're doing right."

"But what about all those people I've wronged? I've made a list of at least twenty people I need to ask to forgive me."

"Go for it, H. H. Go to each one of them and ask. You may be surprised how they'll rejoice with you," I answered.

"But there is one family on my list that may not forgive me. You didn't know this, but I used to be in the Klan when I was a young man, and we did some bad things to people back then."

"The Bible teaches when we've wronged someone to go to them and make it right, if we can," I answered.

"There are some Klansmen still living who'd kill me and my family if I confessed all we did," H. H. said. He lowered his head toward where June sat.

"H. H., in the next two weeks, why don't you visit everyone on your list you can see with safety? I'll start praying for you every day while I'm on the mission trip. I'll ask God to help you find a way to confess to any others. If you've done things illegal, you may need to go to the law enforcement folks, too. June, I know you'll keep praying."

"I sure will. And whatever it takes, even if it means a prison term, it's okay with me because now H. H.'s heart's clean, and I know God will use his testimony in a powerful way if he'll live the rest of his days for the Lord," June said.

After agreeing to meet together with me after my return from the mission trip, H. H. and June left. They walked from the office holding hands and laughing, and I left astonished, glad I'd given extra time to rejoice with them. Who knows, if God can forgive H. H., maybe He'll even forgive S. A. and the other officers.

I twisted the key in the ignition and heard the motor start. At the same time I intuited God's response, "My arm is not shortened that I cannot do great things. If any one will use the key of faith, I'll crank his engine and give him new life."

32
AFTERNOON BEFORE THE MISSION TRIP

I picked up some Angus burgers from Hardees before returning home. Over a quick lunch, I shared with Darla what God had done in the life of H. H. and June Smith. I can still see the broad smile on her face and hear the clap of her hands. We prayed, thanking God, Who never ceases to surprise, and asking Him to use H. H.'s testimony in powerful ways.

Then we went to bed and napped a while, so to speak. We knew we'd not get the chance to be with one another in Tanzania, since the women roomed with the women and the men with the men. That was one of the greatest sacrifices of our mission trip, as our love runs deep. When we have to be apart, I miss her curling up next to me. Having lived on a foreign country as missionaries, though, we knew a little of what it meant to sacrifice and were willing to pay the price of being apart a week or two.

After a while Darla rolled over and said, "Brent, do you love me?"

I hated that question because it meant two things: one, I hadn't reassured Darla enough, and two, I just entered quicksand. No matter how much I'd struggle, I'll still be at the mercy of Darla's rescue.

"Of course I love you, honey"

"How do you know?" she asked.

"Well, about six years after we married, when Tom was three and Brian was one, I looked into the night sky. It was full of stars and it hit me—POW! Right here in my forehead. I love Darla. I do. I love Darla. And from then on I just knew it." The quicksand deepened. I needed rescue.

"Brent, I wish you'd be serious sometimes." This time it did hit me. Am I a little like Early Washburn? He used clichés to avoid communicating. Did I use humor for the same reason?

"Honey, it's just that I don't know what you're looking for. If I knew, I'd give it to you," I said.

"I'm not looking for anything. I just want you to be real," she answered.

"Okay, here's the real deal. I love you and have ever since I came to know you. Your red hair fascinated me at first, but then your spontaneous personality reeled me in. It's funny that I'm a pastor and make my living with words. You mean more to me than anyone else in the world, but with you, words fail me. I don't know how to say it right. Just know I really, really love you." I heard Darla breathe a sigh of contentment and soon we both fell asleep.

We awoke from our after-nap nap to the phone ringing. Dad called to say, "The doctors have some news about Mom and it may not be good." Talk about a wake-up call.

"What is it?" I asked.

"They can't tell for sure from the scans they've read, but they think more may be going on than just a large gall stone blocking the bile duct."

"What do they think it is?" I knew the answer but hoped to be wrong.

"They say they can't be sure but it may be cancer," Dad answered.

"When will they know, Dad?" I asked.

"They say they won't know until surgery. They've got to operate this afternoon anyway to remove the gall bladder. They just wanted us to be prepared in case Mom has something more than a gallstone."

"Can I talk with Mom?"

"Not right now, son. The nurses are prepping her for the operation. I stepped out in the hallway to call you."

"When's the operation?" I asked.

"They'll take her back in less than an hour," he answered.

"Where are you? Third floor?" I asked.

"Yeah, room 344," he answered.

"I'll be there in less than thirty minutes."

I told Darla the news. She grasped both my hands and looked into my eyes. I could see the hurt she had for me and for my mom. No one loves like Darla.

We talked about the possibility of not going on the trip. Our clothes were ready, if not packed, and we decided the best thing would be for Darla to stay home and pack, just as if we were leaving the house at three a.m., as planned. If we needed to cancel, we'd just cancel. Family comes first.

I called Sam on the three mile trip to the Wesley Hospital to ask for prayer, and he promised both to pray and also to call the other mission volunteers to ask them to pray.

I hadn't pocketed the cell phone from talking with Sam when I received a call from Wanda Washburn. It came while I waited at the first traffic light.

"Hi, Wanda. How'd you get my cell number?"

"We shared our cell numbers at the last mission trip preparation meeting, remember?"

"Oh, that's right. I'm sorry. My mind is somewhere else. What can I do for you?" I asked.

Wanda began to whimper. "Pastor, I need you to counsel me. I wonder if I should go on the mission trip after all. I want to go, but this morning I received a phone call from some college girl about a party at my house. I told her in no uncertain terms we don't have college parties at my home, now or ever, and she must have the wrong number."

Wanda sniffled and hesitated but continued with a broken voice. "After I hung up, she called back to say she didn't think there'd been a mistake because she'd watched the number with care when she pushed the buttons this time. I asked her how she'd received my number, and she said an older man had given the number to her boss. He'd set up the party for Sunday night with the escort service she works for." I had a hard time understanding the last part of the sentence because Wanda had begun to wail.

"Now settle down, Wanda. I know it sounds bad, but maybe there's some error. Have you talked with Early about it?" I asked.

"No, not at first I didn't. I figured he'd just give one of his crazy jingles, and I'd not know what he was talking about or thinking. It's been like that with him for years." She sniffled more, but I said nothing as I slowed down for the next traffic light while waiting to see what she'd say.

With a sudden strength in her voice Wanda continued, "I'll tell you what I did, though. I got her number from our caller ID, got her boss on the phone, cancelled the party, and told him I'd call the police on him and his so-called escort service if they ever called my house again or attempted to come on my property."

"Good for you. What'd he say to that?"

"He said, 'Please don't do that, ma'am. Someone must've made a mistake. Sometimes people call us as a prank. Yeah, a prank, I'll bet that's what this is. We'll cancel any party at your home and I'll put a block on our phones so we cannot accept calls from there. We've got a list of a hundred homes or more where things like this have happened and we never again accept any other offers from those places. I'll add your home to the list.'"

"I told him, you better see to it that you do, because I know some high ranking officials, and they'd love to take down any sleazy places in our area. It'd be good publicity before an election." Speaking with a lower pitch in imitation, Wanda continued, "He said, 'No, no, no, ma'am, you don't have to do that. I'll take charge myself to make sure you don't have any trouble with us.'"

"About that time Early walked in and saw me putting the receiver down and said, 'E. T. phone home?' When I didn't say anything he said, 'What's a matter? Rat got your tongue?'"

"I told him an escort service had called about some party. His face turned red and he mumbled something about a 'hand caught in the cookie jar,' whatever that meant. You see what I have to live with? You tell me what a hand in a cookie jar has to do with an escort service.

"Then he claimed he hadn't planned anything like a party or called an escort service. He said, 'A denial in time saves nine,' or something like that. He said, 'Honey, you were meant for me—maybe as a punishment—but you were meant for me.'" Wanda began to cry again and choked out the words. "He told me, 'Honey, we've been married fifty-six years and I plan to stay that way.'"

"Do you believe him?" I asked as I turned into the hospital drive.

"After all these years of marriage, I do," she answered.

"Then what do you plan to do about the mission trip?"

"I guess I've answered my own question. I'll go on the mission trip, and that way I'll have time to pray about this matter some more and talk with Early about it when I get back. Thanks for talking with me on the phone, but I guess I didn't need you to counsel me after all. I've figured it out for myself and I feel much better. God's good like that, you know. He'll help you if you ask. You should ask more, too, pastor. I'll see you in the morning." And she hung up. A good thing, too, because by now I'd parked in the lower level of the parking lot and headed for the front entrance.

When I got to the third floor hallway, I noticed a bed outside the hall. Mom was in it with Dad by her side. "They're taking me for surgery, son. I'll see you when I get out."

"Sir," I asked the aide taking the bed toward the elevator, "can I have a word of prayer with Mom before she goes into surgery?"

"Sure you can. They're waiting for us in surgery but surgery can wait for prayer, don't you think, pastor?" the aide said. I looked up from the bed to see his face and recognized Jim Hardaway, a member of Big Bottom Church. I lifted wordless thanks to God for sending Christians to work in places like this where people need a kind disposition and a caring attitude.

"Mom, I've decided to cancel my mission trip so I can be with you while you recover from surgery," I said.

Mom's brow furrowed and she turned her head a bit. I recognized that move as her signature to express doubt. "Son, if you do I may never make it out of surgery. You know God wanted you on that mission trip. Do you think this surgery is a surprise to God? I'll be here when you get back. Don't cancel your trip."

"But Mom, we leave at three o'clock in the morning. I can't be with you if I go."

"Well, you go anyway. I know you love me and you know I love you. So what's the delay? You've got to go. I've been praying for your trip for two months now. I'll be waiting to hear how it went, too."

"But Mama, how can I go when you're recovering from surgery?"

"The same way Jesus went to the cross and left his Mom and brothers and sisters behind. You can do it. Besides, you know I always wanted to be a missionary. I couldn't go, but you're going in my place. You go on now, you promise? I'll pray for you and you pray for me but you go, you promise?"

"Momma, if that's what you want, I'll do it; but in my heart I want to stay with you."

"You'll see me again, son. You'll see me again. You'll come home and I'll be waiting for you." I noticed Jim Hardaway shuffling and glancing at his watch. I knew the time had come. I prayed for Mom. I kissed her good-bye. For a moment I was transported to childhood when I'd kissed her goodbye as she left for work, and I left for school.

Dad bent down, placed a soft kiss on her forehead, and said, "I'll be here waiting for you, Babe," and they began wheeling her away. Dad pulled his handkerchief and wiped a tear from his eye.

Jim motioned for us and we caught up with him and Mom, boarded the elevator, and rode to the second floor surgery unit. They pushed Mom through the swinging, double doors marked, "No one but authorized personnel beyond this point." We stood alone in the hallway. A wife and mother had gone to surgery through doors we couldn't enter.

We went back to her room on the third floor to wait. Soon the room filled with family members, and we needed the larger waiting area. There I talked with aunts and uncles and cousins. We had prayer again for Mom. One of the neat things about living back in South Mississippi is the proximity of extended family and feeling their hugs in times of need.

The stay in surgery waiting lasted longer than we'd planned. Since they suspected more would be needed than a simple gall bladder removal, this operation would not be the laparoscopic kind. I'd seen scars on people who'd had the more extensive type Mom would receive. There would be a lengthy cut from the belly button to the back and a corresponding, lengthy recovery of several weeks.

An hour after they'd wheeled Mom away, a nurse called to let us know the doctor had begun surgery. Two more hours passed and we'd not heard another word. Relatives became nervous. One asked how long the surgery would take. Another hour crawled by, and the nurse called to say one doctor was closing with stitches and another doctor would be out to talk with us soon.

I didn't take her words as a good sign because the nurses, after surgery, often say something like, "Mrs. Paulson's doing well and the doctor will fill you in on all the details soon." Surgery waiting is not a place where "no news is good news." Fifteen minutes later, the doctor entered. He looked overwhelmed by the large contingency of family members present. He asked if Dad and I and any close family would come with him to a more private room to talk. Dad and I walked into a small room off the waiting area used by doctors and chaplains to give bad news or to counsel people with their grief. As a pastor I'd been with many families in rooms like these, but hoped I'd never have to be in one with my own family.

In the fog of what would soon happen, I didn't get the doctor's whole name but recognized it began with an L. We walked together into a dark room with blue wallpaper. Funny the little things I remember when difficult times come. The wallpaper struck me because blue is the color of heaven. And the darkness struck me because it signified the lack of color in this world.

Dr. L. motioned to Dad and me to sit on the couch while he turned a recliner so he could face us. He sat well back into the chair, as if needing all its cushioning to support him for a hard task. "I wish I had better news to bring you. We removed Mrs. Paulson's gall bladder. As we'd suspected, there was a sizable stone that blocked the bile duct and kept the liver from draining. That part of the surgery was successful.

"After the removal, however, the liver still didn't drain through the bile duct. As we searched for the reason, we found a large mass blocking the bile duct near the point it joins the liver." He illustrated the size by showing us his fist. "We cannot be positive without a biopsy, but in almost every case, these turn out to be malignant. And the bad news is there isn't much we can do with these types of cancers. They don't respond well to radiation or chemotherapy." He wrote down the lengthy name of the cancer so we could look it up on the internet, cholangiocarcinoma, Klatskin's type.

Dad asked the doctor to explain again what they'd done, as he was in shock and, with poor hearing, didn't catch it all. I thought it astute of Dad even to think to do request further explanation. This time the caring doctor found a pad of paper on the coffee table. He turned to a new page and drew a picture of the liver and bile duct and the gall bladder draining into the bile duct. He showed us with the picture what he'd done and where the suspected cancer still blocked the duct. He'd tried to put a shunt through the cancer to drain the liver, but had been unsuccessful. He'd created an artificial drain from the liver to the side of Mom's body. She would now have to wear a bag to collect drainage from the liver.

I asked, "Doctor, might it be possible that what seems to be a mass is just swelling from the gall bladder disease Mom had?" I was looking for some hope, any hope of continued good life for Mom.

He answered, "Yes, it's possible."

I asked, "Have you ever suspected cancer and found swelling of this type before?"

He answered, "Yes, I have, a couple of times. If it's swelling we should know within a few hours. However, in my opinion as a surgeon, I'm sorry to have to tell you but I think your Mom has cancer. The mass was hard and defined with clear borders. It doesn't seem to be swelling to me."

Then Dad asked the big question no family ever wants to ask. "If it's cancer, how long will she have?"

Doctor L. was considerate in his explanation. "Doctors don't know how long patients have to live, and these matters are out of our hands; however, I suspect your wife will have major problems within two years as this type of cancer can spread into the liver, pancreas, and surrounding areas."

We thanked this caring man and he left. I could tell it hurt him to have to share the news. Dad began to cry.

Dad is a man's man who seldom cries. When I was eleven I saw him shed some tears on the ride home from his own Mom's funeral. I remember it vividly because it was the first time I'd seen him shed tears, and I didn't see him weep again for more than ten years. But now he bawled. "If it were me, I could understand it, but she's such a good person. She's so kind to everyone. Why her instead of me?"

This went on for several minutes. I knew it best to let him express his feelings, but I also knew I was delaying my own. For some reason I couldn't deal with my own emotions at the time. I hugged Dad and we prayed for Mom.

We walked down the hall and shared the news with relatives and friends. Some cried. Others hugged Dad and me. Several began attacking the messenger, "Doctors don't know everything. They may be wrong. They've been wrong before."

I recognized the expressions as a show of deep caring for Mom and for Dad, but also the classic signs of denial. When extremely bad news hits, my first response is to say, "No, that can't be." The second response is shock. The third is guilt. These three interplay back and forth for many people.

The guilt stage hit me. Mom had been diagnosed with cancer and my response? To fly out of the country for ten days. Some son I am. But I remembered her words and my promise.

Soon another doctor entered the waiting room and told us Mom would be in ICU for several days. I talked with Dad about not going on my trip, and he looked at me with dismay. "You promised your Mom with your own lips. Are you going back on your word?"

"But Dad, don't you need me to stay with you during her recovery?"

"Not as much as I need you to be a man of your word. Besides, it'd scare her if she saw you in ICU. She'd think you'd stayed because she was dying right now."

And so I went home. Darla had done the work of three people somehow. She had all our bags and materials packed for the flight. I shared the news with her, and we sat in silence, side by side, just holding one another's hands and sometimes looking into one another's eyes.

My profound sadness was halved during those few moments. It was as if she lifted part of the burden and took it herself. For several minutes we sat like that. Sometimes Darla and I don't need to talk. Between soul mates, sometimes a simple smile, a tear, or a held hand said all we needed to say.

The day hadn't gone as planned. It alternated between the mountain peak of H. H.'s salvation and the valley of Mom's surgery and the subsequent C word. Why can't C stand for cure and care and character and commitment and Christ? Yet, I felt His Presence. For this, too, I have Jesus.

I loaded the SUV with everything we could pack that night. I felt led to preach from Psalm 23 in Tanzania, and so I filed the sermons

I'd developed into my briefcase. While I glanced at them once more, the thought came that God may have led me to this Psalm more for me than for the missionaries. I needed the guidance and assurance of a loving Shepherd right now.

I double-checked the tickets, shot records, contact information, medicines, itineraries, and passports and insured all were in place in my briefcase. We threw some goodies into a bag in case we got the munchies at the airport or on the plane. Then we crashed into bed, exhausted, for four hours sleep.

33

ALL ABOARD?

We awoke at two in the morning to shower. We'd meet the mission volunteers at the church at three. Tell Connie Barksdale drove the church van with eleven mission participants ninety-seven miles to the Medgar Evers International Airport just east of Jackson. We'd catch a commuter plane to Atlanta and from there a jumbo jet for a seventeen-hour flight to Johannesburg, South Africa where we'd rest overnight. From Jo'burg we'd scheduled another plane to Dar es Salaam, capital of Tanzania. If all worked well, we'd spend a second night recuperating in Dar before riding four hours on rough roads to Iringa for the mission meeting.

Some of the group slept on the two-hour drive from Hattiesburg north on Highway 49 and east on Interstate 20 to the airport. I couldn't sleep. I was seated in the front of the van next to Tell Connie and listened to her take on the latest gossip around the church. I listened not because I wanted in on the gossip, but because I wanted to keep her talking so she wouldn't go to sleep. Connie was a jewel to help with the travel but her conversation wasn't what I'd call inspiring for the mission volunteers.

She went into great detail about the latest blunder by Carter Ross. He gave a devotional during the previous week's retreat for singles from the Twenty-third Psalm. His theme was that the sheep must follow their shepherd. He told them when the sheep sleep not all the sheep sleep at the same time. He said the sheep should synchronize their sleep so that they'd have at least one sheep seeing after the flock. A sharp shepherd supervised the sheep's doing this. His point for the singles was they also have a Good Shepherd watching over them. However, with all the S words his tongue got tangled and he ended up stepping in some smelly-sounding word he shouldn't have slipped in. The singles all knew his problem and laughed about it.

His slip ups became the hot topic of the singles' retreat. Some said he had a woolly-booger of a problem. Others said Carter's difficulties were nothing a good sheep dip couldn't cure. One said the pastor should put the rod to his staff. And on and on it went.

Her story kept me awake most of the trip. I closed my eyes and prayed Carter's gaffe wouldn't make the paper. When I opened them again, I realized I'd dozed for a few minutes. Tell Connie was still talking, but now we were driving through the dangerous round-a-bout that leads into the airport.

Planners copied cities in Europe and England in the circular traffic plan on the entrance road to the airport. Perhaps they'd hoped to give an international flair to the airport; instead it had caused numerous accidents in its rural setting outside Flowood, Mississippi. We made it through without an accident and pulled into the lane for departures.

I've always thought airport people use morbid terminology. People boarding planes have to go to a "terminal" for a "departure" to their "final destination." While thinking about the language of death, a shadow passed over us; and soon I saw the jet and heard the roar of its engines. The expressions they use sound like a fatality waiting to happen.

At any rate we arrived at five-fifteen and the plane was scheduled to leave at seven-thirty. The line snaked back and forth three times but seemed to be moving steadily, so none of us feared missing our first plane. That is until Wanda, just in front of me, said, "Why in the world would they make us take off our shoes? This floor is cold. And besides, do they think a seventy-something-year-old woman is going to be carrying a bomb in her shoes?"

I tried to shush her, but it was too late. At least twenty other passengers in line heard the word "bomb," and several began to fumble with their cell phones. I hoped against hope they were calling family. Wanda wouldn't be quieted, however. She hadn't had her morning coffee and was growing impatient. She snapped at my insistence that she quieten down and said even more stridently, "They wouldn't dare think an older lady like me would carry a bomb."

In less than a minute a security guard came running up, and a passenger in another line pointed our direction. The guard asked Wanda to step out of the line with her suitcase. I explained to the guard that she was with our group of mission volunteers and that I was in charge of the group. He was polite but firm in asking me to step aside with her. I pulled my paperwork and Wanda's from my briefcase and handed the case to Darla. She sighed, but understood what was going on.

I stepped out of line with my luggage and Wanda's. Her voice raised to yet another level. "What's this all about, sir? Don't you know we're serving the Lord? You better let us go through or He'll zap you. We're not carrying bombs."

The security guard's voice remained calm but insistent. "If you don't step aside, Ma'am, we'll be forced to arrest you. You wouldn't want to cause a scene, now, would you? If everything works out, you might still make your flight, but you'd better cooperate or I can guarantee you won't make it."

Wanda had been warned against just such an episode in our mission preparation meetings. We'd even role-played so that volunteers like Wanda who seldom flew would be prepared. In the excitement of the mission trip, and perhaps due to her lack of sleep, she'd forgotten the warning never to say the word "bomb" or to call attention to herself.

The guard, by now accompanied by three others, showed us to a large side room with a concrete floor, two stainless steel tables in the middle, and cameras on two corners. The room gave me the heebie-jeebies because it reminded me of an interrogation room I'd seen on one of the CSI shows, complete with a two-way mirror on the wall.

We were given orders to unload all our baggage onto the tables for inspection. I urged Wanda to be quick and quiet about everything and maybe we could still catch the plane. She followed directions until the guards asked, "Is everything unpacked from your suitcase, Ma'am? I'm about to take it to our x-ray machine."

Wanda replied, "I should say not, young man. A woman's got a right to some privacy and I'll not surrender that."

"What do you still have in your luggage, Ma'am?" the guard asked.

"My harrumph," she coughed.

"What'd you say?" the guard asked. But Wanda didn't respond.

"Come on now, I don't have all day. What's in the luggage?"

Wanda's voice dropped low and she said, "My base outfits."

"Your what?"

"My base outfits," Wanda said in a low voice.

"What in the world are base outfits? Something you wear at an army base?"

"No, no, they are the foundational garments a woman puts on first before she puts on her outer attire," Wanda replied, still talking softly.

"You mean your underwear?" the guard asked with a loud enough voice for everyone in the room to hear him.

Wanda's face reddened, but she replied with a soft, "Yes."

"Well, let's see them, ma'am. We don't have all day, you know," the guard said.

Wanda rose to her full height and said, "Just who do you think you are, young man?"

Before Wanda accosted him further and got herself arrested, I stepped between them and said, "Sir, Mrs. Washburn is a private lady and wouldn't mind at all showing her, uh, her underthings to a lady. Would you mind asking a lady guard to assist you in this part of the procedure?"

"Broootherrr," the guard replied. "What is this, a department store with clerks to assist the customers? Okay, tell you what. I've got a mother and a grandmother, too, and I'd want them to be treated with consideration. I'll call my supervisor if you like. She's a woman. But I'm warning you. It's going to take some time. Furthermore, if this lady troubles us again, I'm going to arrest her. You got that, buddy? I'll arrest her."

"Thank you, officer. We don't mean to cause you any problems. We're law-abiding citizens, and you'll see that when the inspection is completed. We'll cooperate," I promised.

"See that you do," he replied as he turned his back to us and walked out of the room, leaving his two friends to see that we stayed put.

We must've waited twenty minutes when I received a phone call. It was Jane Winfield. I excused myself to Wanda but asked her to "not get in any more trouble," as if that might help. Wanda just looked at me funny, but I walked to the corner of the room.

"Jane, I'm so glad you called," I said with my back turned to Wanda.

"Yes, I heard about your mother and wanted to let you know we'd be praying for her and for you, too. How are you?"

"If I could tell you the whole story right now, you wouldn't believe me. Let's just suffice it to say that we're in the Jackson airport. Wanda used the word 'bomb,' and now she and I are in a holding room while they wait for a supervisor. In all likelihood, we'll miss our flight to Atlanta and who knows from there. Just pray. I think God had you call so you could pray for us."

"I'll do that. I sure will. Just as soon as we get off the phone I'll talk with the Lord for you. I know you are in a pickle right now and are heading out of the country, but I thought I'd ask you to pray for me, too, when you get some time."

"Sure I will. What's wrong?" I'd never known Jane Winfield to call me for prayer.

"I'm not sure anything is wrong, I'm just not too experienced in this sort of thing."

"What sort of thing?"

"Well, John Anderson called me a few minutes ago and asked me to go get some coffee with him."

"I hope you told him you would."

"Not exactly."

"What? You know the Lord has been setting this up, and I know you want to go with him. Why the delay?"

"I told him I just don't want to rush into anything."

"Rush into anything? For heaven's sake, Jane, the man's eighty. The last time you turned him down he didn't ask you again for more than sixty years!"

"I know, I know. Do you think I discouraged him?"

About that time a lady appeared at the door, and I heard her broadcast, "I'm a supervisor. I was told you'd requested me?"

"Just a second, Ma'am," I said.

"I hate to go, but the supervisor just walked in the room. I don't know if I'll get to talk with you again until I get back from Tanzania, but please take this advice from someone who loves you. I saw the schoolgirl sparkle in your eyes when you first told me about John Anderson. Call him back tomorrow and invite him over for some of your hot oatmeal cookies. Will you promise me that?"

"Oh, I don't know."

"I've got to go. Just tell me you'll pray about it."

"Okay, I'll pray about it."

"Well, turn on the oven to get it ready for the cookies when you do, because I think I know what He's going to tell you. Goodbye."

"Bye and thank you."

"Cookies, Jane, cookies," and with that I broke the connection.

"Yes ma'am," I said, turning to the supervisor.

"About time," she replied.

"Sorry about that. I had a phone call and got off as soon as I could. We're mission volunteers on the first leg of a long trip to Africa, and we were pulled from the line to check our goods. Mrs. Washburn here preferred a lady check her personal items, so we asked for you. And," I continued, "I hate to rush you, but we've already heard one boarding call for our plane."

"Oh, you needn't worry about that," she said. "People who call the supervisors never make their planes."

"I beg your pardon?"

"I said, you don't need to be in any rush because the plane you want is about to complete its boarding. You'll have to reschedule for another flight."

"Now see here," Wanda interjected. "I know the mayor of Hattiesburg and our state senator. Who do you think you are, trying to delay us on God's business?"

"I don't care who you know, ma'am. In fact, I hope you know some good lawyers because if you pester my guards any more, I'll send your tail to jail. Hey, tail to jail—that rhymes, doesn't it? I'll have to remember that one. Anyway, I'll bet you could do a lot of mission work in the Rankin County Jail," the supervisor said.

I stepped in again. "Ma'am, we won't be causing you any trouble. In fact if we could aid your work, just tell us how and we'll be glad to do it."

"You'll help me a lot by keeping this lady out of my hair while I search her things." Turning toward Wanda she continued, "Ma'am, if you hadn't used the word, 'bomb,' none of this would've ever happened."

"Well I never . . ." Wanda replied.

"Well you did," the supervisor replied.

"If we'll be delayed a few minutes, would you mind if we tell the rest of our mission group good-bye?" I asked.

"You'll not leave this room until your inspection is completed, but you can step over in the corner and use your cell phone if you wish." And with that sobering news I called Darla and arranged to meet her in Atlanta. Our original plans gave us more than two hours to change planes in Atlanta, so it might be possible we could still catch a flight and join the rest of the party there.

Darla said she and the group would gather before boarding and pray for our safe travel. We agreed to meet in Jo'burg if we didn't get to rejoin in Atlanta. Darla was wonderful about the whole thing. She didn't even say, "I told you not to invite Wanda," or "If you'd listened to me none of this would've happened."

The supervisor was thorough, but efficient; and we soon left the holding area, just in time to see our plane taxi down the runway. "I made us miss our plane, didn't I?" Wanda asked.

"You did, you did," I replied, "but it's not the end of the world. Let's hurry to the ticket counter. Maybe we can still make it to Atlanta in time for our next flight. But this time, please, please, do not mention anything that would cause any passenger or guard to get suspicious." And with that we hastened down the wide corridor to the counter.

As luck would have it, Mike, one of the supervisors of security who was a member of nearby First Baptist Church of Richland, heard from the other guards about our mission trip. He contacted the other members of the group to find our destination and intervened to assist in switching our tickets and luggage to the next flight. We even had time to buy Mike a cup of coffee and pray with him for the safety of the airport before boarding. God never ceases to amaze me at His provision.

Wanda didn't say a word on the flight to Atlanta and that suited me fine. It was shortly after eight in the morning, and I'd already had all of Wanda W. Washburn I could take, and don't forget the W. I nodded off to sleep and woke up as the flight attendant began announcing connecting flights and from which gates they'd be departing. I wrote down our information. Then I informed Wanda what we must do and that she must keep up. We deplaned and found a flight attendant who gave us directions. We half-walked, half-ran down the corridor. I pulled my carry-on with Wanda's attached so that all she had to carry was her purse.

We found the people-mover and used it to quicken our trip to the underground train carrying us to the proper terminal. We boarded it and rode to the right destination. Within an amazing twenty-five minutes after deplaning, we approached our departure gate. There we met the rest of our group, already in line to board. Even though we were sweating from the fast walk and from the stress of all we'd had to do in such a brief time, we hugged every member of the mission team. God had come through for us.

I expected Wanda to apologize to the group for the problems she'd caused them but instead she said, "Can you believe those guards, pulling us out of line like that. They made us miss our first flight and if I hadn't prayed hard, we'd have missed this one, too."

Before she could say enough to raise the suspicions of the other passengers and crew, I suggested, "You know, we're in line to board. If we don't have a time of prayer now, we'll not get the chance again until we get to Johannesburg." And with that the group held hands while I lead them in thanking God for putting us back together and watching over us. I made sure to stretch out the prayer, thanking God for the good weather, our good health, the good airline personnel, the pilots and others who kept planes flying and on and on until I heard the "now boarding" call. I didn't want to give Wanda any opportunity to delay us further.

Once the line began boarding, I prayed again, this time without voice. First I asked God to forgive me for using prayer as an opportunity to keep Wanda quiet. Then I thanked Him, for real this time, and from the bottom of my heart, for moving us through the maze of the Atlanta International Airport in such a quick time and allowing us to make our flight to South Africa with the rest of the group.

On the way into the plane, I heard Wanda say, "That's what we need: a lot less talking and a lot more praying." I'd never thought it would happen, but at that moment, with all my heart, I agreed with Wanda.

34
LEAVING ON A JET PLANE

Our group boarded the 747-400 and found our assigned places. It wasn't easy on the big jet, as each row had ten seats across in the coach section. Two aisles separated the three seats on both sides from the four chairs in the center of the plane. Wanda and I were on the same side of the plane and in the same row. One of us would have an aisle seat and one a window seat, with a passenger in between. I considered how best to keep her out of trouble and handed the ticket for the window accommodation to Wanda. Then I scrunched our carry-ons into the overhead bins.

The plane was almost full, so a few savvy passengers switched seating to gain more room next to the last three open places in the coach section. Two flight attendants demonstrated the safety instructions for us—the usual routine about the seat cushion as a floatation device, the oxygen masks, the exits, and how to buckle the seat belts. We taxied down an auxiliary runway to the holding area. The jet lined up behind two others. After a slight delay, we raced down the runway. The jumbo jet shook as it gained speed and sent vibrations through the seats. Soon it lifted off.

I'd missed something on the flight from Jackson to Atlanta. Wanda lifted her feet on take off. When I asked about this, she said, "Don't you know the most dangerous time in a flight is the lift off? If everyone would pick up their feet just think how much less weight the engines would have to pick up."

The salesman in the seat between us laughed and laughed and tried to tell Wanda the plane was carrying the same weight whether or not our feet were on the floor. She didn't believe him. He had an outgoing personality and seemed to find Wanda fascinating. They began to talk, but I tried to sleep. I was tired of Wanda—tired due to the lack of sleep, tired because of the difficulty at the Jackson airport, and tired of being responsible for the group.

I closed my eyes but Nev's face appeared. Once more I heard him say, "If we don't get you this time, pastor, we'll keep trying until we do." I prayed several minutes, asking God to protect me from the hands of the evil and the self-centered.

I closed my eyes again, and this time H. H.'s dilemma came to mind. I heard him say, "I was in the Klan. Some of those folks'd kill me and my family if I confessed what we've done." I interceded on behalf of H. H. and June. God delivered him for a powerful reason. He had great plans for H. H. I prayed God would grant him safety and give H. H. a platform to share the good news of how God can set people free from the sins of hatred, envy, and bigotry.

Jane Winfield's vision came to me, the one of the six charging bucks who were stopped from harming the church by a sheet dropped from heaven. I remembered a deer untangled from the six, went under the veil, and became part of the church. Was this God's telling Jane that H. H. would become safe in the fold? I knew Jane was wise, but it dawned on me that some of her wisdom was supernatural. It wasn't that she knew some things the rest of us didn't, but also that she knew some things the rest of us couldn't know. They were revealed by God to her alone. Recalling the vision made me feel more secure about H. H.'s decision and God's keeping power.

I thought I'd get some rest. My mind still wouldn't cooperate and pictured the committee room where the mission and personnel committees had met with Hispanic pastor Manual Reyes. I saw Maria Reyes' tears and felt her pain as the betrayals of her husband's commitment to the Lord and to his family came out. I took this as a sign I should pray for them and spent several minutes doing so. I don't know if he'll be able to serve in a pastorate again. God can still use his life, though, if he'll repent and live with integrity.

This time when my eyes shut, I saw the choir members laugh about my phone buzzing up and down the length of the organ. I heard the squeak of S. A. Tanner's shoes and imagined his tongue going in and out like a snake's while he hissed his discontent. The sight startled me so much it forced me to open my eyes. For several minutes I prayed with eyes open.

Soon I closed them again. I listened to the laughter of the boys in the restroom the Sunday I came in view of a call as pastor of Big Bottom Church. I heard their words, "I'm not voting for him." My mind raced. I was jolted again by the sudden strike on the topwater lure, saw the fish leap out of the water, and felt the shake of the boat as Mike battled the monster bass. I watched Mike's lip quiver and heard the shakiness in his voice as he expressed dismay that his parents were headed for divorce.

I smelled the catfish Carter Ross and I consumed while he spoke of the problem with the preschool policy. I hadn't eaten catfish since that time and still didn't desire it. I envisioned the room where the Council of Elders grilled me; heard Nev say they'd started a web site, www.bringingbackyourbigbottom.com; listened to the seal break from the ketchup bottle; and pictured again the thousands of red splotches, each one aimed with God's perfect precision.

I unlatched my seatbelt and stooped to pick up the briefcase I'd stored under the seat. I opened it, found my Bible, and began to read from 1 Peter, "Cast all your cares upon Me, because I care for you." I closed the Word and began casting. One at a time I lifted these concerns to the Lord, these and a dozen others that came to mind. I felt a deep assurance that He'd handle each of these problems plus many others that awaited me.

I wanted to sleep. I felt the need for it. Fresh from the help of God's Word, I expected it, but my mind traveled to the small counseling room in the hospital. I could recall every detail. I'd read of this phenomenon in people who'd had tragic accidents. Some could describe with great accuracy each aspect of the accident and everything surrounding it, from the sound of screeching tires to the look in the eyes of the person who rescued them, as if the scene permanently etched itself within.

I viewed the couch along one wall and the two chairs and the recliner against the other. The two lamp tables framed the chair nearest the door, a Gideon Bible resting on one of them. A box of Kleenex tissues lay on the arm of the sofa. The blue walls bordered with pink-floraled wallpaper seemed to soak in the dim florescent lights from overhead, making the room darker. The doctor drug the heavy recliner from near the door and placed it opposite the couch where Dad and I sat. I heard the scratching sound its legs made on the carpet.

The Doctor's white hair shone and he looked neat and proper, but he slumped in the chair as though tired. I heard the softness of his voice and felt his hand reach over to touch my shoulder as he spoke. "I wish I had better news," pounded in my ears. "I wish I had better news." "I wish I had better news." "I wish." "I wish." Cancer. That damnable word, "cancer."

I thought the initial shock had ended, but now I found myself using my handkerchief. This time it wasn't so much for what Mom faced, but for the hurt in Dad. I saw his white hair and his wrinkled brow and the tears overflowing his eyes. I heard his words once more, "I could understand if it were me, but why her? She's such a kind person to everyone."

I know some people find it harder to pray when they face losing a parent, but I didn't. I knew I'd be with her again and she'd be healthy and whole. Heaven is a prepared place for a prepared people, and Mom's prepared. I thanked God for heaven and prayed her time remaining wouldn't be filled with suffering.

Scriptures began to come to me one after another as if falling from the sky: "Call on Me in time of need." "What time I am afraid, I will trust in Him." "Don't worry about anything; but in everything with prayer and supplication with thanksgiving let your requests be made known to God. And the peace that passes all understanding will guard your hearts and minds in Christ Jesus." "I know the plans I have for you, not to destroy you, but to give you a future and a hope." "All things are possible for those who believe." "Rejoice in the Lord always. Again I say rejoice." "Trust in the Lord with all your heart and do not lean on your own understanding. In all your ways acknowledge Him, and He will direct your paths." "He will call upon Me, and I will answer him; I will be with him in trouble; I will rescue him and honor him. With long life I will satisfy him, and let him behold My salvation." "Come unto Me all you who are weary and heavy-laden, and I will give you rest."

I meditated on those words and repeated them to myself. I closed my eyes and sleep came. The next thing I knew, a flight attendant tapped me on the shoulder. She said, "Please raise your seatback during mealtime. Do you prefer the chicken, the fish, or the beef for your dinner?" It took me a few seconds to regain consciousness; but I adjusted my seat, selected the chicken, and turned to hear Wanda and the salesman order the beef.

Best I could figure, I'd been asleep over four hours, and we were about eight hours into the flight. Wanda said she and the salesman had talked the entire time. He had the same look of enthrallment I'd noticed when Wanda had suggested lifting her feet on take off. "You ought to write a book on this woman. She's fascinating," he said to me.

"Yeah, she's something all right," I said.

"I can't believe she told off the security guards at the Jackson airport when they thought she'd carried an explosive," he said.

I brought my index finger to my mouth to warn Wanda not to say the word "bomb."

"It's okay now; we're already on board. What're they going to do, throw me off the plane for carrying a bomb?" she asked with a volume audible for several rows.

The three passengers in the seats in front of us turned to look over the seatbacks at Wanda. One rose from her seat, stood in the aisle a moment with a deep wrinkle formed between her eyebrows while staring at Wanda, and then walked toward the front. Two passengers from just across the aisle in the center row of seats also looked disconcerted. Within moments a flight attendant stood beside me as if she were busy. I figured she'd been alerted and had come to listen to Wanda. Just as in the Jackson airport, however, Wanda wouldn't be quieted.

"Why would they think an older woman like me would try to harm anyone? Common sense ought to tell 'em terrorists don't dress like me. Why, they ought to be looking for people like . . ."

"Uh, Wanda," I interrupted, "what did you order for supper?"

"Beef. You heard me order, didn't you? What are you trying to do, shut me up from telling how those guards made a mockery of themselves when they tried to find my bomb?"

With those words the attendant turned and half-walked, half-ran to the front. A moment later the captain announced there would be a delay in serving the evening meal. He stammered but said maybe we could get to the meal within an hour or so. The passengers let out a collective, "ugh."

A husky man wearing a suit coat and tie stepped beside me and asked me if I wouldn't mind stretching my legs a minute so he could talk to the man beside me. I agreed, since I'd been sleeping and needed to walk anyway. I rose, stretched, and headed for the restroom. I saw him slip into my seat.

After my restroom break, I determined to walk the length of the plane a few times for a bit of exercise and to check on the other Big Bottom passengers. Two had gone back to sleep, four were waiting in the restroom lines, and Denise and Darla were talking. When I approached Darla, she pointed across the center row toward my seat. The salesman had stood up and the man who'd asked to talk with him took the seat next to Wanda. When the salesman retrieved his items from the overhead bin and walked toward the front, I decided to ask him what had happened.

I drew near him outside the restroom door. "Did you hear?" he asked. "Must be my lucky day. They had an extra seat in first class and offered it to me. Can you believe that? I've been flying to and from Africa several times a year for six years, and I've never had that before."

"How'd it happen?" I asked.

"I don't know. Maybe they knew I flew this route often, or maybe the lady I sat beside brought me good luck," he said and disappeared through the magical curtain that divided business class from the rest of us peons.

I cut my exercise short and returned to my seat in time to see the husky man pull out a pair of handcuffs. The cuffs clanked against the connecting chains. Soon Wanda asked the man what they were.

"Handcuffs," he said. "Ever seen a pair?"

"No, I haven't," she said, "except on TV." Her face resembled a child's at Disney World.

The man tried on one cuff and then snapped on the other. Wanda looked with admiration. "Want to try them?" he asked.

"Oh, no," Wanda replied. "Handcuffs are for criminals. I'd never wear them."

"I don't mean keep them on. I just mean put them on to say you know what it feels like," the man said. With those words he unlocked the cuffs and laid them over his knees.

"I wonder what the ladies in my Sunday school class would say if they knew I'd tried on a pair of handcuffs?" Wanda asked.

"Yeah, it would sure be something to talk about in your class. I'll bet every woman in there would be jealous."

"Do you promise to unlock them?"

260

"I don't know if I should let you. I'm a private investigator and I'm headed to South Africa to bring back a criminal."

"So that's why you had handcuffs. Would you please let me try them on, just once?" Wanda asked.

"I guess it wouldn't hurt just once," the man said, "if you'll promise not to break them."

"Oh, I promise," Wanda said. And with that the man slapped them on her wrists and with a click, click, click tightened them in place.

"These are tight. I'll bet they work, too. Just wait till the ladies in my class hear about this." Wanda said.

"Yeah, they work," the man said, as he unlocked the handcuffs and took them back, "and they've saved a lot of lives. But the neat thing is the restraining belt."

"What are you talking about?" Wanda asked.

"Have you never seen a restraining halter? My, you have lived a sheltered life." As he spoke he picked up the briefcase he'd earlier stowed on the floor, opened it, and retrieved something that looked like a seatbelt with a shoulder harness attached. "Yeah," he said as he eased it over his shoulders and cinched the belt around his waist, "these things are like a mobile jail."

"Wow." Wanda's eyes opened large again. "That's something. Just wait til the ladies hear about this. Can I take your picture?"

"We'll do better than that. Why don't you put it on and I'll take your picture. Then you can show your class when you return."

"Oh, I don't think so," Wanda said. "I'm a lady and I don't know how it would look if I put on a halter."

"Come on, give it a try. You'll never get another chance to do something like this."

"You know, you're right. My husband Early—Early Washburn's his name—he's all the time telling me to loosen up because, 'You only go across once.'"

"You mean 'You only go around once?'"

"Something like that."

"Now you've got the spirit," he said as he stretched out the halter.

"I'm so overwhelmed I don't know what to say."

"Don't say anything. Just pull out your camera and I'll take the picture."

"My camera is in my carry-on bag in the overhead bin."

"I needed to get up for a minute anyway to go to the restroom," he said.

"Yeah, me, too. I'll get my camera when I return."

I rose for the man and Wanda to exit. I faced the restrooms in the rear of the jet since they were the closest. The husky man stepped behind me to allow Wanda to go to one of those restrooms. After she headed that way, he whispered to me, "Sir, this happens once a year or so. I'm an air marshal. Just don't interfere with me or I'll have to cuff you, too. Don't say anything to her and we'll all be better off. I'll explain the whole thing to you in a few minutes." With that he moved toward the front of the plane and through the curtains.

I prayed Wanda would be comfortable and cooperative the rest of the trip and not cause problems for others. My stomach knotted. I could imagine the problem she could cause if she got feisty. Before I finished praying—and worrying—she returned.

"Pastor, would you mind retrieving my camera from my carry-on bag? It's in the zippered pocket in the front."

"Sure. No problem." With that I opened the bin and shifted the bags until I saw Wanda's. By the time I had her camera the marshal had returned and the three of us took our seats again. I handed her the camera and said, "I didn't know you had a digital camera."

"There's a lot about me you don't know. I'm pretty fun-loving. I try new things like this halter." Wanda pointed to the restraining halter on the middle chair. "You should try more new things, too. It'd do you good. You'd have more fun in life." And with that she slipped on the halter and the marshall tightened the belt behind her back.

"Just one thing would make this picture better," he said. "If you'd allow me to snap on the handcuffs it'll look like I've arrested you. Now wouldn't that be a fun picture to explain to your ladies?"

"Yes, let's do it," she said. And so the man snapped the handcuffs in place and with an easy motion clipped them into a loop extended from the belt of the halter. He turned to me and said, "Would you mind taking the picture? I've got to get something from the back of the plane." He handed me the camera as he rose and exited.

"You're coming back now, aren't you?" Wanda asked.

"Of course," the marshall said. "I'd never forget a fun-loving lady like you. I'll be back. Just give me a few minutes."

I took the picture from several angles, and we settled back for the man's return.

"He's such a nice man," Wanda said. It's so special to get to try on a halter and handcuffs. If you'd be friendlier, people would let you try new things, too. It would help keep your sermons fresh and make you more interesting."

Knowing that in the end I'd have to eat whatever words came out of my mouth, I decided on the safe approach and nodded. "Uh, huh," I said and closed my eyes. I hoped against hope Wanda would go to sleep and we could wake up at our destination.

After about thirty minutes, Wanda said, "I wonder what happened to that nice man?"

Before I could reply, the radio cackled and a male voice followed, "This is the captain. I'm sorry to have to report to you. There's been a slight problem, and we are being diverted to the Cape Verde Islands." The passengers gasped.

"The good news is the plane is in good shape, the weather is good and, with good luck, there shouldn't be more than a few hours delay in the Cape Verdes before continuing our trip to South Africa. We're less than three hours out from landing. The evening meal has been postponed, and you'll be dining in the Cape Verdes. I suggest you settle in for a nap if you can and I'll come back over the intercom to fill in the details before we land."

No sooner had the crackle of the speakers subsided than the noise level in the plane shot up. Every passenger seemed to talk at once. The three passengers in front of us turned to get a good look at Wanda in her halter and handcuffs. I heard one curse and then say with disgust, "It's that woman's fault."

Wanda must not have heard the comment because she asked, "Whatever do you think it could be?" They didn't reply.

Soon after the flight attendant had listened to Wanda and then rushed to the front, I'd noticed the blips on the screen indicating the location of the plane had curved toward the Cape Verdes. I suspected the problem was Wanda's use of the B word, but thought it best to mention to Wanda, "I don't travel overseas often. Maybe that fellow going after a prisoner in South Africa has some insight to help us."

"Would you go ask him? And when you find him, ask him about these handcuffs, too. They're starting to get a little tight on my wrists."

I walked to the back of the plane and found the man in an aisle seat near the last row. I knelt beside him and said, "Sir, I'm the lady's pastor and we're on a mission trip with several others on board. I'm so sorry about all this trouble."

"Yeah, I'm sorry, too, but since 9/11 we have to err on the side of caution."

"Can you explain all this and give me some details about what's going to happen now?" I asked.

"It is against the law to talk about bombs or terrorists on a plane in a way that makes other passengers feel threatened," he whispered. "Your friend overstepped her bounds. As an air marshall I had to handcuff her. This happens once or twice a year and almost always with older folks who aren't aware of the kind of world we live in.

"In my professional opinion, there's not a problem, but I can't go on my gut feeling. I have to go on the evidence of what she said. There are strict rules about this sort of thing. We'll have to land in the Cape Verdes, the baggage and plane will have to be checked, everyone will be delayed several hours and maybe overnight. To top it all, we can't tell the passengers the whole story yet because if we did they'd get agitated. They might even riot when they realize they've missed their connections and missed the people expecting to meet them. I've seen people spit on folks like her, curse and even kick. If I hadn't been there, they'd have beaten a man last year.

"I followed protocol and looked after the health of the lady by restraining her. I suggest you tell her you found me and I got delayed a couple of hours helping the crew. The cuffs aren't coming off. Tell her how exciting it'll be to tell her class that she remained restrained while the problem on the plane was being worked out. Tell her I'll come back to the seat as soon as I get some things worked out.

"By the way, I'm a member of First Baptist Church, Orlando. I've been on mission trips, too, and I know the predicament this puts you in. I'd suggest you ask the others on the mission trip with you to start praying for her safety. When the other passengers put two and two together and figure out she's to blame, we'll be lucky if they don't turn on her."

"But what will happen to Wanda and me and our mission group when we get to the Cape Verdes?"

"I don't mean to be blunt, but she should have thought about that before she started talking about explosives. I suggest you handle it the best way you can. If she gets too disruptive, I'll be forced to let her try on a new faceguard they've come up with to keep people from speaking. I hope it doesn't come to that. As for you and your group, I suppose you can go on to your destination, after the plane checks out okay. But with the lady, it'll be a different story. She'll have to spend a night or two in a jail cell until this gets straightened out. It wouldn't surprise me if she had to compensate the airlines for this little side excursion."

I knew if Wanda were delayed for a day or two I'd have to stay with her, but the mission group would go on to South Africa and then Tanzania. I scolded myself for ignoring Darla's intuition. She sensed danger before it happened. Why don't I listen to her? I shouldn't have invited Wanda on the trip. It was just like Sam suggested, I must be a masochist.

I've always been fascinated with how my mind works when under pressure. Sometimes the strangest things emerge. On the way back to my seat, I began to reflect on how my first six months at Big Bottom

Baptist Church had been filled with turmoil. Right away, the thought came that the Bible begins with the lofty words of Genesis One, "In the beginning God created the heavens and the earth." However, the Book of Genesis ends "in a coffin in Egypt."

My start with Big Bottom began with a call from my friend Curt Jones asking to let him submit my resume to a church near where I grew up. It now looked as if these first six months would end "In a jail cell in the Cape Verdes."

That's how life is, though. Lots of ups and lots of downs and lots of tension in between. Along the way are many opportunities, in the main, opportunities to trust and grow in the Lord.

As I walked back to my seat that day, I once again chose to trust Him. I wouldn't give in to self-pity. After all, He didn't promise there'd be no hard times, just that He'd be with us all the time. A sense of peace flooded over me, and I remembered the people of Big Bottom Church were praying for the mission trip. It came to me that God didn't leave His children in Egypt forever. In His time, He rescued them. He wouldn't leave Wanda, or me as her guardian, in the Cape Verdes forever. Somehow He would grant us an exodus, too. I trusted Him to make a way even if I couldn't see it yet.

I thought about how God could make something good happen out of this and a smile crossed my face. It energized me to think it was just like God to divert us so that some good deed might be accomplished. He can take bad things and bring good results. Maybe someone in the Cape Verdes needed our witness. I wondered what God would do.

LaVergne, TN USA
17 March 2010
176227LV00006B/1/P